Reborn Lycan

Holly Hiller

ISBN 978-1-958-711-85-9
Library of Congress information available upon request.

For more information or to place bulk orders, contact the author or Jennifer@BrightCommunications.net.

Introduction

This is my first attempt to write a story of my very own. I hope others will read and enjoy my creation. I wrote this book using pencil and paper because I do my best to get my thoughts down on paper first. I go through *a lot* of paper. Typing doesn't have the same effect on me and my brain flow. My friend Kalynn Lemak edited the first five chapters to help me start this journey.

This book has mature content. I'll try my best to make it good and steamy. It is a lot harder to write than I realized.

Background to Understanding on How My Book Works

Humans are not supposed to know about the supernatural world.

Mind-linking: A form of telepathy, communicating mind-to-mind, getting someone to feel/think/hear without the use of outside sounds. **Mind-linking will be bold italic.**

Werewolf: A human soul and body with a wolf spirit that can transform into a wolf, taking over the human body, but keeping the human soul within and back to a human body.

Moon Goddess: Worshipped by werewolves, the Moon Goddess has powers to invade dreams and to create creatures, animals, or supernaturals of the night. She has given them free will to reject the soulmates she assigns. Because of their human souls She has no power over free will.

Lycans: A human body and soul with a wolf spirit that is stronger than a wolf but transforms into a wolf-human hybrid in a body that walks on two legs instead of four and can talk.

Alpha: The leader of the pack

Luna: The alpha's mate

Beta: Second in command to the alpha, but still under the luna

Delta: Third in command to the alpha, but still under the luna

The werewolves' children (usually the eldest boy) are trained to take their parent's roles when they're ready to retire or die.

Werewolves mingle flawlessly with humans, even taking human jobs if they want. They must follow human laws, werewolf laws, and pack laws.

PROLOGUE

As Zane's eighteenth birthday rolled closer, he finally felt his body getting ready for his shift. Rumors had swirled around the pack that he was a dud wolf because he didn't shift on his sixteenth or seventeenth birthdays—as most werewolves do. He felt like an outcast.

"Rumors are the words of the unknown," Zane's mother told him. "People talk about what they don't know, understand, are jealous of, or are simply just afraid of. Don't let them define who you are; be your own person."

Zane was blessed with his father's tracking abilities. Good thing because he's no fighter—despite also inheriting his father's tall, lanky build of six feet two inches tall. His senses are more elite than most, and he can hear, smell, and see better than most wolves. But Zane's most heightened sense is his sixth sense. Zane can focus his other senses and feel when something is different, whether good , bad, or indifferent.

Zane's best friend is Rocky, the third in command, a delta enforcer. His real name is Robert O'Malley, but he's built like a boulder and can take a punch, then laugh. If you put Zane and Rocky side by side, two of Zane would make up the width of Rocky's frame. The friends hang out at school sometimes and in between their training. Rocky tends to hang out with the alpha's son, Alex, and the beta's son, Mark. He tries to get Zane to hang out with them too, but he is nowhere near their level. They tend to punch each other out of fun, and he can't handle that in the slightest.

Trackers like Zane gather the intelligence to help the pack succeed or fail. His tracker father can be gone for months at a time on missions for the alpha.

Zane got teased growing up because he didn't grow as quickly nor fill out as most wolves. But when he finally started to at least get taller, the teasing shifted. Then he got teased about being skinny. Rocky would throw a few punches, making examples out of wolves who continued to tease Zane. He even did this in front of the humans in school, to get them to stop too.

I feel so excited and anxious to finally feel my body getting ready to shift for the first time, Zane thought. I wonder who my mate will be more. Will she accept who I am and love me for just me? I want my mate and me to have what my parents have. Even if they didn't have their Moon Goddess mate bond, they would still be madly in love with each other.

Chapter 1: The Gut Feeling

Zane woke for school and got ready like every morning. He must not have slept well, because he woke not feeling fully awake. He smelled his mom's breakfast. (She loves cooking, and she cooks all the time because she's the head chef for the pack.)

He heard everyone in the house doing their morning routines, except his dad, who must already be at the pack house. Zane hopped in his private shower (one of the perks of being the oldest), hoping a shower would make him feel more refreshed. It did some good, so he finished getting ready in his room and headed downstairs for food.

"Good morning, Mom," he greeted his mother, who's about five foot five inches tall, fit and bubbly.

"Good morning, son. How did you sleep?"

"Not good. I woke up feeling tired."

"That's no good, dear. Eat up. Maybe you just need some fuel to get you going."

"Ya, probably. Thank you, Mom. I love you."

"Love you, Zane. Now eat, eat."

Zane choked down some breakfast, hoping it would give him energy for the day and headed to school.

At his locker, Rocky paid him a visit.

"Sup, dude," Rocky said, giving Zane a bro hug. "Your birthday is coming up next week. Do you have any plans?"

"I usually spend it with my family. You know that."

"Of course, I know that. Can I come over too? We got you a gift you're going to love."

"Who's 'we'?" Zane asked, surprised.

"A few of us. What's important is the what, not the who. Can I come over?" Rocky repeated.

"I'll ask my mom, but of course, she'll say yes. She probably loves you more than she loves me for Christ's sake," Zane laughed.

"You're right. She loves me," Rocky said, laughing too. "I probably don't even have to ask to come over, but my parents instilled manners in me, so you know. Just tell me what time, and I'll be there."

"What's your hurry? It's like a week away. It's not as if I'm not going to talk to you before then. Why do you seem more excited than me about my birthday?"

"It's not every day your best friend turns eighteen," Rocky replied.

As the piercing bell rang to signal the start of classes, the friends said in unison, "See you at lunch!"

By lunch, Zane was not feeling too good.

Maybe I'm a dud, Zane thought. *Werewolves my age don't get sick. I've only seen the really old ones start breaking down.*

Zane stuffed his morning materials in his locker, grabbed his lunch, and headed to the mess hall. He spotted Rocky with his "normal" crew—Alex, Mark, and some girls who hang on them, both human and she-wolves. As Zane sat, the group greeted him, then went about their business.

Rocky looked at Zane and whistled, "You're looking a little under the weather, bro. You feeling, okay?"

"Ya, I'm okay, man. I didn't get much sleep last night for some reason, so I feel wiped out."

"Should I call the doctor for you?" Rocky asked, sincerely.

"Not necessary, brother, but thanks for caring."

"Man, I love you. You know that."

"And I love you, bro," Zane replied.

At that, the others at the table began to snicker—except Alex, who looks like Zak Baggins in his twenties.

"Hey, take that bromance to the janitor's closet, would ya. No one wants to see that shit," Mark (like a young Sam Winchester) the beta grumbled.

Without hesitation Rocky and Alex both punched Mark (Alex's best friend)—hard, so hard he flew out of his chair and landed on his back. As his metal chair clanged against a table, then hit the floor, the mess hall went silent.

Alex stood, towering over Mark, and said, "Really, Mark? That's a bit disrespectful, don't you think? Do you really think caring for family—blood or not—is a bad thing?"

"No, Al…Al…Alex," Mark stammered, resisting the urge to call Alex "Alpha" in front of humans.

Alex turned to address the entire mess hall, "Go about your business! This does not concern any of you."

Everyone listened, even the humans.

Zane bowed his head out of respect to Alex and replied in mind-link, *You didn't have to do that.*

Zane, you guys are like brothers to me, Alex mind-linked. *You two are a prime example of what being a true pack is all about. As soon-to-be alpha, I must finally grow up to see that as a strength. Seems our beta has to start growing up and see that too.*

Thank you, Alpha. I might not have my wolf yet or even get it at this rate, but I hope you'll still give me the honor to serve you.

Knock off this feeling that you look and feel sick because you're getting your wolf for your eighteenth birthday. It's having a different effect because you're getting it a bit later than most. It happens sometimes. Trust me, you have your tracking abilities, and I have my alpha ones. Go home, rest. That's an order.

Yes, Alpha.

With those alpha orders, Zane grabbed his homework for the day and went to the school nurse (who is in the pack), who sent him home. Once his feet crossed the threshold, his body took over. He stumbled to his bed and passed out.

I pray to you, Moon Goddess, let me be receiving my wolf, Zane thought. *I don't want to be a dud.*

Right before Zane passed out, he heard in the slightest whisper, "You're my special son."

I must be hearing things because I'm so tired, Zane mused before falling into a deep sleep.

A little later, Zane was startled awake by the sounds no kid wants to hear—their parents having sex. He grabbed his pillows, put them over his face, prayed to suffocate, and fell back to sleep.

"Zane, baby, wake up! It's time for supper," his mom called later from downstairs.

Zane headed downstairs to see his family already eating. They wait for no one. His sixteen-year-old brother, Robert, and twelve-year-old twin sisters, Erica and Bernie, sat at one side of the table. His mom (Trudy), and dad (Evander "Evan") sat at the other. Zane joined them. He began slowly trying to eat.

"Are you okay, son?" Evan asked. "The alpha told me that his son ordered you to go home because you seemed unwell."

"Ya, not soon enough, I guess," Zane mumbled under his breath.

"What was that?"

"I didn't sleep well last night, so I'm just so tired, like the life is being sucked right out of me," Zane said.

"Maybe you're finally getting your wolf, son."

"Or I'm just a dud, like all the rumors are saying, and I'm actually sick, like a pathetic human."

"You know that's not true, son."

"Really, Dad? Robert shifted, and he's two years younger than me!" Zane exclaimed, grabbed a bottle of water from the fridge, and stormed back to his room.

"Just let him go, Evan," Trudy said.

Chapter 2: Relief

The next day, Zane woke up feeling worse than he had the day before.

I cannot move a muscle! he thought. *I'm a pathetic dud—just like the rumors that have been going around for two years have said. I can't believe I'm so sick like this.*

Trudy quietly entered his room—with her light brown hair up tight ready for her chef duties at the pack house—to check on him. "Zane, sweetie, how are you feeling today?"

"Like I can't move. I feel weak. Sorry I'm a dud, Mom."

"That's nonsense. Just stay home and rest today. I brought you up some peanut butter toast and water. Try to eat, please. If you're not feeling better by tomorrow, to the pack doctor you'll go. I love you." With that, she left for the pack house for her duties.

Zane passed out once again.

At school, Rocky was waiting for Zane, but by first bell he saw no sign of his friend. Classes came and went, and by lunch there was still no text, not even a mind-link attempt from Zane, so Rocky called his friend.

Zane finally answered after the fourth ring, "Hey, bro, how's school?"

Relief washed over Rocky as he slumped against his locker. (If anyone in school saw how this big burley, black hair, hazel-eyed guy loved his best friend, he would never hear the end of it.) "Man, are you all right? You didn't even give me a heads-up you weren't coming to school today. After how awful you looked yesterday, you really had me worried,"

"Sorry, man. I felt so much worse this morning than yesterday. My mom told me to stay home, and I passed right back out again. I'd have probably slept the day away if you hadn't called."

"Aw, sorry for waking you, man. Go back to sleep and get better."

"It's fine really. I'm glad you woke me up. I need a shower badly anyway. These sweats are gross."

"I'll stop by after training today to check up on you, okay? Feel better."

Rocky hung up his phone and headed to lunch at his usual table. Alex shrugged off the girls who hang on to him constantly and sat by Rocky.

How's he doing, Rocky? Alex asked in wolf hearing.

His mom told him to just stay home and sleep. I woke him up when I called to check on him, Rocky replied.

He's getting his wolf; I can tell. My wolf seems to be getting more protective over him all of a sudden, Alex said.

Have you talked to your dad? He might know why your wolf's suddenly being more protective over him, Rocky said.

He said I'm maturing into the alpha. He shrugged, like it's normal to feel this way. He's the alpha, so it very well might be.

Well, at least he's finally getting his wolf, so he can stop thinking he's a dud—like everyone has called him for the past two years, even you, Rocky said, irritated.

Ya man, I'm going to have to apologize to him and you. You at least put me in my place a few times for it. I hated you for it, but I see why my father didn't punish you for knocking me on my ass when I needed it.

Damn right I did. What kind of future enforcer would I be if I didn't do the right thing? A bad one, that's what.

Ain't that the truth! My father makes being an alpha seem so easy, but I know it's not. I'm not looking forward to those choices at all.

With that conversation over, the friends finished their food, carried on with the rest of the school day, then headed to training.

As Zane lay in bed after talking to Rocky, he felt hotter and weaker than before, like absolute trash. He slowly tried to get out of bed and head for his shower. Besides desperately needing to cool down, he needed to clear his head. He was having some weird dreams about a red-haired girl.

Finally making it to the shower, Zane let the cool water run down his face and his almost hairless slightly muscular chest and feverish body, feeling good on his hot body. He closed his eyes, stuck his face directly in the stream of the shower, and held his breath.

Images of the girl from Zane's dream flashed through his mind. *Her dark, long red hair, and a shorter body frame than most she-wolves, but the fire in her green eyes tell me otherwise,* Zane thought. *I'm definitely certain she's a she-wolf.* His breath hitched. *She's gorgeous,* before Zane even realized his hand was on his cock, he leaned forward, pressing his head on the shower wall his wet hair dangling downward. With one hand on his cock and the other bracing himself, he started stroking to the image of her. His strokes got harder and faster the more her beautiful face became prominent in his mind. By the time Zane finally released, he was out of breath, and her face was gone.

"Holy shit, what the hell was that?!" Zane said aloud—louder than he meant to because his voice echoed off the shower walls and it didn't even sound like him. The water now felt colder than it had before, and as refreshing as it was, Zane got out of the shower. He walked toward the sink to brush his teeth. Glimpsing himself in the mirror, he stumbled back and dropped his toothbrush in the toilet. Momentarily in a state of shock, his toothbrush stayed in the toilet, until he collected himself enough to fish it out and throw it away.

My...my eyes look like they're fucking glowing back at me, which is not normal for werewolves, Zane thought. He splashed cold water on his face and dragged his hands down his face. Then he turned his head away from the mirror and headed downstairs for lunch. Thinking his fever made him see what he saw, he thought he should grab some food.

Quickly realizing no one else was home, Zane made himself a sandwich and drank some tea, trying desperately to clear his head. But her face was all he saw.

Is she my mate or just some random girl? Zane wondered. *What was up with my eyes? Am I getting my wolf, or am I just so hopeless about not having my wolf, I'm making shit up?*

With Zane's mind now spirally out of control, he went into the living room, plopped down on the couch, and turned on the TV. A few seconds later, he was out like a light.

A few hours later, Zane's family had returned, and they all were at the dinner table. His mind wandered back to thoughts of the red-haired girl. *Oh, please for the love of the Moon Goddess, don't let me get a boner now in front of my family,* he thought, then as a distraction, he asked, "Dad, how did you feel when you knew your inner wolf was starting to develop?"

"So, you finally accepted that all your sickness is due to your wolf coming, instead of worrying about being a dud?"

"I think it finally dawned on me after my shower. After I got out I...I looked so different that I dropped my toothbrush in the toilet. My voice didn't even sound like me. I was shocked to say the least. Do you understand?"

"You see yourself differently and hear yourself in a new way. In a way you're the same, but different. Your body is adjusting for your wolf. Actually, all you kids listen: When your bodies start going through changes as you start developing..."

Zane's sisters dropped their forks and shrieked in horror, "Daddy! No, not the talk. Not now, please!"

Evan and Trudy started laughing so hard they could barely catch their breath. Trudy snorted and looked like she was crying because her eyes were watering so badly. Robert and Zane laughed too. They started to calm down, so Evan could finish his thoughts.

"I know you learn all about puberty in school, so I don't need to go into *that* part," Evan continued. "We grow and age at the same rate as humans do, until we start getting closer to getting our wolves, usually around sixteen, or in Zane's case eighteen. We don't know why his waited, but it happens. While we deal with our human side catching up with getting our bodies ready for our wolves, our human bodies prepare for shifting. When our bodies are finished, that is up to the Moon Goddess. We normally start feeling stronger. Our senses get more in tune with our surroundings, and we notice more than we did before.

"Because I'm a tracker, all you guys will likely have inherited better senses than most, though probably not more than an alpha. That's why you needed glasses, Robert, when you were younger."

Robbie nodded in understanding.

"Then around age twelve is when things slowly change," Evan continued. "We don't really notice the changes; we just grow with them. Around that time, kids start looking like they're getting fat, but it's not that at all. It's their bodies soaking up and harboring nutrients—mainly calcium and protein—storing it for their first shift."

The girls looked at each other, gasped, and asked simultaneously, "Are *we* going to get fat now that we're twelve?" Both girls pushed their plates away.

"Really, girls, knock it off," Trudy admonished. "You'll eat to grow and prepare for your wolves, like everyone else. I've had four children, and I'm not fat, thanks to my wolf. I'm very grateful for her."

Thank you, Tru. I love you too, Trudy's inner wolf purred at the compliment.

"Will we get periods like humans do, Daddy?" Erica asked.

Evan gagged on his drink. "Can you field that question, Trudy?"

Trudy smirked, "Oh, well, honey, you're doing a wonderful job so far. I don't want to interrupt."

Evan gave Trudy a playful growl in return for her sass. She gave him an air kiss in return.

"Fine. Girls, we have what humans call a uterus, but we call them wombs. Like your father said before, we develop like humans for a while... Robert, Zane, pay attention!"

"But why? We aren't girls!" Robert whined, then a little louder after Trudy *thwapped* him in the back of the head. "Ow! Mom, what the hell!" Another *thwap*.

"A: Don't curse around me. You haven't earned that yet. B: You need to know what we she-wolves go through. How do you expect to understand your mate or even how she'll be having my grandbabies?"

"Mom! No way am I doing that anytime soon. Pester Zane!"

Zane shrugged, *Don't mind having babies with my dream girl, literally.*

Trudy sighed, then continued, "Enough, let me finish. As I was saying, you girls have recently turned twelve, but to answer your question, yes, you'll have a period until you get your wolf. However, you have not been through a true full moon yet—when the moon is at her highest and brightest, like she's smiling down upon her children at her fullest power. As our goddess' creations only, her power can help us develop. It's her way of giving us blessings. They happen only three or four times a year. Rarer still is the True-Blue Moon. They happen only every twenty years or so, and one's supposed to happen on Zane's birthday this year."

After that educational mealtime conversation of the birds and bees, the family cleaned up. Zane went back upstairs to relax, feeling a hundred times better than he had been. That was a good thing because he was starting to feel pressure to get back to school. *I don't want to fall behind,* he thought. Then he heard his dad coming up to his room.

"Zane, are you decent, son? Rocky said he'll be here shortly to check on you."

"Ya, Dad, I'm decent. Just send him straight up as always."

Zane must have dozed off because he was startled awake by Rocky knocking on his door.

"Hey, man, how was training?" Zane asked, rubbing the sleep from his eyes.

"You know, the usual. Kick ass, get hit, laugh it off. How're you feeling?"

"A hundred times better. I finally feel my wolf. Isn't that awesome? I'm not a dud after all."

If you weren't sick, I'd slap you silly. What have I been telling you, bro?"

"I know. I know. You were right. This is a stupid question since you shifted a while ago, but when you were about to shift, did you dream about one particular girl, over and over?"

"No, but I sure do fantasize," Rocky said, wiggling his eyebrows.

Zane gave him a bro punch.

"Ow!" Rocky said, rubbing his arm. "Wow! I wasn't expecting that!"

"I was being serious, sorry. The dreams started last night. They're always about the same girl, over and over. I can't stop thinking about her now. She seems so real. Maybe it was my high fever. Do you always fantasize about the same girl, or are even my fantasies boring since I don't have any experience?"

"You're a man, you like women, and apparently a specific type. The girl in your dreams might be your mate—or she might not be. You just might have needed something for a release. Am I right?"

Zane nodded.

"I got horny as fuck before I shifted," Rocky nodded. "You'll find her, I mean, your mate; there's no rush. The goddess doesn't reveal anything before it's the right time. Describe the girl you have been dreaming about and maybe we can find one close to her, so you can go play."

"You know I haven't done shit with girls before. Why would I start now?" Zane asked.

"Oh, don't be such a pussy about pussy, eh? Just describe her. Maybe she's in the pack."

Zane closed his eyes, and the girl came to him instantly, then he described her to Rocky, "Oh, she's gorgeous, with long, dark red hair, greener eyes than mine with such fire and determination, short, and tits to die for." He opened his eyes to see Rocky jump up like he was electrocuted.

"I hate to seem startled, but one, you're getting a serious boner, and two, your eyes seem to be glowing," Rocky said.

Chapter 4: Those Eyes

Zane dropped his head into his hands and sighed. He thought maybe he imagined the glowing eyes because of his fever. *Guess not. He saw it too.*

"I thought I was crazy," Zane confessed.

"What?" Rocky asked, exhaling with a whoosh.

"After my shower yesterday, I...I looked in the mirror, and my eyes were glowing. It shocked me so much that I dropped my toothbrush in the damn toilet. I figured I was hallucinating because of my fever. I guess not."

"I'm not going to lie, brother. Your eyes are *not* normal. Did you ask your dad or anyone about it?"

"Um, no, like I said, I thought I imagined it all."

"Well, let's sit and talk it through before we get anyone else involved. Now explain everything from the time you woke up yesterday."

"When I woke up yesterday morning, it felt like I hadn't slept at all. That night, in my dreams, was the first time I had seen her face, but at that time I didn't think anything happened, so I thought nothing of it. I did my normal morning routine. My mom just thought I needed food since I'm so skinny. You obviously saw me at school. And at that point, it just had gotten worse. Then Alex told me to go home and to trust him that I'm getting my wolf. I slept a lot, then I took a shower, and she came to me again. I, you know, relieved myself in the shower with her on my mind. After I was done, she was gone. I got out and tried to brush my teeth, then I saw my eyes. Dropped my toothbrush in the toilet, yelled to myself. Rocky, my voice was so different it scared the hell out of me. Again, thinking I was just imaging things, I went to grab something to eat. Passed out on the couch until supper. I felt a hundred times better after that last nap. Then at dinner, we had a lovely conversation about the birds and the bees because I asked about me looking different to myself in the mirror. That sums it up."

"It seems like every time you think about her, your eyes glow," Rocky mused. "I just mind-linked for your dad to come up here. Maybe he can shed some light on it since he has seen things."

Evan had been downstairs watching *Family Feud* when he received Rocky's mind-link, asking him to come upstairs.

With a quick backward glance at the TV, Evan strode up to Zane's room. "Hey, Rocky, what's the matter?" he asked.

"Tell him everything, Zane," Rocky commanded.

Evan sat on Zane's computer chair and focused his attention on his son. At first, it seemed like normal things: not feeling well, fantasizing about a girl, typical teenage stuff. But Evan's attention piqued when Zane mentioned his glowing eyes. *I wonder if he was trying to ask about it at dinner but didn't know how.*

Once Zane finished his explanation, he put his face in his hands and sighed. "What's wrong with me, Dad?"

"Honestly, I don't know, son. Maybe it's your wolf? Can you show me? Try it again on purpose."

Rocky put up his hands in a defensive position and asked, "Do you understand he'll probably get a hard-on at the same time?"

"Well, that's a natural reaction when you're attracted to someone, and I don't care. I used to wipe his ass, for crying out loud," Evan said with a smile.

"Dad, do you really have to go there?"

"What are parents for if we don't get to embarrass you a little from time to time."

"Anyway, I'll try not to do 'that' okay?"

Zane closed his eyes and began thinking about his dream girl. When he opened his eyes, sure as shit, they were glowing—and the other thing happened too.

Evan leaned closer and peered into his son's eyes. "Isn't that something? Besides being horny, what else do you feel?"

"Tired, drained really, but not sick like before."

"If you feel up to going to school tomorrow, go. But I need you boys to keep all this to yourselves for now. Seriously, don't tell anyone, not even the alpha's son. We need to take this to Alpha Steven *ourselves*. Got it?"

"Yes, sir," Rocky and Zane replied. With a nod to each of them, Evan headed back down to his office and poured himself a BAHA whiskey. He didn't know how to react to what he had just witnessed. His son's eyes *glowed*. Like what the fuck?

I hope it doesn't have anything do to with my past. If that fucking witch... Evan thought, then shook it off. *It can't be.* It was only 8:30 pm, shouldn't be too late to interrupt Alpha Steven, so Evan closed his office door, picked up his phone, and hit speed dial. *I'm too old school for cell phones and it's a tracking device for others when I'm on a mission, so I never bothered to get one.*

"Ah, Evan, what can I do for you at this hour?" Steven asked, picking up after the first ring.

"I...I really don't know if I can talk about it now over the phone. I'm stupid for calling, Alpha. I'm sorry."

"Evan, I know something is wrong, or you wouldn't have called me."

"It's about my son Zane." Evan hesitated after that, unsure how to proceed.

"Yes, Alex mentioned he wasn't well. Alex said he can feel his wolf coming. Is he all right?"

"Yes. No. I don't know."

"I can send the pack doctor over right now if you need her."

"No, no he doesn't seem to be sick anymore like that. It's just... When do you have time to sit and talk with us? It's not an emergency I don't think, so no rush."

"Let's see, tomorrow is Thursday, but I have to go to Strong Hold Pack tomorrow. Can it wait until Friday after school?"

"Yes, Alpha, it can. Thank you, goodnight, Alpha Steven."

"See you Friday. Goodnight, Evan."

At just five feet two inches tall, Valerie might be short, but she's swift—though she's always working against the melons on her chest. Many of the boys in the pack told her that she's pretty. They always compliment her hair color and how it makes her eyes pop, but they won't get anything out of her, and they know it.

Valerie strove for respect, and in her pack the only way to get that is to be a great fighter. She's not big, not full of muscles of any kind, but still strong. She struggled to gain what little respect she had from a few pack members. She's the runt of her family—the only girl with a barely older brother, and their mom is pregnant again. The siblings are so close in age, people think they are twins.

Valerie is the laughingstock of the beta family. She studies hard and trains harder, forcing herself to become great even if it kills her. She hopes her mate will be in a great position, like an alpha or even a beta. She need to prove to her father that the goddess finds her worthy, so he will too. That's why she trains so hard. She can't be worthy of a mate like that if she's weak.

Her best friend is Althea (Bluey) Norris, who is Alpha Van's daughter. The girls share the same struggles. She's a semi-tall, leggy, blond-haired, blue-eyed beauty, but she's a fighter. Of the two friends, Bluey is the brains, and Valerie is the brawn. Bluey is a self-proclaimed beautiful trophy mate, but not in the "I'm better than you" kind of way. She just wants to be seen as more, just like Valerie does. Both girls also share the same family struggles—and the feeling that other wolves view them as weak just because they're girls—their fathers anyway. They push each other to be the best, which is one of many reasons why they're best friends.

This past summer, when both girls turned eighteen, they hoped to find their mates. Truth be told, the she-wolves hoped their mates were in different packs because the pickings in this pack were slim. Valerie was grateful not to be mated to one of Bluey's brothers, though she did have a crush on her older brother Roman. She called him "Romeo" because when she first started having a crush on him, they were reading Shakespeare in school.

But that was before he changed into an arrogant asshole. Valerie wanted to venture out of this pack with Bluey by her side.

One morning at school, Valerie spotted Bluey at her locker. "Hey, girl!"

"I can't wait to get out of school and get the hell away from here," Bluey said.

"Hell, yeah, I'm with you. I want to travel and find my mate, so my father said he would contact other packs and arrange an itinerary to travel across county. He said it's because he wants me to be safe, but *I* think he just wants me out of his hair—probably wants me to find my mate and then be *his* problem. Who cares at this rate. Anywhere is better than *this* pack."

You know I'm coming with you, right? I'll bet you any amount of money our fathers are on the same page. My father wants me out of his hair too," Bluey said agreeably.

"Why wouldn't I go without you?" Valerie joked, and both girls laughed—as always, so in sync.

As if on cue, up walked their brothers: the next in line alpha Roman (Bluey's brother) and beta Ricky (Valerie's brother), with their rippling muscles and panty-dropping smiles. Roman with his dark blond hair lets some bangs hang down to hide his eyes behind. Roman had his dark brown hair with natural red highlights military buzz cut. Just like Bluey and Valerie, Roman and Ricky were best friends.

"Hello, Val," said Roman being Roman, in the most sexual way he could muster.

"What's up, Romeo?" Valerie snickered.

"You know I hate that, Val, yet you still call me that. Why? I know you've had a thing for me for a while now, so let's figure something out."

Val searched for her brother for a little back up, but he was talking to Bluey, so he didn't hear his best friend hitting on his little sister.

"We aren't mates. What makes you think you can get anything out of me? Your title? Psh, bitch, please. That's not everything."

With that thrown in his face, Roman turned a few shades red. This wasn't the treatment he'd grown accustomed to: girls spreading wide for him at his request. "Now, now, Val. We both know why you train to be the best. It's to impress me, so I choose you over my mate. Isn't it?" Roman asked, still trying to appease Valerie with his resolve-weakening smile.

Valerie did her best sultry walk toward Roman and put her hands on her hips and stared into his hazel eyes. Then she slowly raked her hands down his chest, "Romeo, oh, Romeo... No." She reached for Bluey's hand, and they walked away.

Bluey could barely contain her laughter until the girls were out of the building. They had been on the bad end of their brothers' tempers before and didn't want to relive that experience. Once out of earshot, they laughed so hard Valerie thought she might pee.

Bluey tried to choke out words, "Oh...my...goddess...the look on his face...priceless!"

After a few more minutes of laughing, the girls calmed down enough to get into Bluey's car. She drove them home, where they did homework, then trained until dinner.

After dinner, Valerie got a mind-link from Alpha Van, telling her to meet him in his office.

Oh great, Romeo told him what I did to him, and now I'm in trouble, she thought while she headed to his office and knocked. "You wanted to see me, Alpha?" she said, peeking her face into the room.

"Have a seat, Valerie," Alpha Van said, gesturing toward the chairs across from his desk.

As Valerie walked further into his office, she could see Bluey, Ricky, and Roman were already there. *Well, fuck!*

Without preamble, Van launched right into his point, "I'm sending you all on a little trip across country to find your mates, since none of you have found them here like I hoped."

Valerie felt his gaze land squarely on her face. "Together? As in one car?" she asked.

"Yes, all in one car," Van retorted impatiently. "I'll give the boys all the money you need for this trip. I've already planned with some of our allies for you to spend at least a weeks' time at each pack. You are to be on your best behavior on this trip. My son will keep me informed on how the trip is going. You're dismissed."

Bluey and Valerie started walking out together before the Alpha called, "Valerie stay a minute."

Valerie quickly mind-linked Bluey, *I'll come to your room when I'm done here.* Bluey nodded and walked away.

"Have a seat. Your father will join us in a moment," Van commanded.

About a minute later, Valerie's father, Beta Jones O'Reilly, stood beside the Alpha and crossed his arms.

"Daddy, am I in trouble?"

"No, Val, you're not, but Alpha Van and I've talked about a few things that we need to address with you," Jones stated flatly.

"Oh, shit, that doesn't sound good," she accidentally said aloud.

"You'll keep your mouth shut, with no interruptions and no questions. Period," Jones admonished."

"Yes, Father," Valerie said, dreading the conversation before it even began.

"As you know, my son is next to be alpha and has yet to find his mate in this pack. He has been to several other packs for training and business. I know he did not save himself for his mate, as no alpha or beta could, but if my son tries to have sex with someone from another pack and he ruins her, it could be seen as an act of war. We can't have that—especially with our allies—can we? Do you see where I'm going with this?"

Valerie felt her eyes bulge right out of her skull. Tears of anger formed. She knew damn good and well she couldn't take on the alpha nor her father. She straightened up in her chair, looked Van in the eyes, and said, "No, sir, I don't." Then she looked back at her father, standing looking intimidating as fuck. The alpha looked back to Valerie with a smug look.

"I think you do, but I'll spell it out for you. I need you to be the one to prevent war. If he doesn't find his mate on this trip and he's getting frisky, you will help him relieve himself. Bluey has the same instructions for your brother. Now that you have your orders, leave."

Valerie looked back at her father with pleading in her eyes. He stood like a statue, with no emotion in his eyes—no love, remorse, nothing.

My father should feel something for me, not whore me out to the alpha's son, not after how hard I worked. Now it seems all my hard work was for nothing.

Without a word, Valerie walked out, with her back straight and her head high, trying to keep her pride intact.

We need a plan.

Chapter 6: The Plan

As Valerie walked out of the alpha's office with whatever pride she had left, she went right to Bluey. Since they both lived in the packhouse, it wasn't very far from her father's office. Valerie knocked softly on Bluey's door, then entered when asked. Without any words, the friends embraced. Without letting the other go, they sat on Bluey's bed and bawled their eyes out. Valerie slowly released Bluey, and she gave Valerie a semi-smile.

"Why are you smiling?" Valerie asked.

"I think I have a plan."

Like venom out of her mouth, "Yes" was all Valerie could say. Iggy (Val's wolf) was inching closer to losing control. She wanted blood. It took all Valerie's strength to keep Iggy down.

"We have two months left of school, and we were going to take the trip anyway, but now at least it's paid for," Bluey rationalized. "You have a cousin in one of the packs we're visiting, right?"

"My mother's side of the family is scattered; can you be more specific?" Valerie asked.

"Would any of them with higher positions be willing to help us?"

It took Valerie a few minutes to take a mental run through all her relatives, which packs they were in, and what positions they held. "Yes. Actually, my Uncle Curtis is a delta enforcer of the Silver Stone Pack. I have his son—my cousin—Robert's number."

"Well, call him! We need his help," Bluey blurted.

"Okay. But can I know what's going on in that pretty head of yours before I bother him?"

"No, or you might back out of it. Get him on the phone."

"Ugh fine. Let's go to my room where I left my phone."

"No, we have to call from my room because it's soundproof, you know with me being the alpha's daughter. Go get your phone and come right back."

Valerie ran to her room and grabbed her phone. On her way back, she ran into Roman. As usual, he looked down at her, but this time it wasn't because she's short. It was because of lust.

"Hey, Val. How was your talk with my father?" Roman asked with a smile. "Why don't we go to my room and get the party started? I've to help you learn how to be quiet when I'm fucking you senseless." Roman grabbed Valerie's right arm, firmly just above her elbow.

"Let go of me!" she yelled. "You have your whores here. Use them. We aren't in another pack yet. Just keep in mind what our mates will say. If you were *my* mate, I'd have jumped your bones already, but you're not, so I repeat: Let go of me!"

Valerie pulled out of Roman's grip and practically ran back to Bluey's room. By then it was about 2100, and Valerie still had no idea what Bluey's plan was. She looked up Robbie's number, called, and put the phone on speaker.

"Hello, who is this?" asked Rocky, who clearly didn't have Valerie's number in his phone.

"Hey, Robbie, it's Valerie O'Reilly, your cousin from Shrieking Moon. Do you remember me? Would you have time to talk to me and my friend?"

"I'm in the middle of helping my best friend with some things. Is this important?"

In the background, Valerie could barely hear the most appealing voice. Iggy came forward in her mind to get a better listen. The voice said, "It's okay, Rocky. Whoever is calling you probably needs you. You're in high demand."

"If you don't mind, bro," Rocky said.

"I don't. Go ahead," said that amazing voice.

"Okay, what do you need?" Rocky asked, now giving Valerie his full attention.

Suddenly, Bluey grabbed the phone from Valerie so fast Valerie thought she had broken it.

"Hi there, you sound delectable. My name is Althea, but Val calls me Bluey because my eyes remind her of the blue moon. What's your name?"

Oh my gosh, I can't believe her, right now. I've got to speed this along, Valerie thought, then snatched her phone back from Bluey.

"Look, Robbie..."

Rocky interrupted her, "Please call me Rocky. No one really calls me Robbie anymore."

"Sorry, anyway after school ends in two months, Bluey's father and mine are sending us on a trip with our brothers to visit packs to find our mates."

"What's the problem with that?" Rocky asked puzzled.

"Bluey and I were told in order to avoid war between the packs we visit, that when either her brother or mine gets a sexual itch, we have to be the ones to scratch it. But we don't want to be their whores; we're saving ourselves for our mates."

Valerie heard the phone drop on the other end, then a powerful roar. She was scared—and aroused at the same time.

"Holy shit, holy shit, ZANE, ZANE, come back to me, Zane," Valerie could hear tremendous commotion. "Trudy!! Trudy!!" Valerie put the phone back on the speaker so Bluey could hear too. Together the friends listened in horror to the chaos unfolding on the other end of the line.

As Rocky and Zane talked about his eyes and dream girl, Rocky's phone rang. He checked it, looked suspiciously at it, and asked if he could take the call. Zane guessed it must be important because otherwise he wouldn't take it at a time like this. He told Rocky to take the call, then got up to leave and give him some privacy.

"No, dude, stay," Rocky said, then turned his attention to the phone call.

Zane ignored the conversation until Rocky tapped him on the shoulder and covered the phone with his hand.

"Hey, I just had a thought. What if it's her?" Rocky asked, pointing to his phone.

"Who do you mean?"

"My cousin is on the phone. I haven't seen or talked to her for years, so I kind of forgot about her. She fits your description of your dream girl. She's short with long, dark red hair and green eyes, like you described. I'll put her on speaker. Keep quiet."

Zane nodded in response. But as he heard Valerie speaking, her voice sounded to him like heaven. She was telling Rocky about her alpha making take a trip to find mates, blah, blah... Then she started saying something about her alpha ordering her and her friend to have sex with their brothers, because they're an alpha and beta.

Zane's body began to shake, and rage started consuming him. Before he knew it, a blood-curdling roar came from deep inside him.

I think my wolf is pissed was his last thought before he blacked out.

Chapter 7: Rage

I've never seen anything like that before in my life, Rocky thought. *It's like Zane became unhinged. His eyes scared me the most—that is until the death-threatening roar. Not a howl, oh no, a someone-is-going-to-die roar. Sounded like an angry T-rex from the movies, but deeper.*

"Trudy!" Rocky yelled for Zane's mom, not that his parents didn't hear that roar anyway. His mom must have already been on her way up because she was there in seconds.

"Oh my goodness! What the hell happened?" Trudy asked Rocky, breathlessly, running toward her son. She grabbed him and tried to calm him. Her eyes flicked, signaling her wolf had taken control. Her wolf must feel his wolf in distress, knowing he hasn't had his first shift yet.

Soon after, Zane's dad, brother, and sisters entered the room. His sisters looked scared shitless and left. Zane's dad and brother ran over to him and tried to hold him down. His mom asked Rocky again what happened to make him like this.

"Long story short, I think his mate is on the phone, and he overheard her say she was ordered by her alpha to do something unspeakable to the alpha's son while on a trip after school," Rocky said.

Trudy looked around the room, spied Rocky's phone on the floor, picked it up, and asked, "What's your scent, dear?"

The phone was still on speaker, so Zane could hear the voice he found appealing answer, "Eucalyptus and lavender!"

Without giving an answer, Trudy yelled to Evan, "Have Zane's mate talk to him, tell him her name, that she's okay, and stuff like that. I'll be right back." Then she jetted out of the room.

Valerie got back on the phone, and Rocky could tell she was nervous. He picked up and asked, "Did you hear that, Val?" He heard her gulp.

"Yes, but what do I say? I don't even know who he is," Valerie said.

"All you need to know right now is that his name is Zane. We don't know his wolf's name yet because he hasn't gotten it yet. He's obviously developing him at the moment. His eighteenth birthday is next Saturday."

I hope this works, Rocky thought, taking the phone closer to Zane. "Okay, he can hear you now," he said to Valerie.

"Um, Hi, Zane. My name is Valerie O'Reilly. I'm the second born, beta's daughter of the Shrieking Moon Pack. I'm safe, fine, and well, ummm, please come back to the ones you love. Zane, I need you to calm down, so you can actually talk to me. Please? My wolf's name is Ignisara, but she prefers Iggy."

Trudy burst back into the room, carrying two candles and lit them. Val continued to talk to Zane, and the talk combined with the candle scent started to calm him down. As Rocky held the phone close to Zane, he looked around the room. His parents looked bewildered, and Rocky could see his father mind-linking someone.

Within ten minutes, Alpha Steven appeared in the doorway. Zane seemed to be in a deep sleep. Rocky turned his attention back to his phone and told Val she did a great job calming him down and congratulating her on being Zane's mate, because he's a great guy.

"Please keep this, to yourself and ask your friend to keep quiet because we don't know what really happened here," Rocky requested, then ended the call.

Trudy ushered everyone out of Zane's room down to the living room, while she stayed to watch over him.

Downstairs, Evan sat, put his head in his hands, and asked, "Rocky, what the hell happened tonight?"

Before Rocky could even formulate a reply, Beta Jake and Rocky's dad, Curtis, joined them in the living room. Rocky sat along with everyone else and began the short version on what he believed set Zane off. "My cousin Valerie called me, asking me to help her and her friend out with something. She told me something that her alpha had commanded her and her friend to do."

Alpha Steven spoke, "Yes, her alpha called to arrange a week here so they could look for their mates: his son, Roman, and his daughter, Althea, and his beta's son, Richard, and his daughter,

Valerie. Think he said we would be their third stop. Was it about that?"

"Yes and no, sir. The girls were told—*commanded*—that they are to accommodate the boy's "needs" to prevent war. When Zane heard that, he lost his shit," Rocky explained.

"Are you fucking kidding me? I know Alpha Van was despicable, but that is beyond appalling because those two can't keep it in their pants. Do you think she's his mate?" Steven asked.

"After what happened, no doubt, but he doesn't even have his wolf yet. Why would she affect him so much without it?"

"Has anything else happened that I need to know? I know Evan wanted to speak to me about Zane. I know it's late, but this seems important and needs to be discussed now."

How the hell did he know something else happened? It's like he knows something was wrong. It must be those alpha instincts Alex talks about, Rocky thought.

"Before I say anything, Alpha, no offense, I want to know that Zane will be safe from harm. I want this to be kept quiet until we can figure it out and help him," Evan said respectfully.

"If it's that important to you, I'll personally ensure no harm comes to him. As for keeping this quiet until further notice: Everyone present for these events and conversation going forward are hereby commanded, by me Alpha Steven of the Silver Stone Pack, are now sworn to secrecy about the subject of Zane Montgomery and can only discuss the situation with anyone present today or if I swear them into the situation. This is my command of all present today until I release you from this command," Steven said, using his alpha command, unbreakable vow.

Then Alpha Steven turned to Evan and asked, "Now can you explain, Evan?"

"Zane tried to talk to me about feeling different. He said he didn't seem to recognize himself in the mirror, and when he spoke, he couldn't believe it was his own voice. At first, I just thought it was because he wasn't used to feeling his wolf coming because of his age. But when Rocky called me upstairs, he started describing a girl he had dreamt about. I thought it was just boys being boys thinking about girls, but his eyes...his eyes...they...."

"*Glowed!*" Rocky interrupted. "They fucking *glowed!*"

After that, everyone seemed to stop breathing. It got even quieter. Alpha said he'll be cancelling his trip tomorrow, and he told Rocky to stay home from school and spend the day with Zane.

Getting orders like that I can live with. It's not every day you get told to stay home and have a chill day with your best friend/ brother, Rocky thought.

Then they all went their separate ways for the night.

Chapter 8: Findings

By the looks of Alpha Steven, he didn't sleep much the last night. He was usually very kept and professional, but today his usually kept hair still has bedhead, and he was wearing sweatpants and a T-shirt. He had already called Alpha Charles to apologize for having to cancel their meeting, explaining he had a pack issue that needed immediate attention. As a fellow alpha, Charles understood. Steven's love, his mate, made him eat before she would let him go do his duties this morning.

My wolf and I love her so much. I'd probably wither down to nothing if it wasn't for her forcing me to sit and eat before I start my alpha duties every day, Steven thought.

Steven called in his top two that morning to talk about what was going on. As he waited for them to arrive, he started the dreaded paperwork for the day.

Maybe I can get ahead of it, so I can spend time with my mate, Tessa, Steven thought, but a knock at his door told him they were already here. The pair quickly entered and sat while Steven finalized some papers.

"I wanted you all in here today, so we can discuss what happened last night," Steven began.

"All I can really say, Steve, is I was in my office finishing up my daily report, and around 2100, I felt a calming power that made me feel powerless, if that makes any sense," said Beta Jake, Mark's dad.

"It felt like a power burst from a supernatural—like a witch. But the patrol hasn't reported any breaches and said everything was calm for them," agreed Delta Curtis, Rocky's dad.

"I think it had something to do with what happened to Zane. I feel he's different. I felt a sort of power coming from Evan's house at the time of the incident. But it must have dissipated before we got there. Curtis, Rocky stayed home from school today, right?" Steven asked.

"Yes, he's waiting for Zane to wake up, so he can do his thing," Curtis replied.

"Could you have him come here for a moment? I want to ask some questions, since he was actually there," Steven said, watching Curtis space out for a minute, probably mind-linking him instead of using his phone.

"He'll be here shortly, Alpha," Curtis said.

As the three waited for Rocky to arrive, they discussed their routine pack business: security, finances, and the emotional state of the pack. Alpha Steven knew all too well one bad egg would lead to more. In the past, he had to punish and kill a few pack members. Yes, kill, because sometimes banishment only leads to more problems. Steven was not a ruthless leader—just a smart one. With a knock, they stopped the routine talk, and Rocky entered.

"You needed to see me, sir?"

"Yes. Please sit. I wanted to go into more detail about last night's events," Steven said.

"What about it? I told you what happened. No offense, but I don't want to keep rehashing it."

"Rocky! That's no way to speak to your alpha," Curtis admonished. "If he wants you to keep explaining what happened, you will."

"It's all right, Curtis. I understand. I know he means no disrespect; I can feel he's just frustrated," Steven said soothingly.

"I'm sorry, sir. I'm frustrated. Seeing my best friend like that was troubling, especially since I didn't know how to help him."

"I didn't call you here to have another run though of the events. What I need to know is, when he started losing control, did you feel anything?"

"Besides freaked the fuck out? I don't recall. Why?"

"Did you feel like you were suffocating? Any urge to possibly kneel to him?" Steven asked.

"I could feel his rage and panic, like I was more connected to him. I could feel he didn't know what was going on either," Rocky said.

Alpha Steven didn't say anything, just leaned back in his chair and pondered, trying to piece everything together. *Let's see: Jake felt calm but powerless. Curtis felt a supernatural power surge. I felt something powerful was awakening. I'm trying to wrap my head around this. Something is on the tip of my tongue but buried in my brain.*

Steven slapped his forehead to wake his wolf, Sunka.

Sunny, wakey wakey.

Finally need me, Stevie? Sunka asked sarcastically, but playful.

Oh, are you cranky? Do you need a run?

I'm always up for a run, old man.

Do you feel something among us? I can't seem to figure it out.

Something is coming to life, an old power presence.

Do you know what that means?

No, but it's something that hasn't been around in a very long time. I can tell it's not a new power.

All right then, but you gave me an idea. Thank you. I'll grab Tess after this and let you run and have fun with your mate at the falls.

Addressing the men in the room, Steven said, "Sunka gave me an idea on where to start. He said it felt like an old power coming back to life."

"An old power? Like a legendary kind of power?" Jake asked.

"You're a fucking genius, Jake!" Steven exclaimed.

"Well, duh," Jake quipped, making the men laugh.

"Here's today's plan: Jake, you go to the alpha library to look for anything that might give us clues on the power. Curtis, you take over beta duties for the day, including meeting up with patrol members and keeping a close eye on things. Rocky, head to Zane's and wait for him to wake up, spend the day with him, and keep him calm. I promised Sunka I'd let him run with his mate for a little, then I have to make some phone calls and get Zane's mate here for his shift."

With all tasks assigned, Steven went to Tessa so they could spend some time together and their wolves before getting back to business.

Beta Jake headed to the pack vault, which holds the pack's most valuable assets and secrets in the underground floors of the pack house. The pack tracker, Evan, was very good at his job. He could find anything and anyone, and he was also like a lie detector. Steven used this information to avoid a lot of problems. Some packs have tried to extort Alpha Steven for money, information, or even land. He used what he must keep to peace, but he would get his hands dirty like everyone else. He hated it when things got messy.

Once Jake reached the vault, he sliced his hand, placed his bloody palm on the security pad, looked into the retinal scanner, and spoke his name and code word as calmly as possible. (The system detects distress and won't open the door.) All this security seems extreme, but it worked.)

Jake scanned all of Alpha's books. Some were journals passed down from alpha to alpha, and others looked like regular old books. He was uncertain where to start, until an old leather-bound book caught his eye: *Legends of the Luna*.

This has to have what I'm looking for: a legendary power. I don't know anyone more powerful than our Goddess Luna (Selene), Jake thought.

But the more Jake read, the more confused he got about Goddess Luna. This book alone had three different versions of three different mythologies. It's a good lesson to learn about how different people have different points of view on the same thing. However, the goddess could very well be a combination of all three.

After a few hours, Beta Jake had finished just that one book, but he read it in great detail and took notes along the way. He stood to stretch and leaned over the table to review his notes:

- Goddess Luna's parents were Titans. They were also brother and sister (gross), Hyperion and Eurphessa (Theia).
- Her bother Helios is the sun god; her sister Eos is the goddess of dawn.
- She was a lover of Zeus at one time but fell in love with a shepherd named Endymion. He was cast into an eternal sleep for several reasons. She visited him in his cave every night and bore him fifty daughters.
- Zeus turned Lycaon, the son of Pelasgus, and his sons into wolves as punishment. Their forms were known as Lycans.
- Selene possessed the power to create night creatures to watch over them in the night. She grew to enjoy the Lycan form, so she created werewolves. She gave some of her creations different abilities and powers.
- She also created vampires, witches, and something else that was blacked out in the book.
- The last beings she created had the most power of them all, and they were part of a prophecy.

Chapter 9: Prophecy

By about 1130 hours, Alpha Steven returned from his run and fun with his mate at the falls. They needed that time together. Everyone was still off doing the tasks they were told to do. He sat at his desk, leaned back in his chair, and sighed. His task to call Alpha Van Norris was now on his plate. He picked up his phone to make the call.

"Alpha Norris speaking."

"Good morning, Alpha Norris. It's Alpha Steven. How are you this morning?" Steven asked pleasantly.

"Cut to the chase, Steven. I'm a busy alpha. Is there a problem you're calling about?"

"No, sir. I wanted to invite the group that is supposed to visit my pack after school next weekend for a surprise birthday party. I figured since they were supposed to come here anyway, might as well do it when my entire pack is present during this party. Some of my of-age pack members will be leaving to find their mates as well," Steven said, then held his breath. There was a long pause after he finished speaking.

I don't know when Zane will shift, but if we don't get his mate here before his birthday, he might not survive. I hope his wolf waiting so long to surface doesn't kill him, Steven thought.

"That sounds reasonable, Steve. I'll send them in the pack plane after school lets out on Friday."

"No need, Alpha Van. I'll send our plane with escorts since it was a last-minute idea on my end."

"Fine. I'll let you know when they get here and leave," Van said through gritted teeth as he hung up the phone.

Steven sighed in relief and relaxed in his chair.

That went better than I thought. Van wasn't always a hard-ass jerk, but things change. People change. Steven's reverie was interrupted by a knock on his door. He knew who it was immediately with his advanced wolf senses of hearing and smell.

"Come in, Jake."

"I spent hours reading just one book called *Legends of the Luna*. There was so much information and different versions of who Luna is, but I took some notes that might be helpful," Jake said.

Beta Jake sat and gave Alpha Steven the rundown of his notes and explained the book and why he chose that one. Steven listened, thinking hard. His eyes widened when Jake mentioned the word "prophecy."

"Are you telling me after all this time I couldn't remember that we have prophecy scrolls?" Alpha Steven asked.

"Wait, we have prophecy scrolls? Thought those were just folklore?" Beta Jake asked.

"It's supposed to be known to alphas only. We're told about them once in a lifetime. Back to the vault, Jake. Let's go."

Steven and Jake entered the vault, and Steven paused to remember where the hidden vault was. Under the reading table. He pushed the table out of the way, formed his finger into a wolf claw, sliced his palm, and smeared blood around the floor to reveal a hidden witch spell. His father used it as a precaution. Moments later, a crescent moon illuminated one of the tiles. Steven opened it and took out the scrolls, which he and Jake carefully unrolled and started reading. Steven was on his third scroll before he found one that fit the situation. After reading the scroll intensely, he looked up from it and nudged Jake.

"I think I found something. It's called the Prophecy of the Lycan Reborn. It kind of fits some things you found earlier. After Zeus transformed Lycaon, Selene also fell in love with that form. She created other creatures of the night just like him, called them Lycans, gave them all of the abilities and powers she could imagine, and called them the "protectors of the night creatures." But they went rogue on them. They began to resent their duty protecting the "lesser" creatures. Selena didn't give the Lycans mates to love and cherish like all her others. She didn't want them distracted from their duties. However, they started stealing mates of others to try and have them be loved. Wars began, but the Lycans were unstoppable.

"Selene couldn't handle watching her creations that she loved so much killing one another at an alarming rate," Steven continued. "She intervened, stripped the Lycan souls from their human forms, and took them back home, in hopes of nurturing the Lycan souls back to peace. She left them to live out their lives as humans. She did make a promise though: When a divine love produces their first heir, he'll be blessed with a *Lycan* wolf. By his eighteenth birthday, on the day a True-Blue Moon of the spring solstice, the full powers of a Lycan will be reborn. If he's surrounded by love from a mate and true friends, he'll become my most true and powerful watcher."

"Oh my god, Steven! Zane is a Lycan! That means Evan and Trudy's mate bond is severed. What the hell is going on?" Jake exclaimed.

"We knew Evan and Trudy had a rough start. Evan is the reason why I made rules on pre-mating sexual relationships when I took over as alpha. Let's reconvene after lunch. I'm starving."

They headed to the pack dining hall on the main floor of the pack house to enjoy Trudy's food. The pack house is a mansion-size building that holds werewolves and their families if they don't want a separate home on pack lands. Humans would see this as a gated type of community or cult type area. *How does Evan stay so thin and fit?* Steven wondered. They chowed down because research is tiring. They had casual conversations with all the hard-working members of the pack. They saw Evan and Trudy and told them to go to the alpha's office when lunch was over.

Steven saw his mate, Tessa, standing in the kitchen next to Trudy. He slowly snaked his arms around her and whispered, "I had a wonderful time this morning." He felt her heart race and saw her blush. *After all these years, I can still embarrass her.*

"Oh, Steve, stop it. Everyone is here," Tessa said.

"I'll never stop, my love. I'll make you scream my name for all the pack to hear. Let them know what their alpha is still capable of."

"You wouldn't dare!"

"You know I will, love; you know I will." Steven said with a kiss, then headed back to his office. He left his door open because all he was doing was boring paperwork. He was getting caught up—with only pack transfers to deal with. Unfortunately, they take a long time because he researched everyone he didn't know personally. If a pack member requested a transfer out of the pack, he met with them to discuss why. If they don't like something about the pack, then Steven needs to make changes. He got through a few of those when Evan and Trudy walked in.

"Have a seat and let me get Beta Jake and Delta Curtis in here before we get down to business," Steven said, gesturing toward the chairs.

"Is there something wrong, Alpha? Did I do something wrong? I'll take full respon..." stammered Evan.

"Good grief, Evan, relax. We learned something about your son's...wolf."

A few minutes later, Jake and Curtis entered the office.

"Close the door please," Steven said before they sat, then turned to Evan and Trudy. "Do you have your true mate bond?"

Evan and Trudy looked at each other nervously.

"We feel we still have *a* bond, but our *true mate* bond was destroyed long ago because someone couldn't keep it in his fucking pants!" Trudy fumed with anger that had been simmering for years. Evan looked panicked, like a fish out of water.

Steven raised his hand up to let Evan know to let his mate vent. He could feel her wolf surfacing. They both needed it. Steven let her continue.

"I love him, Alpha Steven, so much that I let his indiscretions go because for what it was worth, he came to me in the end. But that witch bitch came to my home after he ended it and tried to break our mate bond with her magic so he would go back to her. She blew powder in my face and chanted something, and I felt our bond snap. I still have a lingering feeling of love, so I know it's not completely gone."

Steven let the couple calm down before he broke the news to them about the prophecy. Truthfully, he needed more time because it was weird for him to say it aloud: Zane is a Lycan.

Chapter 10: Aftermath

"Earth to Val," Bluey said.

"Yeah," said Valerie, still holding the cellphone in her right hand.

"Are you okay?"

"Is saying that call was nuts to much of an understatement?"

"Girl, hell no, that was completely crazy. I think your mate already loves you. He went totally bat shit, from the sounds of it."

"What are we going to do?"

"I wanted to ask your cousin when we got to his pack and hadn't found our mates yet if he could find a few people to pretend to be our mates, but it looks like you already found yours," Bluey said with the biggest grin on her face imaginable.

Since he's my cousin's best friend, he could be of high rank. That would surely prove to my father that I'm worthy of something in his eyes. If our goddess blesses me with a high rank, that means she thinks I'm worthy, so he should too, Valerie thought. This impressed her wolf, Iggy, very much. *I pray Bluey finds her mate in the same pack, so we can finally get the hell out of here— together.*

After all of the excitement, Valerie and Bluey were both extremely tired, so they cuddled up together and slept. Valerie fell asleep with questions about Zane tumbling in her mind.

The next morning before school, the girls were rudely awakened by cat calls from the two they have grown to love but despise.

"Well look what we have here, Ricky," Roman said, standing beside Ricky in Bluey's doorway.

"Go away! This is our safe space. You aren't allowed to come in here," Valerie hollered at them.

"We aren't in her *room;* we're in the *doorway,* "Roman `replied cockily. "If I didn't know better, Ricky, I'd say they were already trying to give each *other* the pleasures we're going to receive."

"Maybe we should watch next time, eh Roman?" Ricky responded.

"Oh, for fuck sakes, get the hell OUT!" Valerie screamed.

"Get the fuck out of here!" Bluey finally said, her wolf coming to the surface. She flew up out of bed and slammed the door in their faces. Turning to Valerie, she asked, "What the hell is with wrong with those two lately? They're beyond disgusting anymore."

"Who the fuck knows what has gotten into them. Now I'm scared to go to my room and get ready for school."

"I have clothes of yours here, remember?" Bluey said comfortingly.

A few hours later, Bluey sat in class waiting for lunch. Val's brother sat, staring at her. She knew he wanted her as he had expressed this many times. She knew he was disappointed when they weren't mates. Val on the other hand, was relieved, not that he wasn't attractive, because he is, but he no longer treats women with respect.

He thinks we should all bow down to him, just like my brother. He probably will get an alpha daughter anyway because he's a strong beta. I'll get a strong mate regardless of rank because I'm an alpha's daughter. I just wanted to be treated with respect. I don't care what rank he is.

Valerie was still stuck in her own thoughts when the bell rang. She was slow to leave because she wanted Ricky gone before she even got up, lacking the strength to deal with him right now. To her luck he came to ruin the day.

"Hey, my blue-eyed beauty," Ricky crooned.

"What do you want, Ricky?" Bluey asked, with as much venom as she could muster.

"Me, you after school, you know, might as will break you in before the trip, right?"

"What the fuck is wrong with you! I'm saving myself for my mate!" Bluey said, slapped him hard, and ran. She didn't bother going to lunch at that point. She mind-linked Val to tell her she was going home and that she left Valerie her car. She threw her stuff in the car and headed to the woods.

Thalass "Sassie," Bluey's wolf, had been on edge since the phone call. She needed to be let out before the kids trained after school. Bluey's wolf is beautiful, strong, and fierce, larger than normal because of her alpha blood. She's white with silver-gray tipped fur that shimmers blue like water when she moves.

Bluey waited to shift until she got into the woods between school and the pack house. She didn't bother stripping before shifting because she had plenty of clothes. Once she started shifting, Bluey took a backseat in her mind and gave her wolf the wheels. She let her run and not invade her thoughts, even though they're one in the same. She ended up going to her favorite thinking spot by the creek. She got a drink, then hopped in.

"Sassie?"

"Yes, Althea?" Bluey's wolf refused to call her Blue or Bluey like everyone else.

"Penny for your thoughts?"

"You can obviously read them. Why would you ask?"

"I can't always, and sometimes I don't want to. I love you enough to give you privacy even in our mind."

"Fine. I'm thinking about our mate, this situation. You know I could rip Ricky apart for you and get rid of at least one problem. I sense something isn't right with him anymore."

"Don't I know it, but that would cause problems. Val would hate us for killing her brother. Don't worry. Once we get to talk to Val's cousin again, I think he'll help us. I can feel it."

"Not to mention he sounds smokin' hot too," Sassie chimed in with a purr.

"He did indeed. I'll convince Val to talk to him after training and ask him to at least help me out, since Val knows she has a mate."

"I can't believe your father would put us in this situation."

"I know, but he hasn't been himself in years. All he wants is our obedience."

"We'll fight together, Althea. You're strong, I'm strong, and we're unstoppable together."

"Yes, we are Sassie. I love you. Let's go home, take a nap, and wait for Val to get home."

Bluey headed back to the pack house, showered, grabbed a small package of cookies, and laid down to wait for Val.

Zane was finally calm after last night—calm, but bored. He could only play video games for so long. He decided to hop in the tub to relax.

He started getting that antsy feeling again, and Valerie's beautiful face was front and center. *At least I now have a name to put to her face.* He lit the candles his mom gave him, got into the tub, and let Valerie consume his mind. *She's so beautiful.*

Zane imagined touching her silky, soft skin and gorgeous, red hair. Closing his eyes, he rubbed the cool surface of the tub with one hand and grabbed himself with the other. He chanted her name and imagined his hands touching her face, cupping her cheek, and running his other hand down her back. Stroking himself, he went in for the kiss...

Bang, bang, bang came a pounding at the door, jolting Zane out of my fantasy so fast he slammed his upper body up, out, and over the tub, and his stomach slammed into the side. Hanging halfway in and out of the tub and on the floor, "Son of a bitch!" was all that came out of him. He scrambled to the door, not bothering with a towel, yanked it opened, and screamed, "*What?!*"

"Fantasizing again, are we?" Rocky smirked.

"My wolf won't let me not. When I'm alone, I can't help it."

"It's okay, man. Just get dressed. We need to talk."

Zane quickly dressed, sat in his gaming chair, and asked, "You were at the alpha's office for a bit—was it about me?"

"Well, of course, we talked about you—my dad, the alpha, the beta, and me. They asked a few questions, like did I feel I had to bow to you at the time. From what I gather, they all felt some sort of power shift, and they think it came from you."

"Why the hell would you bow to me? *I* should bow to *you* if anything."

"I don't know. What do you want to do today?"

"I'm feeling stir crazy. Let's go work out."

"Okay, let's do some warrior training," Rocky suggested.

The friends went to the training grounds toward the outskirts of the southern border of the pack territory line, and Zane was pumped for the warrior training. All he knew was some self-defense and gun training—the rest was about using his senses because of his tracking abilities. Rocky started him off with his warrior training warmups.

"All right, buddy. Let's start off by doing as many push-ups as you can."

"It won't be many. Look at these scrawny arms." Zane held his arm next to Rocky's in comparison.

"Oh, I know," Rocky chuckled. "But I want to see if the alpha and the others were right about you having old power." Rocky dropped into the push-up position next to Zane, and they both were keeping pace with each other—something Zane hadn't previously been able to do. After a few dozen push-ups, Zane started breaking a sweat, while Rocky still looked at ease. Zane felt good to be doing this with his best friend.

In general, wolves are much stronger than humans. However, they don't show it so as not to give away what they are. After about the 200-push-up mark, Zane collapsed with spaghetti arms. Rocky still hasn't broken a sweat yet and pumped out fifty more for good measure.

"Hey, you did better than I thought. You're getting stronger," Rocky said, patting Zane on the back. Zane noticed the hit didn't hurt like it usually would. "Now let's run the perimeter a few times, then do some hand-to-hand combat."

"Run the perimeter a few times? What are you—a robot under that skin?" Zane panted.

Rocky looked at Zane with seriousness in the eyes. "No. I'm an animal." Then he wiggled his eyebrows.

What did I get myself into? Zane thought, taking off jogging and hoping he didn't die with all this unusual exercise.

Rocky set off behind Zane in an easy jog.

Rocky, when do I get to run? asked Rocky's wolf, Carrick, "Rick" for short.

At training later on with the other guys. What's up with you, Rick? You have been quiet lately.

Just hanging out back here, letting you do what you do. Can we talk while you run?

You can talk to me anytime.

Do you remember the call during the fiasco?

Last night was crazy, but yeah Val called.

But there was another girl on the phone too.

That was her best friend, Althea, Bluey they call her, the alpha's daughter.

Oh, an alpha's daughter. Okay, never mind.

Why are you asking about her? Rocky asked.

Her voice perked me up when I heard her. I don't know how to explain it. But she's an alpha's daughter.

Her voice was lovely, and you never know, pal. Zane has a beta's daughter for a mate, and he's a tracker.

I hope we get to meet her in person, so we can find out if her wolf calls me.

All we can do is ask our Moon Goddess to pair us with a loving mate, Rocky said.

True, my friend, true. Do you realize Zane isn't getting a wolf?

Of course, he is! Humans don't roar like he did, Rick.

You do know the goddess gave us more than just strength, right?

Yea, we also have awesome looks and the best of friends anyone can ask for.

He's powerful, Rocky. Tap into your senses. You felt his rage. Just think, Rocky.

Carrick ended the conversation. Rocky had fallen far behind Zane during their wolf talk, so he ran to catch up.

"How are you feeling so far? We're almost already done with lap one," Rocky said.

"I feel pretty good actually. Want to race?"

Rocky took that as a challenge, and he booked it, leaving Zane behind.

"Hey, you cheated!" Zane called.

Rocky laughed as he crossed their starting line. Zane started to pass him for lap two, so Rocky stopped with, "Hey! Let's do combat skills now."

"Are you afraid I'll win a fair race?"

"Not at all, bro. I'm just a bit distracted and want to throw punches."

Rocky started the skills training with what Zane already knew, then kicked it up a notch. A few hours later, they headed back to the pack house for lunch and rest. Zane passed out on the couch and Rocky the recliner. A few hours later, Rocky was woken up by his phone. A quick glance told him Val was calling.

"What's up, Val? Everything okay?" Rocky answered groggily.

"I wanted to talk to you about a few things. Do you have time?"

"Yeah, give me a moment so I can go talk in private. Zane passed out on the couch. He isn't used to the training I put him through today. Alright, what's up?"

"I want to understand why me talking to him calmed him down. Bluey thinks he's my mate."

"I think you're his mate too."

"How can you say that? You can't tell if someone is your mate without meeting them. Our wolves have to connect in person."

"There's no other explanation, Val. Between talking and his mom's candles of your scent, he calmed down."

"This is confusing. Can you tell me anything about him?"

"What do you want to know?"

"Can you send me a picture? What's his rank? Is he a good man?"

"Hold on," Rocky said while he took a picture of Zane sleeping on the couch. *Why would she care what rank he is?* Then it clicks: *She's a beta's daughter, and her father sucks. I hope she gives Zane a chance.* Rocky sent her the picture of Zane sleeping and a few others he had of them being goofy, then waited for a reply.

"Awww! He's adorable. He looks so thin compared to you."

"Well, he's a tracker—a great one at that, so he hasn't bulked up. As you know, they're sleeker for the sneak-in, sneak-out operations."

"He's only a tracker? Seriously? You guys think he's my mate? I'm a beta's daughter."

"Look, Val. He's the most compassionate, strong-willed person I know. I might be friends with the alpha and beta, but I'm his best friend for who he is, not for his rank."

Val was silent, then Rocky broke the silence. "Why did you call that night anyway?"

"We wanted to ask you to pretend to be our mates once we arrived at your pack."

"You seem to already have a mate, so no pretending on your end. As for your friend, I'll protect her while you're here. You have my word."

They ended the call, and Rocky made himself and Zane more food. *He'll probably be hungry again when he gets up. At least it's the weekend now. Worrying about him until his wolf breaks free is a different story.*

Chapter 12: News

After getting off the phone with Rocky, Valerie went to her room to think. Consumed by her thoughts, she began to cry. She worked so hard to be strong; she felt like she deserved more, yet she felt selfish about those thoughts. *Rocky said he's a good man, compassionate. He just isn't strong. He's adorable, but I can tell he doesn't have much strength. I don't have many muscles, but I'm strong. It's important for me to feel like I'm not the only one able to take care of my future pups.*

Deep in thought, Val headed to the kitchen. As she thought some more, she started wallowing in self-pity. *He said Zane got worked up hearing what I was ordered to do, but why? How can someone get that worked up over someone they've never met? Bluey and Rocky think he's my mate, but he doesn't even have his wolf yet.*

Val mind-linked Bluey. *Hey, bestie, how are you?*

Bluey replied with such hatred, *I fucking hate our brothers my father, and this god-forsaken pack!*

Where are you?

My room."

Val grabbed some snacks and drinks and headed to her room. Without a word, she emptied her hands on the bed and hugged Bluey. After the friends hugged for a while, Bluey let go and grabbed some of the snacks Val brought up, then she said, "Your brother keeps trying to get me to give myself to him. I can't deal with this anymore. Not to mention my father telling us we basically have to be whores to our brothers; things have just gotten worse. I won't let him touch me, Val. I'm only for my mate. I'll let Sassie out if I have to. Why can't we just be loved and respected? We work so damn hard, for what? For fucking nothing, that's what. I wish we could just leave and never come back. Maybe someone will put my father in his place. My mother doesn't even talk to me. What kind of mother does that, what kind of Luna is she? A shit show that's all. She's so beautiful this and that. I get my looks from her, blah, blah, blah. But she's a shitty Luna to sit there and ignore her own daughter and treat others better and look at my father with love. How can she love that monster?"

Val sat and let her friend rant and cry. *She needs a chance to work through things, and I'll be here for her.* Bluey laid her head on Val's lap, and Val soothed her by running her fingers through her hair. *I know she loves this. At this rate people probably think we're lovers, but we don't care. We're more than sisters.* Bluey calmed down and fell asleep, then so did Val.

A few hours later, the girls slowly got up from their nap to see their brothers standing in the doorway again. Val no longer saw Roman as a sex symbol.

"You're the creepiest brothers us girls could ever ask for," Bluey said with disgust.

"Dad wants us in his office," Roman replied, with a creepy smile toward Val.

The four headed to Alpha Van's office.

Alpha Van got right to the point, "Alright, guys, here's the deal. I got a call from Alpha Steven of the Silver Stone Pack. He's throwing a big birthday party next weekend, and you're going to his pack to look for your mates. Apparently, not all of his pack will be there when you were scheduled to visit this summer. While you're there, you're allowed to explore and sniff out your mates if they're there. Remember your duties to this pack: They're peaceful, but powerful. Let's keep the peace. Dismissed."

Bluey and Val practically ran out of the office and up to Val's room, where this time they shut and locked the door. Like little schoolgirls, they grabbed hands and twirled with happiness.

"Oh, my goodness, we get to leave here next weekend! This is exciting, Val. You get to meet your mate, and I get to see you happy," Bluey screeched with excitement.

"Yeah, that's great," Val muttered, excited, but not as much as Bluey.

"I thought you'd be happy about this. Now we don't have to wait until school is over."

"I'm too nervous to be excited. I talked to Rocky again today and asked about his friend. Zane is only a tracker. I'm a beta. Why would I get a tracker for a mate? The goddess must hate me." Val showed Bluey Zane's pictures.

"Awww he's adorable. You guys will make the cutest babies. Come on, why is rank so important?"

"Rocky said he's a great guy, but as you can see, he's scrawny. I worked so hard to learn how to fight, and it looks like I'll have to protect him too. How can I have pups if I'll have to do all the protecting?"

"*Valerie O'Reilly!* You listen to me and listen good! As your best friend, I want to slap the shit out of you right now. That man went all hulk just hearing about what my father wants us to do, and he hasn't even met you yet. He might look weak now, but he hasn't gotten his wolf. His wolf wanted out to kill, Val—kill for you before his time to be here. Now you actually get to be with him and help him through his first shift. Not many mates get to do that. He's only turning eighteen. Give him a fighting chance. Your rank is not who you are. Your father treats you like shit. Why would you care so much about what he thinks of your mate? My father treats me like shit too. I don't care what he thinks of my mate. Whether I get an alpha mate or not, I just want to be loved."

Val hang her head in shame. *Her opinion of me matters so much. I can't stand to hear the anger coming from her.* She tried to defend herself. "How am I supposed to face my father with a tracker mate? He already thinks so little of me because I'm the runt. I'll never hear the end of it. All I ever wanted was to be loved by him and have him care. If I'd have been worthy of a higher-ranking wolf, it would make him see me in a different light. I guess I'm not worthy in the Moon Goddess's eyes." Val felt so defeated she started to cry.

"You think you're not worthy in the Moon Goddess's eyes?" Bluey looked at Val with tears in her eyes. "I can't believe that for one second. She might have given you him as a mate for a far greater purpose then you think. Please just give him a chance and don't give your father any thoughts when it comes to you and your mate. Okay? Now let's go get dinner with our heads held high. Remember they have no idea you have a mate. Let's keep it that way."

That night, the girls slept in Val's room with the door locked. As Val fell into a deep sleep, she felt like she was being whisked away to a peaceful place.

Valerie... Valerie...

"*I wanted to come to you before you met your mate,*" *a dreamy and angelic voice pulled her into a deeper sleep.* "*Althea is right, Valerie. Zane is your mate for a greater purpose than just making pups. I chose you for him because you're strong-willed and will challenge him.*

He'll need you for what's to come.

He'll doubt himself.

He'll fight who he's meant to be.

What he's becoming is going to be a great challenge for all.

He knows happiness and love.

That is why I chose him for you.

Don't fight what's meant to be.

You both will love one another for eternity.

The next morning, Valerie had a chat with her wolf, Iggy.

Iggy?

Good morning, Val.

You're awfully chipper this morning. Did you have the same dream I had?

Yes. The Moon Goddess paid us a visit last night. She told me some things I have to be prepared for.

Like what, Iggy? She didn't warn me about anything.

I can't tell you. It's for you to figure out, but I'll be here to help you when the time comes. Your human side has things to do on its own to become stronger than you already are. This is why you were chosen, why we were chosen. As your wolf soul, I have a vital part in what's to come. We'll get through this together. Just make the right choices.

Iggy...Iggy!

But Iggy had retreated back. Val could sense her mind going a mile a minute, just like hers.

Chapter 13: Before Birthday Jitters

After everything that had happened with Zane, Alpha Steven had a sit-down with everyone involved and explained he believed Zane was getting a Lycan instead of a wolf. He explained about the prophecy and how it all fit together. Alpha commanded that while they all wait for Zane's shift, they were to keep their mouths shut and go about their normal lives until his birthday.

Rocky stayed by Zane's side as much as possible, even started him on warrior training. Rocky learned that Zane was getting faster and stronger than he had ever been. Rocky was excited about Zane's birthday because he and the other guys pitched in to buy Zane a used SUV. Plus, he knew Zane would be shifting and Valerie would be visiting. That was the best kept secret to keep.

All week, Valerie and Bluey secretly prepared for their visit to the Sliver Stone Pack. They avoided their brothers like the plague. They slowly packed items they couldn't bear to be without, which wasn't much because they weren't materialistic girls. They also figured they could get after-school jobs in the nearby city to make money and buy what else they needed. Their brothers kept their distance for most of the week.

On Friday, departure day, Bluey sat in class. *The anticipation is killing me. I can't wait to get out of here, but I can't jeopardize this trip. I hope Val's cousin comes through for me. I never want to come back to this hell. I can't concentrate worth a damn. At least I'll be with Val for the rest of the day after lunch.*

Lunch finally arrived, and the friends went to their alone spot for privacy.

"You're awfully quiet, Val. What's up?"

"I'm just thinking about my uncle. I haven't seen him in years because of my father. What happens if he's disappointed with me too? Like I'm a disgrace to the family?"

"Would you stop that! He's literally coming with Zane's father for crying out loud."

After a lovely week without having to deal with their brothers, Ricky and Roman plopped down in front of the girls.

"Hey, sis. What's shakin'?" Roman asked.

Bluey looked at him puzzled. *He hardly socializes with us, and he's never happy to see me. What's going on in that sick, twisted mind of his?*

"What do you want? We're eating, trying not to get sick from your presence."

"Ouch, that really hurts, sis. Can't I just come over and sit with you?" Roman asked.

"No," Bluey stated flatly.

"Fine. I just came over to remind you both of your duties since we're leaving tonight."

"And there it is. Roman, you and Ricky make us sick. Leave us alone."

"Whatever you say, Althea. I know Val here is looking forward to it," Roman said, then he and Ricky walked away.

Fuckin' evil prick, always thinking about getting his dick wet, Bluey thought, then looked over to see Val smirking. "Why are you smirking?"

"Because that bastard thinks we're going through with this!" Val answered, laughing,

Once school was out, the girls headed home, grabbed their luggage, put it in the garage, and waited to be taken to the airport. In the meantime, Bluey asked, "How do you feel about maybe meeting your mate soon?"

"Maybe, maybe not. I'm nervous regardless. So, we'll see what happens. Yes?"

"Here they come. Let's get a move on," Bluey said, as Val's father pulled up in the car to drive them to the airport.

The car ride to the airport was silent. The friends surmised two guys they didn't know must be their escorts from Silver Stone Pack. *One of them must be my uncle,* Val thought. *How bad is it when you don't know who your own family is?*

Once they arrived at the airport and got out of the car, Alpha Van walked up to one of the men with a smile. They started chit-chatting like they were best friends.

Val was caught off guard when one of the men said, "You must be Valerie. I'm Evander, Zane's father, but you can call me Evan." He stuck his hand out to shake, and Val shook it.

"Hello, sir, you can call me Val. This here is Althea Norris, the alpha's daughter."

Bluey went right in for a hug. "You can call me Bluey or Al or Althea. It doesn't really matter. We're so grateful you're here." She pointed to their brothers. "These two boneheads are our brothers, Roman and Ricky."

"I've met them before. How are you boys doing?" Evan asked, shaking their hands. "Go say bye to your father so we can get going."

"Not necessary. Let's go." Val grabbed Bluey's hand and ran up the plane's stairs.

Once they were all settled and safely in the air, Val's uncle came over and sat by her.

"It's been a long time, Val. How are you?" Curtis asked.

"It has been way too long. I hate to admit it, but I didn't even remember who you were."

"I know. I'm sorry. When we get to my house, we can talk a little, then get some sleep."

"I get to stay at your place, not the pack guest rooms?" Val asked.

"My alpha knows we have been apart way too long. He agreed it would be better if you stayed with family. Even though your brother is family too we thought it best to put you with me."

"Can Bluey stay with me? I'd rather keep her close if that's okay."

With a big smile and a hug to follow, Curtis said, "Of course, she can. You can sleep in Rocky's room, and she can have the guest room."

That same day, Friday, was the day before Zane's birthday. He had left school early because he'd been feeling edgy again. He figured he'd work off that feeling with a run. On lap two of his perimeter run, Zane still hadn't broken a sweat. He heard someone about 200 yards behind him. A quick glance back, Zane spotted the alpha. *He'll catch up to me in about twenty seconds. He's very fast and strong. Guess that's why he's our alpha.*

"Do you mind if I join you?" Alpha Steven asked.

"Of course not, Alpha."

"How are you feeling today?"

"I was feeling quite edgy, so I left school and figured a long run would cure that. It feels like a different kind of edgy than what I've been feeling lately."

"Different how?"

"My mind is racing again. I feel stronger, and my senses are more alert that usual."

"Well, son, your body is adjusting later in your teens than most. You could be feeling that; however, I said last week with the prophecy, I believe you're a Lycan not a wolf. You'll be the first since our Luna took them away because they couldn't handle the power. She has the power to create beings like us and other creatures, and she can give us soulmates to control our beasts. She also has the power to take away, but we all have free will and won't interfere unless necessary. She wanted all her other creations protected but didn't give them mates like her others."

"That's overwhelming. Why me? Can I ask you a favor?"

"I'll do what I can, but no promises."

"When I shift, if it starts to go wrong and I seem like a threat to anyone, can you kill me? I will ask Rocky too. I don't want to hurt anyone."

"Zane, you need to understand that shifting for every wolf is scary. Getting a Lycan is even scarier, but guess what? We're not scared of you nor what you might be becoming. We're concerned for you. You have too much compassion to hurt anyone. We only know about Lycans from what was written, but our goddess wouldn't have brought them back if she thought you were going to be how they were. Also, she's given you a mate, which she didn't do for Lycans before. As a man and a beast myself, I know that we need another half to reel in both the man and the beast. We have two souls, but we're indeed one."

Chapter 14: The Departure

After Valerie was done talking to her uncle, she got up and stretched. She walked around the small private plane, then saw the bathroom and decided to splash water on her face to freshen up a bit. When she got out, Roman was standing right in front of her, blocking her exit.

"I can make your first-time part of the mile-high club," he said, trying to be seductive.

"Can you not right now? My uncle is right…"

"Behind you, boy," Curtis cut Valerie off gruffly. "I suggest you go sit back down before the first place you visit in my pack is our dungeon."

Before Roman went to sit back down, he gave Val a glare that said, "This isn't over."

Once his back was turned, Val mouthed "thank you" to her Uncle Curtis, who nodded. Val went back to her seat and looked out the window at the moon, which looked so touchable from there. *It's big, bright, and beautiful, and it feels like it is staring at me. That makes me feel safe.* Val remembered the dream she had, which Iggy said was a visit from the goddess. She leaned her head against the window and started drifting off to sleep.

Then Bluey shook her awake, "Get up, Val. We've landed. We have about another hour's drive to their pack."

Outside the plane, Valerie saw two cars waiting to drive them to the pack. Roman and Ricky went with Uncle Curtis, and Valerie and Bluey went with Evan. Val was too excited now to sleep.

"So, Evan how did you get stuck driving us?" was her opening question.

"We figured since Curtis is the enforcer, he should drive your brothers in case they get out of hand. I'm just a tracker. I've been taught how to fight yes, but I don't have the muscle—just the speed."

With a smirk Bluey asked, "Are you sure it's not because Val here is your daughter-in-law?"

Evan smiled, "Oh, is she now? I didn't even realize."

"I assume you know everything then?" Val asked, deciding to change the subject.

"I do. That's why Alpha Steven insisted Curtis and I come get you, so you have escorts to protect you."

"Thank you so much. We're so grateful. I can't imagine what the flight would have been like if you hadn't been there."

"I think Val and I'd have unleashed our wolves on our brothers. We're beyond sick and tired of their sexual advances."

"You're both safe now. Rest assured. We, as in the entire pack, don't stand for that bullshit. Pardon my French, ladies, but that shit is infuriating. Even if you weren't my son's mate, Val."

"Thanks again."

"Does Zane know she's coming?" Bluey asked.

"Nope, didn't want to ruin a great surprise. He's going to love you, Val. He dreamed about you, before he even knew you were actually a real she-wolf."

"I'm nothing special, just the Beta runt," Val said humbly.

Bluey slapped her on the shoulder, and Val yelped, "Son of bitch, Bluey. What was that for?"

"Say stupid things; win stupid prizes."

The trio talked about random things for the rest of the drive to their pack, such as how things run, whether or not they're accepting of outsiders, jobs, and school. The time passed quickly, and before they knew it, Evan was pulling up in front of Curtis's home.

"Here we are, ladies," Evan said, helping them with their bags. "I was told to tell you if you need anything wake up your Aunt Blaze. Go explore and get some sleep. Curtis is dropping your brothers off at the pack house, and he'll be here in a little bit. It was a pleasure meeting you and being your escort here."

At the same time, Val and Bluey said, "I'm starving," giving everyone a much-needed laugh, then, "Great minds think alike." Then everyone roared with laughter. Val grabbed Bluey's hand, and they sniffed their way to the kitchen. While the girls peeked in cabinets and the fridge, they were startled by a "Why hello, girls." Val's Aunt Blaze gave both girls a warm loving, hug. She had the most awesome features either girl had ever seen—like opposite highlights. She had sharp cheek bones and dirty blond hair with reddish-black streaks but otherwise boyish features like broad shoulders. *Perfect fit for my uncle. I haven't had a hug like that in a long time from my mom,* Val thought. *I feel loved by someone other than Bluey. It's nice.*

"We're sorry for waking you, but we're starving," Val said.

"It's quite all right, girls. I was waiting up for Curtis, and I heard Evan bring you in. Curtis will be hungry anyway. Let me whip up a midnight snack."

"You don't have to do that," Val protested.

"Nonsense! You came along way, and besides you'll sleep better on a full belly."

"Your home is beautiful, and it smells fantastic," Bluey said.

"Thank you, dear, but I haven't started cooking yet. What do you smell?"

"Pine and lavender. It's simply amazing."

"That's interesting, dear, very interesting. Are you the alpha's daughter?"

"Yes, ma'am. I am," Bluey said.

With a very big smile, Blaze said, "That's riveting, and none of that ma'am business. Now how about some greasy cheesy goodness before bed?" She started making cheesy bacon burgers. It might be too much for a human midnight snack, but for werewolves, it's perfect because their metabolisms are much faster.

Not long after Blaze started cooking, Curtis came into the room. "Why hello, lovely ladies. Having a midnight snack?" He veered right to his mate and dipped her in a deep kiss. Bluey and Val said, "Aww."

"I love you too. Now get off me before you don't get any," Blaze joked.

"Yes, dear. So, girls, are you excited to meet everyone tomorrow?" Curtis asked.

"I'm more excited to see Val's reaction tomorrow," Bluey said, wiggling her eyebrows.

Blaze filled plates with the burgers and some sides, then handed a plate to each of them. Val and Bluey shoveled down the greasy meaty goodness, helped clean up, then followed Blaze upstairs to their rooms for the night—Val in Rocky's room on the right, and Val's on the left. However...

"Oh my gosh, there's that aroma. Switch rooms with me, Val." Bluey said, sniffing the air.

Val beamed, "Of course," and the friends went their separate ways for the night.

The next morning, when Bluey woke, she realized, *I haven't slept that well in a long time. I must have been exhausted.* Her nose smelled food, and her stomach grumbled on cue. She followed her nose downstairs, where she saw Val and her family sitting at the table already eating, "Good morning, everyone," Bluey said.

Val smiled wide, "Good morning, sunshine. Slept well, I presume?"

"Yes, I did. Why are you looking at me like that? Is my bedhead out of control?" Bluey asked because her long, almost white, blond hair looked like it got zapped by electricity.

"Well, of course, it is, but it's a lovely look on you. Sit, eat, talk. I'm going to shower," Val said.

"So, Althea, would you like to become part of this pack, since Val found her mate, and we know how much you hate your pack right now?" Curtis asked. He only asked because his mate, Blaze, told him about Bluey's reaction to Rocky's smell.

"Hell yes, but how can I stay here? I don't have a mate here like Val does."

"Deary, Alpha Steven has his ways," Blaze said mysteriously.

Bluey wasn't awake enough yet to figure out what they were hinting at. She ate and waited her turn for the shower.

"So, when do we get to go to Zane's party? I'm dying with anticipation," Bluey asked.

"We're going to leave soon to help set up the party in his backyard. His birthday party will be a small celebration, and the pack barbecue will be tonight, I believe," Blaze explained.

About an hour later, everyone was ready to go. They stopped at the pack house for party supplies, and then headed to Zane's.

After waking up to go on a run with Zane, Rocky decided to take a shower in his own house, and the friends parted ways until about 1600. Rocky also wanted to take a nap before the birthday celebrations. *We don't really know what will happen when he shifts tonight.*

When Rocky entered his house, he smelled a fresh ocean breeze. *It smells like heaven. Wonder if my mom got some new candles from Trudy.* Rocky headed to his room to grab clothes for after his shower, when *bam! The scent is even stronger in here.* Rocky mind-linked his dad:

Son, are you okay?

I'm not sure. Who slept in my room?

A couple of people who needed our help. Since you were at Zane's, didn't think you'd mind. Is there a problem?

Rocky heard a smirk with each word. *Is there something you're not telling me, Dad?*

You'll figure it out soon enough, son, soon enough.

Rocky shut off the mind-link, grabbed his clothes, and showered, with Rick panting in the back of his mind. Rocky ignored him, got out of the shower, and took a nap.

Chapter 15: First Sight

As Blaze, Curtis, Bluey, and Valerie headed out of the pack house and toward Zane's, Valerie started getting really nervous—so bad she wanted to throw up. Bluey and Blaze seemed to be hitting it off, chit-chatting away as Val stewed in her bundle of nerves. Aunt Blaze led the girls to the backyard, where they saw an array of decorations, and a man lifting a woman to hang some streamers. Blaze went over to a table and dropped off a box that she brought from home and waved the girls over to do the same. Blaze whispered something to Bluey, who grinned from ear to ear. Then Blaze walked over to the man and woman and started talking.

Val's back was turned at this point. A slight breeze shifted, and she got a whiff of the delightful smell of a fresh forest after it rained. It made her want to drool. She stuck her nose out and into the breeze, and it made her spin around. She locked eyes with the man who was helping the woman.

Val's wolf, Iggy, bounced around, thinking, *Mate, mate, mate.* It felt like everything was going in slow motion, and being hypnotized by his eyes didn't help matters. Bluey gave Val a slight shove toward Zane. Val probably would have been stuck if she hadn't. His eyes were green with a slight shine.

Val didn't feel her legs moving, but she saw him coming closer. She inhaled deeply, and her nerves slowly calmed. Once they were face to face, well face to chest because Zane was so tall, Val looked up and saw his eyes. *They're so green! They can't be real.* In his eyes, Val saw love, admiration, and astonishment.

Zane slowly cupped the back of Val's head like she was in a dream and kissed her. It was her first kiss. *I feel like I'm floating. I never want to stop.* Then Zane released Val, both of them out of breath.

"Hi, beautiful," Zane said, making Val blush.

I never see her blush, thought Bluey, watching from across the grass. *I knew she would come around and put all her fears behind her once she met him. I'm so damn happy right now I could burst.* Bluey had recorded the meeting with her phone. *Such an amazing moment, but I had to give her a push to get her moving. I saw his mom had to do the same. It was like watching one of those slow-motion moments from a romance movie, but I got to watch it unfold in front of me. It's so damn exciting I could just pee right here, right now, but I won't be doing that.*

Watching from the other side of the grass, Trudy thought, *It took me a few moments to realize what was happening, but once I did, I had to give my boy a push to get him to move. My baby boy has his mate! She's finally here. I'll have to make all the alpha's and luna's favorite dishes for a week for making this happen.* Trudy started to cry out with happiness. She noticed Blaze and Bluey recording the interaction. *I'll need a copy to have for eternity.*

Meanwhile, Zane pulled away from his first kiss with Val, oblivious to all of the eyes on them. *That was more amazing than I could have ever dreamed,* Zane thought.

"Hey, handsome," Valerie said, sounding to Zane so adorable and sweet.

I feel like I'm not even in this world right now, like just in the presence of beauty. I feel the need to ease the tension and try to make her smile, Zane thought. "My name is Zane. What's yours, or should I just call you beautiful?"

"Hi…hi…I'm Valerie, but you can call me Val," Val stuttered, still in shock.

"What a lovely name for a beautiful woman," Zane purred.

"So, happy birthday!" Val said, snapping back into reality and throwing her arms out dramatically, with a huge grin. "Surprise!"

Zane pulled her back in, held her tight, lifted her chin, and kissed her again. "Thank you." *This is so surreal; I feel like passing out.*

Zane and Val finally let go of each other and put space between them. They looked around to see they had an audience they didn't have before. Everyone boomed with claps and whistles. Trudy was still in tears. Rocky and Bluey stared at each other. Zane noticed the two unfamiliar guys. *They look livid.*

Rocky felt like time had stopped. All he could focus on was Val's friend. His wolf, Rick, jumped up and down in his head.

Even with all the chaos that had broken out around them, he couldn't break away from her eyes. *They're so blue, ocean blue, blue moon blue. Is this Bluey? Could she be our mate? But she's an alpha, and I'm just a delta. Oh, thank you, moon goddess, for this precious gift. I must be doing good things in your eyes to deserve such a treasure.*

Then it happened: All of a sudden, Bluey ran across the grass toward Rocky, who caught her in his arms. Bluey wrapped her legs around Rocky and started kissing him. He embraced her and returned the kiss. *She's the missing puzzle piece I didn't know I had lost,* Rocky thought. Then he realized all eyes were on him and Bluey—rather than on Zane. *I don't want to steal his thunder,* Rocky thought, slowly putting Bluey down, to another round of applause and whistles. *Zane looks so happy for me. This is why he's my best friend.*

"Yes, yes, yes, I found you. Oh, my goodness, you're a gorgeous hunk of a man!" Bluey burst out excitedly.

Rocky couldn't help but laugh at her demeanor. He could barely get out a thank you. Everyone started to calm down. Zane came over to Rocky and gave him a man hug.

Ick, what's that? Rocky thought, feeling wetness on his shoulder. *Is he crying?* A quick glance at Zane told him it wasn't tears—but sweat. *Uh oh.*

"Rocky, I'm not feeling well. I think it's coming. What do I do with all these people here?" Zane asked quietly.

Rocky jumped into action, mind-linking the alpha straight away, who came right over with his dad and Zane's.

"Come here, son. Let me wish you a happy birthday," Alpha Steven said.

Zane released Rocky and gave Alpha Steven a man hug as Alpha whispered something in his ear, who gave an ever-so-slight nod.

"It seems like Zane is a bit overwhelmed, but the surprises aren't over yet. Rocky, would you like to give Zane his gift?"

Rocky reached into his pocket, pulled out a set of car keys, and handed them to Zane. "Happy birthday, brother."

Zane looked at Rocky like he had two heads. "I can't accept that. It's too much."

"You have to. It's yours. It's in your name and everything. Can't take it back now. Let's go for a spin."

Zane took the keys and walked with Rocky to his dad's garage. Everyone followed them to the garage to see the SUV. It was nothing fancy and it was used, but it was Zane's.

"Alrighty, Zane, let's go for a ride. Who is coming with?" Rocky already knew the answer to that question, but he knew they couldn't let everyone else know what was going on with Zane.

Without a moment's notice, his brother and sisters hopped in, then their dad. "Get out you three. He'll take you for a ride later," Evan said to the younger siblings. "Val, would you like to accompany your mate by taking the front seat?"

She blushed and got in the front seat. Evan got in behind her and Rocky, and Curtis got comfy in the back. The alpha linked, *I'll meet you there.*

"Hell no! My sister isn't going with all those guys in the car. She won't be going anywhere with any of you ever!" yelled Ricky. "This is her future Alpha," he said pointing to Roman, "and I'm the future Beta. She has orders to obey us!"

Suddenly Rocky felt the SUV shaking. He looked over Zane's shoulder to see his hands on the wheel, and they were sprouting fur. *No, no, no, not now. This is not good.*

Sensing her mate in distress, Val placed her hand on Zane's thigh, leaned over, and gave him kisses. "I'm going wherever you go from now on. I'm never going anywhere with them again. I'm yours and only yours. I'm here to stay."

That calmed Zane down a bit. *I don't think it will last long,* Rocky thought. Alpha Steven came back to the car and reassured Zane, "I'll deal with those two. Drive to the waterfall in the middle of our pack territory."

Then off they went.

The prophecy stated: At first position of the True-Blue Moon, he'll receive his Lycan. Second position, he'll sleep. At the highest position, he'll receive his beast.

When Zane met Valerie for the first time, unbeknownst to him, the moon was moving to its first position, triggering his shift. Only the select few who knew what he was truly turning into knew that they're racing against the moon that makes its appearance in the still bright sky.

Of course, my stupid brother had to open his big mouth, Valerie thought. *I already had to calm my mate down. But I get to be here for him, and that's all that matters. I hope his wolf likes me and Iggy, because she can't shut up about how excited she is to meet him. By the looks of it, we're driving to the middle of their pack territory. Why? Shifting is supposed to be celebrated.* Val looked over to Zane and placed her hand on his thigh. *He's not looking too good and is close to shifting right now.*

Zane eased the SUV to a stop at a beautiful waterfall. He opened the driver's side door and practically fell out. Evan, Rocky, and Curtis ran to him and started to help him walk closer to the falls.

As Zane was being half dragged, half carried deeper into the pack territory, he thought, *Glad to be here. I can barely focus. Valerie's hand on my thigh helped more than she realized. I have to make it to the falls fast. Alpha said we don't know what to expect, and the falls is the safest place to muffle the screams. Valerie, my beautiful mate, has no idea I'm not a wolf. I pray to the goddess that she won't run off.*

The group stopped when they heard Zane's first bone snap. He groaned. *This shit hurts like a bitch.* Everyone backed away, staying close enough to Zane just in case. Val dropped to her hands and knees. *She's shifting,* Zane thought, watching in awe.

More of Zane's bones dislocated with a *pop* and a *snap*. He was screaming in pain. He heard faint voices encouraging him not to fight it, saying, "Yes, it hurts, but just let him come." He felt his face getting wet and managed to open one eye slightly to see an attractive wolf licking him. *She's so brave; I love her already.* After a few more agonizing snaps, Zane's face was transforming. *Never in my life have I felt such pain. I'd rather have Rocky punch me.* Zane released a blood-curdling roar of power and strength, shocking even himself.

His body was human no longer, and he felt his conscience now being shared. He was now at the back of his own mind, and he heard a new, foreign voice.

It's nice to finally be free!

Who are you? I mean, do you have a name?

My name is Pyrox. I'm your Lycan.

I don't understand what a Lycan is and what it means to have one. We thought they were myths.

Myths come from somewhere, right? I'm proof of that, but there's no time to chit-chat. We need to move around in our new body. I'll explain things soon.

Zane felt Pyrox attempt to move, slowly getting to their feet. *Two feet! Am I not supposed to be on all fours?*

Relax, Pyrox said, while he stretched their limbs. He didn't completely shut Zane out, instead letting Zane see what he sees. Pyrox inhaled deeply, and Zane felt his emotions with that one breath—excitement and love. Pyrox spotted Valerie, then slowly approached her, letting her wolf know he meant no harm. Zane smelled her bravery on top of her other calming scent.

Iggy wagged her tail and yipped. Pyrox bent down, and she licked his face. Pyrox chuckled.

I've never heard a wolf laugh, Zane thought, surprised.

Iggy did the mating pose, letting her mate inspect her. He sniffed around her, inspecting her and sniffing her privates. *Pure,* he purred, and Zane felt arousal strike. He felt Val's emotions as well, and she was delighted he approved of her.

"Hello, my mate," Pyrox said.

Holy shit we can talk in this form! Zane thought, and Pyrox internally laughed. He knelt in front of Val and nuzzled her, stroking her fur. She purred and wagged her tail; he also purred. He headed toward the guys, Rocky first. *It's strange to actually have to look down at him,* Zane thought.

"Thank you for being with us and showing no fear of this form," Pyrox said.

"He's more my brother than friend. There will never be fear of him, nor you. You're part of him, so now you're a brother too," Rocky said.

Pyrox embraced Rocky in a man hug of love and appreciation, then backed away to address Evan and Curtis. "I'm Pyrox, a Reborn Lycan. We have the same creator. I'll never harm those who are with us, only against us. Never be afraid unless you cross us."

The group had been in the pack territory for quite some time when Zane noticed the sun shifted. Zane and Pyrox collapsed to the ground, then he shifted back to human form, a process that hurt so much worse because they were both exhausted. Right before passing out from exhaustion and pain, Zane felt Val lick his face.

She felt she needed to do *something*. She felt as if she had been in suspended animation as she watched her mate change into his wolf form for the first time. *I'm nervous. He seems to be having a hard time, but that is normal. His bones are not breaking like they should for a normal wolf though.*

Iggy told Val she wanted to shift to greet his wolf. Agreeing it was only fair, Val stripped into her undergarments and released her. Val was frankly glad to let Iggy take control because she became more and more puzzled watching Zane shift. *What is he turning into? By the looks of it, he's no wolf. His bones are elongating more than a wolf's, and they're thicker too. Why is his jaw jutting out of his face with long sharp teeth? His paws look like hands—with claws.* While Val was frightened, Iggy was thrilled. Val felt her need to go to him, but she waited.

Iggy, he isn't normal!

I know! Isn't it exciting?

How are you so calm? He's scary!

Val, he's sexy, not scary. Can't you feel his power? I bet he can go all night and then some. You wanted an alpha, but we have received something better and so much more.

Zane's blood-curdling roar surprised Val as much as it did him. It was so loud the ground shook. It felt like a release of power and exhaustion. As she watched, he rose to stand on two legs. *That's no wolf!* As the two animals greeted each other, Iggy thought, *"I hope he'll be pleased about what the goddess has destined him with."*

Spent, Zane fell to the ground and shifted back. The men carried him back to the SUV, and Evan drove them all back to his house.

Meanwhile, Alpha Steven was back at Zane's house. *Instead of being there for Zane, I have to deal with these two idiots from Shrieking Moon,* he thought, walking over to the idiots as calmly as possibly. "Ricky, what was that for? She found her mate, and you want to deny this. Why?"

"Val and Althea have obligations to us while we're not in our pack," Ricky replied smugly.

"Is that so? Now what kind of duties do they have to the two of you while in *my* pack? Aren't you guys supposed to be looking for your mates?" Alpha Steven questioned sternly, already knowing about the disgusting order their alpha gave.

Ricky's face paled with anger as he tried to keep a straight face. Alpha Steven mind-linked his son, asking him to bring the betas.

"That's none of your concern, Alpha Steven. They have direct orders to accommodate us while we're here," Roman said, trying to sound authoritative.

Alpha Steven could hardly contain his laughter. *That was as truthful an answer as I'm going to get out of either one of them.* Then he said, "These girls have found their mates in *my* pack, and you're currently on *my* territory. They no longer have any duties concerning your needs. Now that we have that cleared up, we'll be hosting a barbecue tonight for the True-Blue Moon celebration. You might want to mingle with all the unmated tonight to concentrate on finding *your* mates, instead of being infatuated with those two girls."

Alpha Steven felt rage boil in his blood. *My wolf wants heads.* He spotted Tessa with Trudy, wrapped his arms around her waist, nuzzled her neck, and purred in her ear. She instantly calmed his beast. As he waited for his son and company, he ate the food Trudy put out for her son's small birthday party.

Still raging, Alpha Steven decided to go for a run. Halfway to the falls, he heard it. *Goddess be damned, that was powerful. I'm not afraid of what he has become. I'm afraid for **him**. The few people who know the legends of the Lycans will want him for their own gain or to kill him out of fear.*

Chapter 17: Mental Preparations

Evan pulled the SUV up to the front of his house, with Zane still fast asleep. Most of the pack believed his shift was over. The pack still didn't know he shifted into a Lycan; they just knew he shifted. Even Alpha Steven and the others who knew about Zane being a Lycan didn't know he was in phase two, about to go into the third and final phase, receiving of the beast, which will affect more than just Zane. The third phase was described on a separate scroll they did not possess as, "Those the moon goddess has chosen to become have already proved to her that they're loyal, fierce, and worthy to stand by her Reborn Lycan's side will each receive special gifts to help her Lycan perform his intended duties."

Watching the SUV pull up from the window, Trudy was on edge. Not even Evan explained to her what happened, but she could see that Zane was out cold. Rocky carried him over his shoulders, into the house, and up to his room like a sack of potatoes. His mate, who Trudy hadn't formally met yet, was right behind them. As a mom of four, Trudy was always worried about someone most of the time. But experience had taught her to put it out of her mind, so she shoved the worry aside to clean up the backyard, then headed to the pack house to prepare for the night's barbeque.

Trudy's mind kept wondering about everything, and she found it hard to concentrate on her duties. She was preparing the fresh kill of meat the hunters had brought back from this morning's hunt when the alpha entered the kitchen. The Silver Stone Pack was very modern and humanized. Cooking for more than a hundred werewolves was like cooking for small high school. The busy kitchen boasted modern appliances, black-and-white backsplashes, with black marble flooring because it was easy to clean and hid the blood stains from wildlife preparations for meals.

"How are things going for tonight, Trudy?" Alpha Steven asked.

"Everything is going well, sir. We are almost done with the prep work so the kill can be grilled."

"Excellent work as always. Might I see you in my office for just a few minutes?"

"Of course, Alpha," Trudy said, then turned to address one of her kitchen helpers, "Remmy, would you be a dear? Once you're done with the veggies, put the already prepared meat in the outside coolers."

"Yes, ma'am."

Finally, an update on my son, Trudy thought, following the alpha to his office. She spotted Evan inside and wrapped her arms around him. He kissed her forehead, and they both sat.

"I wanted to speak to you both about everything happening. After running to blow off steam because of the boys from Shrieking Moon, I felt and heard Zane's power. I assume that meant he was completely shifted at that time. You and Curtis said he didn't seem hostile, which is a good thing. He was training to take your place, Evan, but now we have to get him into warrior training. Should we train your son Robert to be head tracker or one of your girls?" Alpha Steven asked.

Trudy looked at Evan with worry at the thought of Zane, such a gentle soul, becoming a warrior. "To be honest, Alpha, we were grooming the girls to take my place in the kitchen."

"Trudy, my love, I know this affects all our children, and you have every right to be a part of this discussion..."

Trudy interrupted, "I know. I know. I'm leaving." She gave him a kiss.

"Thank you, my love," Evan replied, then turned to Alpha Steven, "Alpha, Robert has already shifted, so we know he's not a Lycan too, but what are the chances one or both of my girls will become one?"

"I was wondering the same thing, but the prophecy doesn't mention any more than one, so we might be okay with them. However, we don't know all the Moon Goddess's plans. Robert has already been doing some tracker training, correct?"

"Yes, sir."

"We have to ease him into more tracking training, the advanced stuff. If he starts asking questions about why he's learning to be head tracker, tell him that his wolf is not up for the task. That should help without fully disclosing what he truly is. If he doesn't like that answer, add that Zane wants to try training to be Rocky's go-to man, now that he has his wolf."

"Robert will probably not even ask many questions. He wants to prove his worth as most werewolves do, but he's not power hungry."

"You have amazing kids, Evan. Let's hope tonight goes well. We'll have to sit down and talk about when we'll introduce him to the king and council. We'll talk about that later though. Could you bring Zane, his mate, and the others to my office? I need to prepare them for what tonight could bring."

"Of course, Alpha," Evan answered, then went home to check on Zane. As he pulled up, he noticed Rocky cuddling with his mate on the porch swing. "Hey, son, is he awake yet?"

"Everything has been quiet, sir. I wanted to keep watch out here just in case. This is my mate, Althea," Rocky said.

"Please call me Bluey. It's nice to see you again."

"Likewise."

"Rocky, please none of that sir business. You're like a son to me."

Rocky smiled and went back to cuddling his mate. Evan went inside the house, up to Zane's room, and cracked his door open to take a peek in. He saw Val curled up beside Zane, both fast asleep. *I'm so happy for both of them*, Evan thought, tears forming in his eyes. *They both have beautiful mates.*

Unfortunately, Evan had to break this up for the moment. He nudged Zane, careful not to touch his mate and leave any trace of his scent on her. *I don't know want his Lycan would do. It could get ugly—fast.*

"Zane! Zane, wake up please. We need to see the alpha."

After several minutes of nudging, Zane groggily asked, "Dad?"

"Hate to do this to you, son, but we have to see the alpha."

"All right, Dad. Does Val need to come too, or can I let her sleep?"

"You all need to be there. I'm sorry."

"Okay then, let me get her up, and we'll meet you downstairs."

After Evan had woken Zane, he looked over to see his beautiful mate curdled up next to him. ***Goddess, she's mesmerizing***, Pyrox purred. ***Can we mate and claim her before tonight? I want everyone to know she's ours.***

Really, Pyrox? I want our first time to be special. You know, make love not sex.

Hrmph, Pyrox grunted in frustration.

Zane gently woke Val, who looked confused and blinked her tiredness away. He smiled down at her, "Hi."

"I didn't mean to fall asleep on your bed, but Iggy needed to be near you."

"My beautiful mate, you never, and I do me never, have to apologize for wanting to be near me. It was delightful to see your beauty upon awakening. Besides, that was the best sleep I've had in a long time, and it was because of you. Sadly, we have to go see my alpha right now."

"Where is your bathroom so I can freshen up?"

Zane pointed to the door.

"You have your own bathroom?"

"One of the perks of being the oldest."

Val did her business, and the pair headed downstairs, where Evan was grinning from ear to ear.

"Hey, Dad. Why do you look so happy?"

"Just seeing you and your mate look so peaceful together, sleeping. She's beautiful like your mother, and I know we raised you right—to do well by her. Let's go grab Rocky and his mate and go to the office."

Heading to the pack house, Zane's mind wandered. His senses seemed to be more heightened and intense than usual. It was making him dizzy, but he tried to hide it, so he didn't seem like a weak mate. *I don't want Val to reject me and take off because she thinks I can't protect her. After all, she's a beta, and I'm just a tracker.*

At the pack house, Evan, Zane, Val, Rocky, and Bluey entered Alpha Steven's office. Without preamble, he said, "Have a seat everyone. There are some things we have to discuss about Zane. As Zane, Evan, and Rocky already know, girls, Zane is not a werewolf. He's a Lycan. Valerie, this will be a trying time. He needs you close at all times at the moment to keep his Lycan at bay. Therefore, I've sent your father and your alpha pack transfer papers and made sure the council received a courtesy copy of the request. Effective immediately. I know you and Althea are joined at the hip, and she has also found her mate in my pack, so I sent papers for her as well."

Val and Bluey both let out sighs of relief.

Alpha Steven continued, "Before you young ladies even worry, I know what you were both ordered to do. It makes me sick to say the least. Once your brothers find out about you now having mates, they will more than likely cause problems. Only a handful of people know about Zane. We need to keep it that way until further notice. The plan for tonight is to let everyone mingle and relax, while Ricky and Roman see if their mates are in my pack. To keep Zane's Lycan at bay, Valerie, you need to stick by his side. If anything should go wrong, Rocky, I need you to cause a distraction, a fight or even complete chaos. You won't be punished, even though I might have to act like I'm punishing you. Any questions?"

Zane took a deep breath after the alpha finished. Rocky gave Zane his "I got your back" pats on his back, making Zane cough because he was holding his breath. Zane was still nervous his mate might go to run out the doors.

Bluey was the first to speak, "Alpha Steven, let me be the first to say, well holy shit, for one. Two, Val and I'll do whatever it takes to keep this secret. Three, thank you, thank you, thank you." Then she excitedly jumped out of her chair to hug him. Rocky growled at that.

Without even a glance Rocky's way, Alpha Steven said, "Oh calm down, boy. It's a sign of gratitude, and I've known her longer. And you're welcome, Bluey."

"What happens if my father or alpha won't allow our transfer because of our blood line?" Val asked.

"We have history, some good, some bad. Some things stay between alphas to keep the peace. He won't want to disturb that. I've also warned him on the outcome of him trying to deny the transfer or if your brothers get out of hand."

"What do you mean? Is something happening tonight?" Zane asked.

"Zane, I'm sure your mate and Althea will vouch for this when I say that their brothers are known for being ill behaved. Trouble follows them wherever they go. They're spoiled brats, really. Their unhealthy obsession with these girls is probably what led their fathers to order them to do such nonsense. I don't doubt they will be anything but good."

Zane let out a low, hateful growl.

"See, Zane, this is what had gotten you in those issues a week ago, and you didn't even know her yet. Could you imagine what would happen if they started trouble now? You have just newly shifted, and even if you were a normal werewolf, you'd *want to* rip them apart. You're a Lycan, and if legends are true, you'd shift and *actually* rip them apart. That would cause many problems that we want to avoid. If there are no more questions, you're dismissed."

As the group left the office, they saw Alex enter, and they all did the nod hello. They headed down to the pack house gaming room to relax before going outside.

You doing all right, brother? Rocky mind-linked Zane.

Ya, I'm just trying to remain strong, so Val doesn't think I'm weak and reject me. My new heightened senses are making me dizzy. I want to be the worthy mate she deserves.

I love you and all, but you're stupid if you think she'll reject you. Don't push her away because of your insecurities.

I can't help it, Rocky. I don't know how you all control yourselves. This is new to me.

Let's try and relax tonight and pray to our goddess that nothing happens. Just remember if she was going to reject you and run for the hills, she would have done it at your shift. We have your back, brother."

Chapter 18: Party Time

A little while later, the barbecue was in full swing. Ricky and Roman seemed to be enjoying themselves. But to Alpha Steven, they seemed too serious for a couple of kids. *I think they needed this time away from their fathers. I know it's their fathers pushing them to take over at such a young age. They seem to have gotten worse as the years have passed, dragging their sons down the wrong path with them. It's a real shame because they both have great potential. Makes me feel bad for them.*

Steven stood in the background, keeping watch over the party, always on the alert for trouble. He saw his dearest, Tessa, looking like a beautiful angel, the perfect Luna that she is. *Thank you, Moon Goddess, for pairing me with a woman with such grace and beauty. Don't make her angry though because she can be a badass when necessary. She must feel my emotions through our mate bond, as she looks at me in a sultry manner. Hope she knows, she'll be sore in the morning.* Steven winked at Tessa, and she blushed. *It's amazing that I still have that effect on her.*

Steven continued to keep a watchful eye. Usually, he would mingle with his pack, but there was too much at stake at the moment. He saw Rocky and Bluey with his son, Alex. Steven had filled Alex in on everything. At first, Alex was worried Zane might want to fight him for the Alpha title. Steven pulled them both into his office to talk through their differences. It became a nonissue because Zane didn't want to deal with alpha duties. *I don't need jealously destroying my pack. I've seen it too many times throughout the years. That's why one of my pack laws is if they're not your mate, you're not to engage with them. I'm not stupid. I know it happens, but it better not cause any problems for me or my pack.*

Steven held his breath as he saw Zane and Val make their way toward Alex and Rocky. At that moment, Roman and Ricky didn't seem to care about their presence. *Good.*

After the quick talk with Alpha and Alex, Zane sought out Rocky. He was waiting for Zane with the girls in the pack house living room. *I'm not sure how I feel after that little talk,* Zane thought. *Alex thought I was going to challenge him for the alpha title. How dumb is that? Lycan or not, I was not born to be a leader.* As soon as Zane came out of the alpha's office, he caught Val's scent. It relaxed him instantly, and he made his way to her. Pyrox was purring in his head, telling him to mark and mate her now. Zane told him to shut up: *It's not happening now.* He walked up to Rocky and the others and said, "Hey guys." He didn't know what else to say.

"Zane, brother, how'd it go?" Rocky asked.

"Alex thought I was going to challenge him for the alpha title. We had to talk through that because I don't want to run a pack, just protect it. He wants me to train by your side and become your right hand. He warned me it's not pretty."

"Fair enough, it's really not, but I enjoy it. I was groomed my entire life for it though. Have you looked in the mirror since your shift?"

"Well, no. You know I was never one to check myself out."

"Well, you might want to. Your body has changed to handle your new form."

"What! No way!" Zane said, then ran to the nearest bathroom to check. The moment he saw himself, he was shocked. *I'm no longer scrawny. Natural muscles where I never had muscles before are now front and center.* "Holy shit!" Zane screamed like a girl. He ran back out of the bathroom to see Rocky laughing so hard he was crying. Zane slapped him on the back of his head, pulled up his shirt, and screamed at him.

"Look at this shit, Rocky! I never had muscles like this before. I won't lie and say I'm not excited over this—because I so am. You go from what I had to what I have now, masses of muscle. I'm in shock."

Bluey was the first to comment, "Hot damn, that's sexy as hell. I don't know what you looked like before the shift, but you're hot."

Rocky immediately punched Zane, who landed on his ass. Zane laughed because he landed close to Valerie, almost taking her down with him. *She smells so good.* Zane did a slow upward gaze while he was down there, drinking in her beauty. *Yup, sexy mate, sexy, sexy mate I have. I want her right now.* By the time

Zane's eyes made their way up to her pretty face, it looked like she was holding her breath. He got up slowly and faced her. He didn't know where his burst of confidence came from. He leaned down to graze her hair with his mouth until he reached her ear and whispered, "You're so beautiful."

Without hesitation, she captured his face in her hands and kissed him.

"Hey, you two, get a room," Bluey said, interrupting their kiss.

Val pulled away and blinked. "Sorry, I don't know what came over me. I'm not normally so speechless, but you're sexy, my mate."

Zane felt his cheeks heat up. He had never been called sexy before. He smelled a very sweet smell coming from Val. His eyebrows raised: *She's aroused.* Now it felt like his entire body was heating up. Her eyes traveled down, and she said, "Seems like we have a problem, Zane. That will be mine very soon." He looked down to see a tent. With that, he bolted to the bathroom.

By that point, Bluey and Rocky were laughing very hard at Zane's issue. He couldn't see if Val laughing, but then again, he had bolted. He hoped she wasn't laughing too. He made it to the bathroom in a panic and leaned against a stall door. *What the hell am I supposed to do about my boner? I can't go to the party like this. UGH!* As Zane pulled his hands down his face, he slid down the door. *I've never been so embarrassed in my life.*

As Rocky had watched his friend sprint to the bathroom, he tried hard to catch his breath. "Oh my god, I've never seen him like this before."

"Val, wow that was hot as fuck with you two, but hysterical at the same time. You might want to go check on him. It's only fair since you're the cause of the boner. We're going to head outside in the meantime. Catch up when you're done." Bluey ended with a wink.

Val had to sniff her way to Zane because she didn't know the layout of the pack house yet. Iggy bounced around in her head, giving her a headache.

Mate wants us so bad. Let's just give it to him. Did you see him? I can't wait.

We'll not be doing that just yet. Would you calm yourself?

How can I? He thinks we're sexy. His Lycan is calling to me. Wants to bend us over and..."

"I said shut it, Iggy! I can't control what happens, and almost the entire pack is outside, so just fucking stop. I won't give myself to him in a bathroom like some slut, and that's final!

Val put a wall around Iggy in her mind to get some peace in there. She thought she had found Zane, so she slowly opened the door. She got a hot shock. When she opened the door, she saw her mate with his pants down, looking sexy as hell with one leg slightly bent, leaning on the sink with his cock in his hand. He was trying to rub it out to get rid of his boner. With all the courage Val could muster, she walked over to him and asked, "Can I help you with that?"

Just before Val shocked Zane by her presence in the men's room, he thought, *What am I going to do about this situation at hand? Hmmm, hand, right. I could resolve this and get back to everyone.* He dropped his pants and leaned on the sink with one hand and stroked himself with the other. *With my gorgeous mate on my mind, this won't take long.* He was in his own head, with images and thoughts of her swimming naked. With his dick firmly in hand, Zane didn't notice her come in.

When "Can I help you with that?" was whispered in Zane's ear, he froze mid-stroke and stood there in shock. He felt tingles on his hand and then he felt her put her hand on his. Intertwining her hand with his, she helped him stroke himself.

"I seemed to have caused this, so let me at least help you finish it, sexy mate," Val said.

As they stroked, Val's lips were on Zane's neck, traveling down his chest and making her way down his standing body. As she kissed her way down, he relaxed, enjoying his first sexual encounter. He noticed her hand retracting from his, and she pushed his hand away completely. What followed was also very new to him: She put her plump lips on the tip of his hardness. Using only her tongue, she licked and twirled around his tip. It was heavenly. Stroking, licking, up, down, and in and out of her mouth, Zane was in complete bliss, so close to his release. He let out a low rumble to warn her it was coming. She continued like a champ, and it came out with a fire. She choked a bit, then continued to swallow his cum.

Zane was frozen in shock, awe, and relief. He took her hands and raised her up so he could gaze into her eyes. Without hesitation, he crashed their lips together. Pyrox purred at her actions in approval and accepted her more now without any doubts—even more than before. Zane blocked him out so he could enjoy this moment with his mate. Out of breath, they released themselves from their kiss. Zane put his forehead to hers.

"You didn't have to do that, beautiful, but thank you so much."

"I don't know why I did that. I've never done anything like that before. Did you enjoy it?"

"That was the most amazing thing I've ever experienced in my life. Maybe I should return the favor. I've never even hugged a girl outside of my family before, so it might take me time to learn how to pleasure you, my mate."

"I like the sound of that, but another time. We need to catch up with Bluey and my cousin. To warn you, she might make a scene when she sees us. By the way, your pants are still down. Let's wash up and head outside."

The pair cleaned themselves up and headed out.

"Oh, by the way, seeing you like that when I walked in was sexy," Val said with a wink.

Zane wrapped his arms around her and inhaled her relaxing scent. Zane smiled and almost told her he loved her already, but he didn't want to ruin what just happened.

With the party in full swing, everyone seems to be having a good time. Zane scanned the crowd, quickly spotted Rocky and headed his way.

"Took care of your problem eh, brother? You were gone for a while," Rocky smirked.

Zane looked at Val, who blushed a little but ignored the comment, glided over to Bluey, and started chatting.

"What problem did you have, Zane? Is it something I need to be aware of?" Alex asked.

Zane's mouth dropped open, making him look like a fish out of water.

"Oh, Alex, we can't help those unexpected issues that pop up out of nowhere and turn into a bit of a sticky situation later," Rocky chuckled.

"Would you shut the hell up please. It's dealt with, as you can see," Zane muttered.

"Oh, and I can smell it too," Rocky said.

"We didn't do that okay. She just helped me. Now please drop it, would you?"

Rocky put his arms up in defense, "All right, all right it's dropped." He looked down at Zane's crotch, "Obviously."

Alex looked down, confused for a minute, then looked back up and laughed. "Now I get it. Val is your mate, Zane?"

Zane filled with pride and stood a bit straighter, "Yes, yes she is."

"God, you guys are lucky. Your mates are hot. I hope mine is fine like yours," Alex said, earning a low growl from both Zane and Rocky.

Alex's eyes widened. "Oh my god no. I didn't do anything to them or with them. I'm sorry I said that. I forgot about possessiveness when mates are first together without being marked. I haven't met my mate yet. I'm sorry."

I want to rip his tongue out! Let me, Zane! Pyrox was now front and center.

No, Pyrox, absolutely not. We can't reveal ourselves. Stop! Zane said.

He called our mate hot! He wants our mate. He's going to try to steal her!

"Pyrox! Calm down now! She's hot, beautiful, and strong, and she's ours. Did she not just prove she wants us back at the pack house just a little bit ago? Have faith in our mate please. She's so strong; can't you sense it? I can, and we'll protect her when she needs us, but I have a feeling she likes fighting her own battles. We'll only cause problems if you force me into a shift. It's not needed. She'll hate us if we do.

Zane closed his eyes and took deep breaths to calm down. He felt an instant at-peace feeling. He opened his eyes, and Valerie had her arms wrapped around him and her head lying on his chest. He saw Bluey doing the same for Rocky. Their mates defused the situation.

"Alex, are you seriously that dense? I've known you for a long time, and I know you're not that stupid. We all know about the talks that have occurred today. Now why would you go and say something so fucking stupid?" Bluey was trying to remain calm and yelling at him at the same time.

Alex straightened up, like he was bracing himself for something. "I'm really sorry, trust me. It's hard seeing these two guys with two upper ranked beautiful women. I mean come on, a tracker gets a beta mate, and a delta gets an alpha mate. Like really, Moon Goddess?" Alex scuffed.

Both Val's and Bluey's eyes grew wide with disbelief and anger. Before Zane or Rocky could stick up for their mates, the girls both punched him in the face, knocking him on his ass.

Oh, shit these girls are fucking awesome! Zane thought, watching Alex go down. Then he heard Roman behind them. He turned to see Roman coming, looking livid. Zane turned back around to see an angry looking Alpha Steven headed his way.

"All of you, in my office *now*!" Steven said.

Now we're in trouble, Zane thought.

Chapter 19: Receiving of the Beast

As Valerie spotted Alpha Steven walking toward them, Roman grabbed her from behind and asked, "What's going on, Val?"

"He said some rude things. Why are you sniffing me?"

"Why do you smell like another wolf! You're promised to *me!* You're *mine!*" Roman yelled.

Val quickly spun around and punched him too. *What the hell is everyone's problem right now? I hope no one else disrespects me. I'm not in the mood,* Val thought, standing over him.

"First off, I'm not yours. The Moon Goddess has chosen my mate, and it's not you. It's him you smell. I'm his, and he's mine. Stop hanging onto your fantasies of us. There was never and will never be an us! I don't know who promised me to you, but the only person who matters is our goddess!" Val said, walking away and heading over to face the music for punching her future alpha. She didn't get very far before Roman grabbed her again. She went to punch him again, but she was stopped by Alpha Steven.

"My office, now!" he yelled.

Val gave Roman one last look of disgust and followed Alpha Steven to his office where the others were waiting. Zane instantly pulled her onto his lap and held her tight.

"No one is in trouble if that's what you're all thinking. Like I said before, do what's necessary to keep Zane's Lycan at bay," Alpha Steven began.

"That was all a ploy then, Alex?" Val asked.

"Before you and Althea punched my son, he had already linked me that Roman was looking ready to cause trouble. I arrived quickly because I had been on watch. Told the rest to go to my office while I dealt with the rest of the situation. Zane was looking like he was losing control," Alpha Steven said.

"I did what I had to and said what I said only because I had to. Once I saw Roman's face, I knew." Alex said.

"I don't understand one thing. He said he was promised I was to be his," Val said.

"Val, you're beautiful, fierce, and strong. You'd make a fine mate to any Alpha. Roman and others probably see that too. Bluey, I mean no disrespect, but your mom is a weak wolf. Beautiful yes, but weak." Alex said.

"Don't I know it," Bluey said.

Spoken like a true Alpha, Steven thought, nodding with pride.

My old pack never treated me or Bluey with respect before, Val thought.

Then out of nowhere, Val fell to the floor in agony. She saw everyone else in the same state—right before she blacked out.

Mid-conversation, everyone in the room started screaming and rolling around on the floor, looking like they were in pain.

What's happening? Alpha Steven wondered, then saw a bright aura and felt a calming presence. As he watched, the figure touched them all between their eyes. Now they all looked calm and appeared to be sleeping. It only took Steven a few moments to realize who she was: Moon Goddess. He instantly bowed before her.

"Please rise, my child. I need to explain. Please sit," Moon Goddess said.

Steven rose as requested and waited for her explanation, honored to be in her presence.

"You were not aware of this phase of the prophecy. Your collections are incomplete. Zane was always going to go through this phase. The others, however, had to prove loyalty with love in their hearts. I've been watching closely. Alex only just earned the gift he's receiving tonight with his good intentions. You may choose only one other to share this information with but be brief in explanations.

"I'll start with Alex since he's your son. He's receiving a gift called Receive/Deceive. He'll be able to see through any kind of lie. He will be immune to magic, medicines, and potions that are used to get information. Rocky's gift is called Eternal Fortitude/Endurance. He'll have an almost unlimited amount of stamina, be able to withstand torture. Althea will have control over water and wind and match her mate's abilities to withstand torture and heal. Valerie will be able to produce and control fire and heat. Zane is a Lycan, and he's meant to be the protector. He can't be affected by the other powers. Zane will have control over all elements earth-bound and supernatural. He'll have immunity against silver, wolfsbane, and magic intended for evil and harm. He'll have one other gift, but it is not for me to say what it is yet. I don't want him falling into the wrong hands, and they know about it. They all will be called *elementals* because they will have control of the earth's natural elements. Everything will be tied to their emotions. The sooner they understand that, the easier learning their gifts will become.

"It is up to you to help them grow into this how you see fit. I leave it to you, and I trust you with these gifts. They will dissipate once they all learn control of their new gifts. There will be severe consequences if you misuse these powers. Don't let them consume you, turn against you, or be greedy for them once they're gone."

The goddess touched Steven's forehead, then vanished.

Zane partially returned to consciousness, in a dreamlike state. He groaned in pain. He heard his name being called, so he opened his eyes to find the darkness was now bright.

"Hello? Is anyone here?" he called out, not expecting an answer. Pyrox sensed a familiarity in the presence Zane had yet to see, but suddenly he heard.

"Hello, my child. You and Pyrox are very special to me. All of those who are meant to help you with this path have proven loyalty with love in their hearts. You're my Reborn Lycan, the protector of all my creations. I made mistakes the first time I created Lycans. I thought giving them mates would distract them from their sworn duties, but it just made them more distraught and dangerous. That was my mistake. That's when I set forth the prophecy. I needed a couple to still love like they had a mate bond, even though it was gone. You're the product of such love. I gifted you a mate who will love you like that and friends who feel like family to help you along the way. Embrace each other; love one another. Be well, my child," the goddess said. Then she was gone, and Zane fell back into darkness.

Once Zane finally came to, he sat up and saw Val. He held her tight and asked, "Are you okay?" She nodded against his chest.

"Welcome back," Alpha Steven said, prompting them all to look toward him. "You all were out for like an hour. How are you all feeling?"

In unison, they all groaned.

"I set up rooms for you on the alpha's floor for tonight. Roman and Ricky don't leave until tomorrow, so it's safer for you all there. Now go rest. We'll talk tomorrow about what all this means," Alpha Steven said.

The group left the office, and Alex led them up to their rooms. Bluey broke the silence, "We'll get through this and handle whatever is thrown our way." She clutched onto Rocky.

The others nodded.

Val and Zane entered their room, finally alone. Zane was tired, but he knew sleep wouldn't come. He felt like his nerves were trying to burst through his skin. *Val has shown me she's almost fearless, and here I sit like a wound-up ball of nerves,* Zane thought, when Valerie startled him out of his thoughts.

"Zane, are you okay?"

"Yeah, I'm nervous."

"Why?"

"Honestly, you make me nervous."

"Why?"

Zane turned to her and gently placed his palm on her face. "You're so beautiful. I fail in comparison. You're strong. I'm not. You come from ranks. I did not. I don't deserve someone who possesses so much when I offer so little."

Val kissed him so fast she took his breath away. He felt passion flowing through her kiss that he was more than happy to return.

"You offer me something I've never had before, except from Bluey. You have already shown me more respect and love than I've had before. Don't sell yourself short on your looks either, my mate. You're a fine specimen of a man."

With a hearty laugh, Zane hugged her. He looked into eyes for a few moments, soaking in her beauty and passionately kissed her again. He pulled away and placed a finger under her chin. "Thank you, beautiful." He kissed her forehead. "I need a quick shower. I'll be right back."

Val nodded and started shuffling through the dresser. He made his way down the hall to the shower and hopped in to do a quick wash up.

Would you stop being so shy around our mate?

You scared the hell out of me, Pyrox! Zane yelled, practically slipping in the shower.

Ya, I was napping, adjusting to our new gifts.

What gifts?

Only time will tell. Let's go back to our mate. I want to be near her wolf.

I still don't feel like I'm good enough for her, like she deserves better.

You were never proud enough of who you are. Your body was going to change regardless of if I was a wolf or a Lycan, but you got the better one. We're stronger than anyone else. Start embracing our new selves. Be proud of us and show our mate she can be proud of us too. You have to do this alone. Once her wolf calls me to mark her, I'll take over in that moment.

I'll try, Zane said.

Zane finished up in the shower and headed back to their room with just a towel wrapped around him. With a deep breath, he took in Val's wonderful scent of eucalyptus and lavender, which was simultaneously calming and intoxicating. He walked over to the dresser and pulled out some clean provisions. He braced himself and repeated *confidence* over and over. He dropped his towel and almost instantly he smelled her arousal, making him feel weak in the knees. *If I wasn't already holding onto the dresser, I'd have fallen for sure.* Zane slowly strode over to her naked, already hard for her, because of her.

Losing not only to himself, but to the beast inside, with confidence, Zane cupped the back of Val's head, tilting it slightly to him. He started with a slow kiss, his desire for her building with every passing second, He kissed her. He felt her melt into the kiss, and she cupped his face with her strong, but delicate hands. Zane slid their bodies on the bed without breaking the kiss, leading her to the pillow.

Zane was lost in this action, wanting nothing more than to take her. Inhaling deeply, her arousal was prominent, a low growl came from within. He straddled her, released their kiss, and slid down her neck, taking his free hand to glide down her body, which shivered. He felt his canines start to elongate, wanting to claim what's his, but he just used them to grace the skin over her neck. Taking his chances of the moment, his fingers brushed her hipbone, softly touching her smooth, flawless skin. Her hips bucked upward slightly. Zane looked deep into her eyes to see desire and want. Once he had seen that, he was lost in her eyes, body, and soul. *I'm all hers.*

Zane nodded at her silently, asking permission to continue. *I want to make sure she's comfortable with me.* She nodded in return. He kissed her body and took off her panties, exposing her wet core. He kissed his way back up to her lips, catching them with his. His fingers slid to her core, so wet, ready, juicy, slipping one in amongst her wetness. Another low growl of pleasure came from Zane and her as well. *She's so tight. I'm almost afraid to continue.* Gliding his finger slowly in and out elicited another moan from her. He slipped in another finger and slowly pumped them in and out of her, and the wetter and wetter she became.

Kissing her with hunger Zane never felt before, getting lost in the action, they almost forgot to breathe. One more time, they released from the kiss.

"Are you sure?" Zane asked.

Val moaned yes. Pulling his fingers and bringing them to his lips, Zane sucked her juices. His eyes rolled to the back of his head, never had he tasted something so delectable before. *And she's all mine.* Moving the strands of her dark red hair out of her face and in the same motion holding her to Zane, he positioned himself for entry.

They were both new to this, and Zane was painstakingly slow, wanting to remember this moment forever—the feeling of making love to his mate for the first time. Feelings and sensations built up that had never been there before were making his body already erupt with pleasure.

Pushing in his first inch, feeling her wet warmth, Zane gasped. She gasped. Slowly sliding in further in her tight juicy walls almost made him release instantly. He grew harder inside her, because her tightness was squeezing his dick, and he knew her wetness was for him.

Val winced. Zane whispered, "I'm sorry." He felt her pain through their bond. *I never want to cause her pain.* Sliding in deeper ever so slowly, letting her adjust, Zane was finally all the way in, and she moaned. Zane stayed still until she gave him an indication to continue.

When Val wanted him to continue, she pushed her hips upward. Zane was carefully pulling out and sliding back in again.

She relaxes more beneath me the more my dick rubs her walls. She spreads her legs wider for me to go deeper, and I do. Val grabbed at Zane's back and ass. Her walls got tighter, pulsing, wetter, and she tensed. Zane's canines were elongated fully now, and they marked each other in the same moment of release.

Emotions that were not only Zane's invade his mind, and he welcomed her in. He was in complete ecstasy, colors, stars, and release. They panted, and Zane heard Val in his head now that they were fully connected. ***I'm forever yours and always. I love you.*** Zane could only reciprocate with the same. Val laid her head on Zane's chest and fell asleep, and he did the same.

Chapter 20: Subtleties

As morning approached, Val slowly woke up—a bit sore from the past night's events. *I've no regrets being fully mated and forever bound to this man.* Val had to pee, but her mate had her fully engulfed in his grasp. She smelled some blood and knowing it was hers made her cringe. *The evidence I'm no longer a virgin is on the sheets.*

Val wiggled out of Zane's hold and made her way to the bathroom, making sure to grab clean clothes on her way. With weak legs, she finally made her way down the hall. She did her business, then got in the shower, relaxing as the water beat down on her. Thoughts of last night flooded her mind. *I didn't think I'd give in so easily, but once he dropped his towel, that was it.* Val was grateful to be in the shower. *I don't want my arousal to wake up Zane. Stop it,* she repeated to herself over and over.

Iggy! Stop giving me visuals of last night!

What?! I can't help it.

You have to stop; we're in the pack house, and he's still sleeping. We can't stay in the room all day and hump each other's brains out.

Last night was just a small taste, and I can't wait for his wolf to take me too.

He's a Lycan. How will you even do that; won't he tear you apart?

The Moon Goddess wouldn't have made him for us if I couldn't handle him. I won't be able to think straight until we fully complete our bond too.

I love you, Iggy. I'd never deprive you of your mate. Just hang in there.

I love you too. By the way, we won't be alone for much longer.

Mere seconds after she said that, Val stiffened up when she smelled her ever-intoxicating mate.

"You have no idea how wonderful your arousal smells, Valerie," Zane's husky voice came through the bathroom door.

Val quivered a little and gulped. "I'm sorry, Zane. I didn't want to wake you."

His voice went deeper. "I can smell your sweet scent of arousal, Val."

Her dam broke. Zane pinned her to the back of the shower, lifted her leg on his hip, and penetrated her once more. She groaned out of pleasure and pain. She braced herself with one hand on Zane's shoulder and the other on the wall. Her head tilted back as he pumped in and out of her—slow but hard. Together, they were a jumble of moans. *I feel like such a harlot doing this in the bathroom on the alpha's floor, but he feels so good.*

Zane's body slicked with water running down it, making Val all the wetter with his sexiness. His thrusts became harder, pushing her to her release. A hot gush came inside her. *My release mixing with his is a cooling sensation I could get used to.* Both spent, the mates rested their foreheads together and breathed heavily.

Moments later, Bluey pounded on the door. "Hey, you two! Others are waiting to piss and shower!"

"Piss out a window, Bluey!" was the first thing out of Val's mouth. She didn't want to end her moment with Zane just yet. *I guess it's already ruined.*

"Get your panties on, you little hussy, before I barge in there!" Bluey said.

Looking at Zane, Val said, "We better hurry. She will come in here."

Quickly, they dried and dressed. They opened the door to see Bluey smirking at them as she and Rocky entered the bathroom. Val and Zane parted ways. Val went back to the room to wash her blood out of the bedsheets.

Zane went to the kitchen to start breakfast, knowing his mom wouldn't be there on a Sunday making food. He started the coffee and preheated the oven and pans. Then he gathered all the food to cook on the counter, arranged from longest to shortest cooking times—a trick he learned from his mom, so all the food would be ready at the same time. *I need to cook enough for like ten wolves.*

As Zane prepared the food, he heard Val talking to Alex on her way down to the kitchen. *This entire situation has brought me a little closer to Alex. We were kind of friends before because of Rocky, but now I'm more comfortable around him without*

Rocky. I'm happy that we're fully mated, otherwise Pyrox would've torn Alex apart, but he's at ease with our mate.

Val headed to the fridge and bent over to grab something. *If she doesn't watch how she bends over, I'll take her here and now, even if Alex is here.*

Val sensed Zane's emotions, spun around, and said, "Oh no you don't, mister. My lady bits are sore."

"I'm sorry for hurting you, Valerie. I should have controlled myself better."

"It's what happens when you take a mate's virginity. Females get the pain first."

Zane swiftly scooped her up, planted kisses on her, and took her to the table. "I still feel terrible. I should have been gentler. You're my forever love. Now sit here, my feisty little mate, while I make breakfast."

Alex smiled listening to their banter, then looked up to see Rocky enter the kitchen, talking with Alpha Steven with Bluey in tow. Bluey sat next to Val as Rocky walked over to Zane manning the stove.

"How was your night? I know how your morning went," Rocky said conspiratorially.

"As good as yours I presume, since I see you're marked too."

"Althea is great. So far this mate thing is amazing. Besides sex, I feel stronger than I ever felt before. She's bringing out the best in me already."

"Valerie makes me feel the same way, but I'm sure getting Pyrox at the same time is making me better too. I don't feel sick anymore. It's such a relief."

"I'm happy you're finally feeling better, brother. Is the food almost done?" Rocky asked as he picked up a spatula to help Zane finish up and serve.

The group enjoyed a peaceful breakfast. The air was calm, and everyone seemed to enjoy Zane's cooking. After the previous day's events, they needed this peace to bond.

Alpha Steven broke the silence. "I sent Roman and Ricky back to their pack early this morning. No offense, girls, but I wanted them gone as soon as possible."

"Good riddance. We can't stand them anymore. They've gotten really bad with who they've become," Bluey said, nodding.

"They seriously have," Val echoed. "We don't understand why they've changed so much in such a bad way."

"I blame your fathers," Alpha Steven said. "Don't worry too much about it for now. How does everyone feel today? I see matings have happened."

The pairs glanced around at each other, and Zane saw looks from Rocky and Bluey.

"I feel clearer headed, like my senses are more open. That's the only difference I feel," Alex said.

"I feel stronger since we are now fully mated. I assume it's because Bluey and I share each other's strength," Rocky said.

"I have no idea really. I just shifted, so I figure I have to get used to being different now," Zane said.

"Very well. Just keep everything as normal as possible. If you need to discuss anything about you know what, have Alex take you somewhere private. I have to go north for a couple of days. Alex can contact me, but Beta Jake will handle things until I return," Steven said.

"Should we inform Mark about the situation? He's my beta after all," Alex said.

"We can discuss that with Jake when I return. He's still a bit immature, and his immaturity might lead to jealousy," Steven said.

After the alpha left, Bluey nudged Rocky. He knew what she was referring to and gave her a go-ahead nod.

"I think we need to talk in private, Alex," Bluey said.

Alex nodded and led Bluey and Val and Rocky and Zane to a more private room. Once inside, words tumbled out of Bluey. "I understand we all went through something yesterday, but I didn't think anything like this was even possible. I know no one here will see me differently. It's the larger pack I'm worried about. This is a new pack for Val and me. How will they see us?"

"While we were in the shower this morning, during my climax, the water engulfed us," Bluey explained.

"Engulfed you?" Alex asked.

"Before that even, some water droplets seemed to stand still, then started collecting around us like a water bubble," Rocky described.

"That's totally amazing, Bluey! You can control water! That makes so much sense since your wolf, Sassie, has those amazing colors," Val said.

Sassie perked up with pride.

Val hugged Bluey and asked, "Has anyone else done anything amazing?"

"Val, you were getting hot in the shower," Zane said.

"Gee, I wonder why?" Val asked with a grin, making everyone laugh.

"Bluey, you can control water. Control your emotions, and we'll take everything as it comes. Your new school schedules are in my dad's office, so if we're done here, let's get them," Alex said.

Bluey whined, "School schedules? Really, Alex? I thought you were cool."

Rocky growled, but everyone else laughed.

"Your schedules match Rocky's and Zane's just in case there's any trouble, being new to the school and needing your mates under control. We all graduate soon anyway, so it's no big deal. Just chill for two more months," Alex said, shrugging.

With sass, Bluey said, "Oh all right, Mr. Alpha."

The friends followed Alex into the office to pick up their schedules. Then Alex gave them a tour of the pack house and introduced them to Mark and a few others. They all relaxed for the rest of the day.

The next day in school, Rocky held Bluey's hand as they walked to their lockers, trying to ignore the whispers and stares.

Today is going to be rough, Rocky thought. *I marked Bluey, but she's so beautiful. Most people—wolves, humans, and even witches—know not to mess with me or with someone I'm close to, but that doesn't mean shit sometimes.* Rocky grabbed what he needed from his locker and headed with Bluey toward Zane's as usual. Zane looked stressed, and Rocky felt power radiating from him. Bluey joined Val while Rocky quietly spoke to Zane.

"How are holding up? You need to tell Pyrox to pull back on his power a bit. We need him under control."

"I'm trying. My senses are in overdrive, and it's giving me a headache already. I hear all the whispers about our mates, and it's making Pyrox edgy."

"Keep in mind that we're already mated and that they're fighters. They have alpha and beta blood. Remember how they punched Alex without even thinking twice—just because he insulted us. And that was even before we fully mated," Rocky said, noticing Zane relaxed and his power was no longer emitting.

"That's true. Thanks for the reminder. This is so new to me. I wish I had your control."

"You'll get there, bro. It's going to be more of a struggle for Val than for you. You already have a slight crowd whispering about you over there, about how much you changed and how much more muscular you look."

"They're gawking at you not me, bro."

"If you say so."

Zane and Rocky grabbed their mates and headed to their classes. Throughout the morning, Rocky mind-linked Zane to keep tabs on how he was holding up. At lunch, they met up with Alex and Mark. Alex moved away their usual groupies to make room for the four.

"Hey, Alex. Hey, Mark. Anything good going down today?" Rocky asked.

"Same old crap; different day," Alex grumbled.

"Val, how's your first day going?" Mark asked.

Rocky raised an eyebrow at Alex, hoping like hell Mark wasn't that stupid. *Mark had always viewed Zane as weak, but he could clearly smell Zane's scent mixed with Val's. I guess Alpha Steven was right about Mark*, Rocky thought. *He needs to start going up.*

"Mark, is it? School sucks no matter where you go. I was enrolled in excel classes along with Bluey, so it's boring when you have already learned the same thing," Val said.

Rocky laughed inside at her response; she nuzzled Zane's neck right after. *She's as smart as my Bluey.*

"I love redheads," Mark said, prompting a low warning growl from Zane.

"That's nice. Go find one," Val suggested.

Althea and Valerie high-fived, and Mark reddened with embarrassment. Alex patted him on the back and said, "Nice try, Mark. I told you she's proud to be Zane's mate."

"I see that," Mark said.

All Zane could think of was getting out of there. *My senses are in overdrive. If Val wasn't giving me affection and calming me down, I'd have lost my shit on my future beta.* The mixtures of sounds, smells, and emotions was making Zane's head spin and his stomach nauseated. He tried concentrating on Val and Rocky's advice to help this pass. But not being able to hold back any longer, Zane dashed to the toilets and threw up. As he was hugging the toilet, the damn fire alarm started blaring, compounding his nausea—and now panic.

Mate! Mate! She needs us. Find her now, or I'm coming out! Pyrox screamed in his head.

The desperate urge to get to his mate kicked in, and Zane almost broke the bathroom door, bolting out of it. When he reached the lunchroom, he saw smoke and fire coming out of all the trashcans—but his mate and friends were nowhere in sight. Zane tried mind-linking Val but got no response. So, in a panic he tried Rocky, *Where is she?!*

We're outside on the north edge of the forest, just outside the school," Rocky replied.

For the first time ever, Zane tapped into his Lycan's strength and speed to get to Val—not caring about consequences. When he finally found them, he saw Bluey holding Val. With a nod of thanks to Bluey, Zane took over and held Val close, so close he could feel her breathing and her heartbeat.

"What happened?" Zane asked.

"Not soon after you left, a human approached her. She gave him sass and told him to get lost, but he grabbed her, then all the trashcans burst into flames, and Val collapsed," Rocky said.

Zane held Val, caressing her hair and face. He had Pyrox try to reach her wolf, but all he got in return was, *Tired, so tired.* Bluey sat next to them, still holding Val's hand and looking very worried. Rocky and Mark had their guards up. Zane saw Alex approaching.

"How is she?" Alex asked.

"All I could get from her wolf was she's tired. Why is all this happening?"

"I don't know how I know this, but I think that guy is a warlock. Once the fire department gets here, we're allowed to leave. I've informed my father of the situation, but he's still at his meeting up north."

"If that guy started the fires, let's go get him," Rocky growled, spoiling for a fight.

"I looked all over the school, but I couldn't find him anywhere," Alex said. "We can't let him know we don't think he's human. We must tread lightly. Once he provoked Val, the fires started. Given the state Val's in, I'm assuming it was her," Alex said.

The friends got comfortable on the ground of the forest next to campus, waiting for permission from the fire department to be released. Zane noticed Val coming to. He kissed her lightly on the cheek. "My love, are you okay?"

"Yes, I'm so tired. What happened?"

"Just rest, my love. I got you. You're safe."

It felt like forever before the Silver Line City Fire Department finally arrived. A few pack members worked for them alongside some humans. As the friends watched from their safe distance, the firefighters entered the building to clear it. Before long, the department head, a werewolf named Henry, a middle guard's pack member approached. He was average by werewolf standards, but above average in the human world. He was middle aged, lost his mate at a young age, and fell in love with a human. He approached Alex to give the okay after he looked Val over. He did human protocols to keep their secret safe. He released the teens, and they returned to the pack house.

Chapter 21: Piece of Prophecy

Earlier that morning, Alpha Van growled in his office in frustration after getting off the phone with Alpha Steven. *Damn it! This wasn't supposed to happen. My boy couldn't even get my beta's daughter to fall for him.* Van cleared his desk with one sweep of his muscular arm. *FUCK!* He called for Jones.

"Yes, Alpha?" Beta Jones asked, scurrying to his alpha's office.

"Fuck! Just fuck! Steven called, asking for immediate transfer for the girls. They found their mates in his pack."

"Son of a bitch!"

"Now that our sons failed, we need a different plan."

"Couldn't you delay the transfer?"

"No. They told him about our order and used it against me."

"Fucking good-for-nothing daughters."

"Let's pray Steven doesn't know about the prophecy."

"Now that our initial plans for power are sunk, we must trick him into giving us them back."

"I like the way you think. Go get Opal."

Jones hot-footed out of the alpha's office in search of the powerful pack witch, as Van started brainstorming ways to get the girls back under his control. *If I make sure the girls cause more trouble than they're worth to Steven, he'll want to send them back. But I've got to make sure none of this points back to me in the end. I've got to clean up this mess.*

Van was desperate to keep his pack from knowing what was going on until he could announce that the pack was moving to the Royal Kingdom. *Then they'll praise me not only as their alpha, but as their king.*

Knowing it would take a few hours for Jones to find Opal and bring her to Van, Van went to his mate to give her a good fuck, then on a run to release his anger. Once Jones mind-linked Van to tell him he was five minutes away from the pack house, Van headed back to his office—a little more clear-headed.

But his calm didn't last long. Van's blood pressure spiked when he saw Opal. *What? She looks six months pregnant! This complicates things.*

"Opal, what's new?" Van eyed the witch warily.

"For one thing, I'm pregnant," Opal said, gesturing at her expanded belly. "What can I do for you, Alpha Van?"

"I need you to pose as a high school student," Van said.

"I'm a bit old to pull that off, and I can't change appearances right now. My powers are all focused on protecting my baby. I can produce a potion here and there, but that's all."

"I can solve that problem really quick," Van threatened.

"Don't you fucking dare!"

"I need what I need. Do you have a solution to my problem?"

"I have a sixteen-year-old son with powers, but I won't send him into danger."

"What I need done isn't dangerous. I need him to go to Silver Line City High School and provoke Valerie. That's it."

"Not possible. One, the wolves and supernaturals there will sense immediately he's a warlock. Two, she's strong and could hurt him."

"Do you have a better idea?"

Opal sighed in resignation. At Van's instruction, Jones took Opal back home. She lived in a modest style home on the outskirts, but within pack territory, near the human town of Howlston so she had better access to farms for her witchcraft supplies. She sat down with her husband and their son, Quin, to explain what needed to be done. Quin's gift was the ability to teleport—or flash—anywhere, anytime. The family planned that he would flash to the school, provoke Valerie, then flash the hell out of there. Opal prepared a masking and cloaking potion to change his appearance and disguise his warlock aura.

Meanwhile, Ricky and Roman were stressing on their flight back to their pack.

"This is a disaster, Ricky. My father is probably flipping his shit right now," Roman said.

"Mine too. They weren't our mates. What did our fathers expect us to do? They're both strong-willed she-wolves with minds of their own. They are not like our mothers. I wasn't going to screw your sister anyway. She's beautiful and smart, but she isn't my mate, nor was she willing to be."

"I hear you, buddy. To try to force Val and Bluey to be with us was just wrong. At least they got away from the bullshit we put them through. I don't want to be an asshole alpha like my father. Sure, he keeps the pack healthy and wealthy, but our warriors are starting to get weak and lazy. For a large pack of 250 wolves, we are sure weak. I need to get stronger to challenge and replace him," Roman asserted.

"We'll have to work on that. If it wasn't for you being here, I'd find another pack to run off to. I don't want to face our fathers' wrath, but I wasn't about to force myself on their daughters either. The thought of it makes me sick," Ricky said.

"I'm going to chill for the rest of the flight. I'm sure we'll need our strength back at the pack."

What felt like minutes later, Roman was jolted awake by the announcement that the plane had started its descent to land. The pair got into the car for the drive to the pack house. Roman dreaded facing his father. *I hate having to act like a pompous asshole all the time just to please him.* As Roman headed into his father's office, he breathed deep and put on his asshole face.

"How could you fail to fuck the one girl I needed you to!" Van yelled at his son.

"I've been trying for two years!"

"You should've marked her and raped her until she was pregnant!"

That startled Roman. *I know he's a bastard, but that's cold even for him.* "I'd never rape anyone, Father! Why did you want me to be with her so badly? We weren't chosen to be mates!"

"That's none of your concern."

"Oh, the fuck it ain't! You wanted me to rape Val until she got pregnant, and you wanted Ricky to do the same thing to your own daughter, I presume. It most certainly does concern me!"

"Fine. I'll tell you why. Val and Althea are part of a prophecy."

"What the hell are you talking about?"

"I'll let you read it for yourself. Let's go to the vault," Van said, leading Roman to the alpha-only vault and handing him a scroll. "This is for your eyes only."

Prophecy of Water and Fire

The wolves of water and fire are destined to guard the king of wolves and the Royal Kingdom.

They're to be the keepers of peace among all creatures created by Moon Goddess.

Once mated, their powers will slowly grow, and their mates will receive great strength to help them with their destiny.

With Moon Goddess's blessing, the pairs will produce the strongest heirs the world has ever known. They will train each generation's powers needed to overcome any obstacles.

When Roman finished reading, he understood why his father wanted him to be with Val so badly. *My father completely glossed over an important point: with the Moon Goddess's blessing.*

"Well, I'll be fuckin damned," Roman said quietly.

"You see why now: Your sister has to be the wolf of water, and Val the wolf of fire. Think about it: Their wolves' color schemes said it all—it was hidden in plain sight. If you two would have done what I told you to, we would be heading toward royalty right now. Because King Dominic Sidious has no heirs nor even a mate, and you're of alpha blood, you would be a shoo-in to be king."

"That's a lot to take in. You should have told me sooner, Father. I'd have tried harder."

"Well, now you know. I have a plan to get the girls back to this pack, but it's going to take time."

"This is heavy shit, Father. It all makes sense to me now. Now I understand why they're so much more determined and stronger than the other she-wolves," Roman said, leaving the vault and his father with a scattered mind. Lost in his thoughts, he blindly grabbed some dinner, which on tonight's menu was steak and potatoes from the pack kitchen, then spotted Ricky already eating in the dining room.

"Hey, Roman. How did things go with your father?" Ricky asked.

"Um, bad at first. There's something we need to talk about in private."

"Sounds good. After we eat, I'll meet you there," Ricky said with a knowing look.

The friends ate and interacted with the pack, then Ricky was the first to get up and leave. Roman knew where he was headed. The friends had discovered a hidden room years before near Van's office. Roman met up with Ricky there about fifteen minutes later. Shrieking Moon's pack house was an old, small, but strong, hold castle. It has many secrets yet to be discovered.

"There's something important about our sisters I have to tell you," Roman said.

"That doesn't sound good."

"I'm not sure."

"Don't keep me in suspense!"

Needing no further prompting, Roman told Ricky about the scroll of prophecy and how their fathers twisted it in their own minds to their own benefit. Ricky sat silently, processing this new information.

"You okay, Ricky?"

"Wow, that's a lot."

"What should we do? Would you rape my sister to become royalty?"

"No way, man. I don't even want to be royalty. But I would follow you, no matter what."

"I don't want to be king. Just running one pack would be hard enough. Should we warn Alpha Steven? Or should we let our fathers destroy their destiny and everyone else's who's involved?"

"How could we warn them without our fathers finding out and then probably killing us for treason?"

"Honestly, I don't know. Not to mention the girls hate our guts right now. We can't talk about this outside of this room. I don't trust my father not to listen in to our conversations."

"Sounds good. Let's get out of here," Ricky said, then the friends crept out of their secret room and went to bed.

Earlier that morning, as Quin got ready for the day, he thought about what the alpha tasked him to do. Even though he was a warlock and not technically part of the pack, he still had to follow Van's orders. *I just do as I'm told and hopefully won't get my ass kicked in the process.* Unlike his mother, Quin didn't like using his powers to hurt people.

As Quin got ready to teleport to Val's new school, with his mother's potions safety tucked inside his backpack, he tried to devise a plan. A few years younger than Val, he didn't know her, just knew *of* her. *She's beautiful, genuine, and smart. She sticks up for people. Yet she's strong enough to reject Roman's clumsy advances. She seems to hate his flirting.* Quin realized that was the ticket: *I'll use that angle to provoke her.*

Quin took the potions to camouflage his identity—otherwise Val would likely recognize him. After teleporting to her new school, he looked around. When he found the lunchroom to be empty except for the kitchen staff, Quin went to find a nearby bathroom to lie in wait.

When the lunch bell finally rang, Quin waited for a crowd to build in the hallway before venturing out of the bathroom. Quickly, he spotted Val with her mate and Bluey with her mate, wolves he assumed were their pack's alpha and beta's sons, by the power around them. Quin could sense the ranks amongst wolves, which was an odd ability for a warlock. He got into the lunch line to get some food to blend in and found a nearby table. Before long, he saw Zane leave. Quin approached Val and tried flirting with her, but she was being nice about turning him down at first, so he pushed harder, grabbed her wrist, and insulted her mate.

Then all hell broke loose. Every trashcan in the room burst into fire, creating mass panic in the cafeteria. Mission accomplished, Quin let Val go, blended in with the chaos, then flashed back to his room.

That was intense to say the least. I thought I was going to get my ass kicked. Good thing the fires started, or I probably would have, Quin thought, assuming that was what the alpha wanted him to cause. *She isn't a witch, so how did she do it? Wolves don't have powers.* It felt so wrong to Quin to do what he did, but he did what he was told.

Back at the pack, Van dispatched Jones to bring Opal to his office to see if the deed was done. He kept the witch at a distance both literally and figuratively. She lived on the outskirts of his territory, and he didn't trust her. *I think Jones has a thing for her; he always enjoys being ordered to go to her.* Van worked on pack bank paperwork until the pair arrived. *Money does the talking in this necks of the woods.* He was nearly finished when Jones finally arrived with Opal.

"Did your son succeed?" Van asked Opal without preamble.

"From what I hear yes. He provoked her into starting the cafeteria on fire. How is that possible? Is she part witch?"

"She's no witch, but she is special. You'll be greatly compensated for that. You know how I operate, so keep your mouth shut. Remind your son and husband of that too. Take this and leave," Van said dismissively, handing Opal a check.

"I'll remind them, Alpha. Thank you."

Before Opal was out the door, Van was already lost in thought. *She set the school on fire. That's pretty troublesome, but I know Steven. Just one incident won't have him sending those girls back on the next plane. I have to come up with something else. This time, I'll focus on Althea.*

Roman, get in here! Van mind-linked his son.

You need me, Father? Roman asked politely, though annoyed by his father's demand.

I need information, then you can head to training. What are the girls' mates' ranks? Did you meet them?

Not really, but Bluey's mate, Rocky, is only a delta, but he's a big son of a bitch. Val's mate, Zane, is only a tracker, and he's scrawny and quiet from what I could tell. Once the girls met their mates, they started avoiding Ricky and me.

That's embarrassing to say the least—an alpha blood getting a delta and a beta blood getting a tracker. Thank you. Head to training now.

Roman headed toward the training grounds, eager to blow off some steam and up his game to beat his father in the near future. He was starting to suspect Van was sabotaging his training to retain his power. A plan began to formulate in Roman's mind, and he vowed to meet up with Ricky to discuss it.

Chapter 22: Letting Loose

With a heavy heart, Beta Jake sat in his office musing. Alpha Steven instructed him to brief Mark on the situation and swear with a blood oath. *I pray to the Moon Goddess that Mark understands why he was left out and won't hold it against me. Maybe it's my fault he hasn't grown up yet. I pushed him in his strength training, but I never really gave him true beta duties nor responsibilities. I wanted him to have a childhood and not burden him with the harsh realities of protecting and serving a pack.* Jake knew all too well how responsibilities had robbed Roman and Ricky of their childhoods.

Jake mind-linked Mark and the rest of the group he deemed the chosen ones to come to his office. It took about an hour for Mark to arrive, with Alex, Rocky, and Bluey trailing behind—without Zane and Valerie.

"Look at you all! I got more than I bargained for," Jake said with a smile. "But where are Zane and Valerie?"

"After what happened, Val needed to rest, and Zane wouldn't leave her side," Alex explained.

"That's understandable. Alpha Steven told me to swear Mark in on our secret," Jake began.

"Tell me what?" Mark asked.

"Before I can explain, Mark, you need to swear a blood oath because Alpha Steven isn't here to command you into secrecy. Are you willing to do that for your friends and the pack?"

"Not going to lie, Dad, it's kind of scary to hear I have to take a blood oath just to hear a secret, but I've been preparing for more beta duties for a while now. I've been waiting for you to trust me enough to give me more responsibilities, so yes, I'm prepared to take a blood oath for my friends and the pack."

Jake embraced his son with pride, his trust growing. His choice with his mate, Nora, to let their pups have a childhood had been validated.

Rocky gave Mark one of his atta-boy back slaps. Mark winced. Rocky didn't know his own strength sometimes.

"Let's get this show on the road, shall we?" Alex said impatiently.

The group circled around Mark. Jake got the red and blue diamond-encrusted ceremonial dagger from the vault.

Alex started the blood oath ceremony. "Do you, Mark O'Connor, son of Beta Jake and Beta Female Nora O'Connor, our future beta, swear on your life protect Silver Stone Pack from our enemies and also to protect the secrets we hold? Do you understand breaking this blood oath is an act of treason, punishable by torturous death?"

"I swear on my life to uphold this oath for Silver Stone Pack and for my family and friends. I'll uphold this oath until my death," Mark said solemnly.

Jake sliced Alex's palm with the dagger, then his own, then Mark's. Alex grabbed Mark's hand, then Jake's, sealing the blood oath.

For the next hour, Jake explained what had transpired to Mark, who soaked it all in without interruptions, as did the others.

"Do you have any questions or concerns?" Jake asked.

"So, Zane is a Lycan—the most powerful being on Earth that we know of. Why can't we feel his power like we can feel Alex's and Alpha Steven's?" Mark asked.

"Zane has to keep his power in check because we don't know what him being a Lycan really means yet." Jake explained.

"You were all visited by the Moon Goddess, Val can start fires, Bluey can control water, and Zane is a Lycan. Dad you're the beta of this pack, but the Moon Goddess didn't visit you. Doesn't that make you a little upset?" Mark asked, after processing the news for a few minutes.

"Son, believe me. She might not have come to you nor me directly, but we're in the path of destiny, of those she *did* visit. If we weren't meant to be, we wouldn't even be here. She has her ways. She gave Alpha Steven and the rest the choice of who is trustworthy and most honorable to be the first few to know the path."

"I trust our goddess," Mark said.

The friends went back to the assigned room on the alpha's floor of the pack house after being released. Lying with Val in his arms listening to her breath calmed Zane and Pyrox, so they fell asleep with her.

When Zane awoke, Val was staring at him. "Hello, love."

"My fiery redhead can actually start fires, it seems."

"Yeah, I guess so."

"You feeling better?"

"I am, but now I'm starving."

"Let's see if my mom is here yet. If not, I'll make you something to eat."

The minute Zane entered the kitchen, his mother engulfed him in a hug. She let go, then embraced Val.

"Oh, my baby boy, how have you been? Come sit. Tell me everything while I prepare a little something for you two before dinner," Trudy said with a joyful smile.

"As you can tell, we're fully mated, but please no asking for grandkids yet," Zane teased.

"Why don't you just take all my fun away. Val, sweetie, how do you like it here so far? Has everyone been good to you? Just let me know if anyone hasn't been, and I can give them diarrhea for a week," Trudy joked.

Val and Zane laughed. *I miss my family so much, but it's not safe yet for me to move back home,* Zane thought.

"Thank you for that, Trudy. So far everyone here has been great. There's much less pressure here, and I feel so safe with Zane by my side."

"You can just call me Tru or Mom. You're family. I'm happy to hear my son is being a good mate. He didn't pressure you into mating, did he?" Trudy asked, standing in front of Zane and threatening him with a big spoon at her last statement. That got another laugh out of Val as Zane raised his hands in defense.

"He never had to pressure me into anything once I saw him naked. Everything was mutual. He's been nothing but wonderful, and I'm so happy our goddess chose him for me."

"Glad we raised him right. When do you plan to come home? Robert is already trying to take over your room," Trudy said, looking at Zane.

"I really don't know, Mom. It's hard to control Pyrox right now, and I don't want to be a danger to anyone."

"I seriously doubt your wolf would hurt any one of us, my dear. I haven't even gotten to see him yet. I'm dying to know who you take after me or your father."

"It's not that I think he'll hurt anyone. It's just..." Zane trailed off, not knowing how to explain himself to my mom, unsure if Trudy knows he's a Lycan. *I don't want her to be afraid of me.*

"It's just what, dear?"

Val jumped in to help Zane out, "He doesn't want everyone in your house to hear us constantly mating. We're having such a hard time keeping our hands off each other right now, if you know what I mean. Here the alpha gave us a soundproof room on his floor. Bluey and Rocky too."

Zane blushed, but he admitted it was a logical explanation to give to his mom.

"Zane, why are you embarrassed about that? She's beautiful, and she's yours. I'm glad she's not shy around me. Here is a little something before the pack dinner, eat up. Welcome to the family, honey," Trudy said, handing each of them a plate of hoagie sandwiches and chips.

Trudy hugged Val again before returning to the hustle and bustle of making dinner. Zane and Val ate, then headed to find Rocky.

Where're you at? Zane mind-linked.

At Alpha's office, Rocky replied.

When Zane and Val entered the office, they saw Beta Jake, Alex, Mark, Rocky, and Bluey gathered.

"Um, hey, guys. What's going on?" Zane asked.

Bluey ran to hug Val. "Oh, my love, how are you feeling? Anything I can do for you?"

"I'm fine, sweetie, no worries. I was just extremely tired and hungry."

"So, Zane, a Lycan eh? How's that going from little power to complete power?" Mark asked irreverently.

The group went silent at Mark's comment and growled at his demeanor—except Alex.

"Honestly, Mark, it's hard dealing with all the changes at once—shifting, mating, and all the power," Zane said.

"Relax, guys. I'm just joking around. Geez. It's pretty cool actually, and I'm glad to finally be let in on the secret. Have you given him a chance to be let out yet?" Mark asked Zane.

"I've been afraid to."

"Regardless of whether you're a Lycan or a wolf, you have to let him out, or you'll be unprepared and lose control of him in a bad situation. Knowing what I know now, I'm shocked it didn't happen this afternoon," Mark said.

"It almost did."

"Mark is right, Zane. We need to find the proper time to let him out. I feel terrible for not thinking about that. Tonight around 2200, let's go to the waterfall where my dad had you shift. Sound good, everyone?" Alex asked.

"That's why you have me, buddy," Mark said, with a bro slap.

The friends agreed on that plan and headed down for the pack dinner.

Later that night, they met at Zane's house to pick up his SUV and head to the falls. Beta Jake made sure to switch his patrol route, so no one who didn't know of Zane's Lycan would witness him. Even with people he knew, loved, and trusted, Zane was still nervous to let his Lycan out. When the group arrived at the falls, Zane took a deep breath. Everyone gathered around him, reassuring him that everything would be fine to let him out. Pyrox was ready to be let out to stretch and meet his mate. He didn't want to hold back any longer.

Zane didn't fight the shift, but it still hurt like a son of a bitch. As his human body transformed into his Lycan and his conscience moved to the back, Pyrox pushed his mind forward.

It feels so good to be free! Pyrox thought. The others fell to their knees in submission to his aura all except Val. She stood tall and proud even with her tiny stature. Pyrox approached her, bowed to her, looking for her approval of his presence. When he bowed, they were face to face. Val gently cupped his snout and kissed it. She got down on all fours, then transformed into her own glorious wolf, such a sight to see. Despite being surrounded by friends, all Pyrox could see was her.

"Ignisara, my beautiful mate," Pyrox said.

She licked him and rubbed her scent all over him, circling him multiple times. Then she stopped in front of him so he could do the same. He took full advantage, rubbing his scent all over her, nice and slow. Suddenly, she darted away, yipping happily. He gladly pursued her. *What a silly mate.*

Pyrox saw her fiery coat darting all around the forest. She tried to hide behind a big oak tree. He stalked her like she was prey, snuck up on her, then said, "Well, well, well, little mate. Are you trying to hide from me?"

Strong and feisty like her human, Iggy gave him a wolfish grin, then pounced on him, taking him down. In an instant, Pyrox reversed their body positions, startling her. "Seems I've turned the tides, little mate. What should we do about that?"

Without a moment's notice, Iggy rolled onto her belly, lifted her hind legs, and wagged her tail provocatively. Pyrox caught a whiff of her. *She wants to mate! I'll give my mate whatever she desires.* Pyrox stroked her fur with his hands. Iggy purred. Pyrox latched onto her rear, mounted her, and took her as his as gently as possible for her sake so as not to tear her apart.

When he was about to let loose, his canines were out and on her neck, connecting her soul with his Lycan soul, and he released inside his mate. Satisfied emotionally, spiritually, and sexually, Pyrox let out all his power in one loud roar that shook the trees and ground. Iggy took her turn to sink her canines into him, marking him forever hers and releasing a satisfied howl of her own. A surge of completeness coursed through Pyrox.

Rocky had watched his best friend once more take his form as a Lycan. It was a sight that will take time to get used to. The sheer power Pyrox emitted was too much to bear, and Rocky was on his knees with the others. After Pyrox and Iggy scampered off in play, everyone let out the breath they seemed to be holding.

"She's so brave. That would scare the hell out of me, but they're adorable together," Bluey whispered.

"Holy shit! He's fucking huge! Absolutely incredible. Did he actually speak in that form?" Alex asked no one in particular.

"Never in my life have I seen anything that large. The absolute power radiating from him was incredible. Wow. I'd never have believed you if I hadn't experienced it for myself. What do we do now?" Mark asked.

The group discussed ideas about what would happen if Zane ever lost control. They stopped midsentence when they heard a roar and felt the ground shake.

"Well, we know what game they're playing," Bluey said with a chuckle.

It took Rocky a minute before he blurted, "Oh, shit! They're mating!"

"My sexy mate is a quick one, isn't he? We might be here for a while, until they get their time together in. Any suggestions?" Bluey asked.

"It's a warm night. In case anyone heard that roar and comes to investigate, we should be prepared with a cover story. Let's go skinny dipping," Alex suggested.

The friends enjoyed their late-night skinny-dipping session, bonded more closely now that Mark was in on the big secret. About an hour later, Zane and Val returned, joining the swimming fun before they all went back to the pack house for the night.

Chapter 23: Secrets Within

Earlier that day, Alpha Steven had been meeting with one of his cousins, Alpha Charles of the Stronghold Pack, in Charles's office, when Alex called to tell him about Quin provoking Val into lighting the trashcan fires at school. Returning his attention to Charles, Steven said, "Sorry about that, Chuck. Never a dull moment running a pack, right?"

"You got that right, Steve," Charles chuckled. "As I was explaining, I've been having issues with the Royal Kingdom. I'm not trying to take on the royals, because we both know how they are. I've tried to reach out to the council, but I'm not having any luck."

"Don't worry, cousin. I'll send you warriors. How many do you need for now?" Steven asked.

"I can comfortably take care of fifty extra warriors for now. I'm prepping for the alpha/beta rotation this summer. Building a bigger barracks at the moment."

"You aren't going to house them in the pack house?"

"Nope. I decided to train them as normal as possible, like true warriors. They're lucky I just didn't decide to put up a tent city to give them a real feel for war conditions. Some of those spoiled ones will learn the hard way. The program was way too lax five years ago, and this rotation everyone signed up. It was extended to second and third borns."

"Alex and Mark are in it this year. Don't go easy on them. Are you sure just fifty extra warriors will be enough? If it's like anything twenty years ago, you'll need more," Steven warned.

"I'm worried about that, but for now, fifty more fighters will be enough to ensure our safety until we figure this out. I won't go easy on them. I promise."

"Great. Consider it done. I'll round them up and start sending them in waves not to raise suspicion with the royals nor surrounding packs. If anyone questions you, say they've been sent to look for their mates."

"Perfect. That's why you were the king's favorite. You're always thinking strategy," Charles said.

Alpha Steven gathered his men and journeyed home. Only two people outside the royal court knew that Steven, Charles, and Jake were once part of the Royal Guardsman. They left the guard after they stumbled upon a secret council meeting—without King Dominic Sidious. They only caught the end of the meeting and heard, "...he's keeping us well fed and our pockets heavy. Who cares if he isn't a true werewolf? His secret is safe with us." They heard cheers and pint glasses clinking. Because Steven, Charles, and Jake left the guard on good terms, no suspicions were thrown their way.

When Alpha Steven finally got home, he exchanged information with Beta Jake. Steven started arrangements for the first wave of warriors to head toward Alpha Charles's pack. After being back for a few hours, he desperately sought his mate to finally relax and spend time with her. Happy alpha, happy pack.

It had been a few days since Roman's father had unloaded all his secrets on him. Roman and Ricky talked multiple times about everything, and they came up with a plan. Now Roman just had to convince Val it would work. He practiced the conversation in his head with his wolf as he walked toward the alpha office.

Before Roman could even knock, he heard his father bellow in his always-annoyed voice, "Come in, son. What do you want?"

"I have a failsafe plan to get the girls back here under your thumb."

"You have my attention."

"What if you sign Ricky and me up for the alpha/beta training? I know the girls are on the rotation for the program. We'll put on our best charm, and no one will be the wiser."

Van leaned back in his chair thinking it over, making Roman nervous. *He thinks his and Beta James's training is enough. It would be great to get away for a while if nothing else. We need to make amends with our sisters.*

"Roman, I must admit that's fucking brilliant. Do you understand that the program will send you all over and is part of the Royal Guardsmanship? It's not for the faint of heart. Are you both up for the challenge?"

"Ricky and I discussed it, and we think it's the best way to get a different kind of training and also insight to how other packs operate and fight. We would even get to scope out King Sidious and put a little bug in his ear about the girls."

"I've trained you well enough already. It's time to let you spread your paws and lead us toward royalty," Van said vainly.

Roman left his dad's office and went straight to Ricky's room. Bursting through the door, he said, "He not only went for it and is signing us up, but basically he thinks we'll be the ones to lead us to royalty."

"Awesome! Shut the door and sit," Ricky said.

Roman knew by Ricky's tone something was wrong. Ricky put on the heavy metal strains of F8 and leaned on his desk.

"Our sister's new school caught on fire last week. No one was hurt badly. I heard Val collapsed, but she's okay. I think our fathers were behind this," Ricky explained.

"Why wouldn't they fucking tell us about that? Why would they try to harm the girls when they think they're the key to royalty? It could have been Val who did it. She's more than likely fully mated now and could have her powers."

"Perhaps, but it doesn't add up after our fathers saying they had a plan. They haven't exactly included us in on it, except to make us fuck them."

"Valid point. But I don't think they would actually put them in harm's way."

"What if I told you I've seen Opal a few times in the past week coming from your father's office? My father wouldn't pass up an opportunity to use her," Ricky divulged.

"She does have a son who's two or so years younger than us. We could find him and corner him at school to make him squeal."

"We can't just go and start being nice, now, can we?" Ricky joked, trying to distract his friend from some secrets he'd been keeping. He hadn't told Roman that if they fail to protect their sisters, he's not coming back to the pack. *I'm just done.* The other secret is that Quin is his half-brother. Ricky's wolf confirmed it when he was fifteen. Even though Ricky didn't get his wolf physically until he was sixteen, the wolves' minds awaken prior to their first shift to guide the humans through it. Ricky mused, *Our Moon Goddess determines just about everything for us. Opal seems to have some kind of connection to King Sidious, I just can't figure it out. I'm going to snoop when our rotation in the alpha/beta comes around to the Royal Guardsman.*

Ricky skipped his classes to search for Quin, which quickly paid off when he spotted Quin in the hall. Ricky stood in the middle of the crowded hall, arms folded across his chest, and stared right at him. Quin didn't notice until someone tapped him to look at Ricky. Quin slowly approached Ricky.

"Follow me," Ricky commanded, leading him into the faculty lounge and locking the door behind him. "How's it going, Quin?"

"Please don't hurt me," he said quietly.

"I'm not going to hurt you, brother."

"I'm not your brother. I'm a warlock not a werewolf."

"That might be true, but trust me when I tell you, you're my brother. That conversation is for another day. I need you to tell me what your mother has been up to."

"Why?"

"Why has she been brought to the pack house? I know Alpha Van is up to something. He only calls on her when he's up to no good." Ricky smelled fear radiating from Quin, and his wolf, Thorn, wanted to protect Ricky from Quin, but he knew they needed this information to protect Val. "Tell me now!"

"Alpha Van wanted her to go to Silver Line City High School and pose as a student."

"You're leaving out the fuckin' why," Ricky said, getting very irritated.

Quin could read that on Ricky's face. He sighed, sat down on the couch, and put his head in his hands.

"I don't want to die, Beta Richard, but I fear that is my fate anyway. I'll tell you what I know on one condition."

"What's that?"

"Can I at least ask for this to stay between us? Please believe me when I tell you I didn't want to do it."

Ricky pulled a chair up in front of the couch as Quin explained what happened that day. *I figured I was right about the fire and my father being part of it. I think he's more evil than Alpha Van. Roman might not believe me. Quin is going to have to tell him himself.*

"I tell you what, Quin, I'll keep this between us; however, you'll have to tell Roman. I'll call upon you when the time is right. You come regardless, no questions asked. Am I clear?"

"Yes, Beta Richard. I understand."

Ricky checked the time and headed to where he needed to be.

It had been a little over a week since the fire at school, and Alpha Steven had been working hard with Val and Bluey to gain better control of the powers the Moon Goddess bestowed upon them. He had decided to keep Val's and Bluey's powers secret from the pack and also the council. Zane was having a hard time understanding how to keep everyone's power under control when he could barely control his own. He loved watching Val and Bluey train—where Val made fire and Bluey contained it. It was magical to watch.

Alpha Steven had been having Rocky and Zane flat-out beat the shit out of each other. He wanted to see how long they could fight and how much of a beating they could withstand.

"You never know when you might need to be able to take a punch and try to show you're weaker than you appear," Steven told them.

Zane thought, *I guess it's because I'm just supposed to be a tracker, and we can't tell anyone our secret yet. Pyrox is telling me to be on alert because he can tell his Alpha (Sunken) is on edge and has been ever since his return. Makes me wonder what secrets are being withheld now. It's not my place to question anyone above me, but just to trust them until they betray us.*

Zane felt badly for Alex, who discovered how many people only wanted to be his friend because he's an alpha. A few fights had broken out, but Mark smoothed them over. Alex had an emotional breakdown, so Zane let him pound on him and yell at him to get it all out. Val made Zane a bath and tended to him after. Having her take care of Zane after was well worth every cut and bruise.

Chapter 24: Reveal

More than a month after the fire at school, all seemed calm and quiet. Preparations for graduation were well under way. The seniors were in the auditorium for their graduation photos, line up practice, and to get their caps and gowns. Rocky and Zane people watched, leaning against a wall near the bleachers. Some of the guys were horsing around, and some girls were crying. Bluey and Val went to roam around. Rocky and Zane had gotten used to them being outgoing, friendly, and feisty.

Rocky could feel Zane's anxiety radiating off him. "Why so glum, brother?"

"Being here really throws me into the reality of having to be an adult, to provide and protect my mate, all that grown-up stuff," Zane said.

"Holy shit! Did you knock up Val already?"

"Really? No, no, she isn't. That's another worry of mine. Thanks for reminding me."

"Don't you want a family?"

"Well, of course we do. Don't you? With me being you know what and her being normal, maybe we can't even have kids because we're different."

Rocky finally understood. *We don't know enough about Lycans to understand if his worries are valid. I really pray our goddess wouldn't do that to such a wonderful couple. They deserve happiness. If they're really part of the prophecy, she should bless them and not forsake them. I'll refuse any bidding of hers if that is the case. He's my brother, blood or not.*

"I don't think you'll have anything to worry about. Now get your ass moving. Let's have some fun. Stop thinking so hard."

"You're so pushy sometimes, like a girl."

"Oh, you got jokes now. Let's go."

Rocky loosened him up a bit. The friends roamed the auditorium, photo bombing as they went. Their chosen group has grown closer together, and Alex and Mark too were starting their alpha/beta training this summer. They all did what they could to help Alex control his temper when he knows someone was lying, because of his goddess-given gift.

Rocky spotted Bluey before she saw him. She decided to wear a delicate sundress that showed off her long legs. *I just love having them wrapped around me,* Rocky thought. Carrick's tongue lopped to the side drooling. She bent down to tie her shoes. Rocky had to work to hold his composure as not to mount her in front of the entire graduating class, his jean shorts helping to conceal his now-massive boner. Like the predator he was, Rocky stalked over to her like she was his prey. He engulfed her from behind, hearing giggling from the other girls, and growled lowly in her ear, "You have done something very naughty." She instantly shuddered against him. Rocky gave her a kiss, then left to find Alex.

Alex was never hard to find; he drew in crowds because of who he was. When Rocky reached Alex's group, Alex pushed other people aside to greet him and said, "We need to see my father as a group when we get out of here."

Nodding, Rocky shouted to move the grad practices along faster, "Let's finish up here and be free of this day!"

The graduating class finished their practice ceremony and just needed to take their farewell photos for the yearbook.

After leaving graduation practice, the group reported as requested to Alpha Steven, waiting for him to get back from the lunch Luna Tessa forced him to have.

Zane finally felt better because Val had reassured me their future would be fine. "Anyone know what the alpha needs us here for?" Zane asked.

"Nope," the group chorused.

Steven walked in soon after. "Sorry to keep you all waiting. I wanted to talk about your first summer after graduation. As you know, Alex and Mark will be leaving for six months for the alpha/beta training. Well, I just received the final roster, and you won't believe whose names showed up: Roman and Ricky."

"What? No, I'll fucking kill them!" Zane protested.

"Zane, you'll do no such thing. This is why I needed you all in here," Steven admonished.

Zane felt Pyrox already at the surface, ready to release his anger. Rocky bear hugged him, and Alpha Steven used the powers he still had from the Moon Goddess, trying to calm him down. Alex stared into Zane's eyes with his wolf, reassuring him nothing will harm the ones he loves. Val had to bite Zane to get Iggy to make Pyrox submit to at least her. Zane was breathing heavily and hugged Val tightly. "I'm sorry," he said.

Alpha Steven, Rocky, and Alex released their hold on him.

"You good?" Steven asked.

"Now we have time to train your Lycan, Zane. They leave at the end of May to start. Our pack is in the middle of the rotation. Alex and Mark will have time to see what they're up to and keep us notified of any ill will. By the time they get here, if I feel Val, Althea, or Zane are at risk, I'll send you to Strong Pack until they leave. Any questions?" Steven asked.

"Are we ever going to disclose info about Zane's Lycan to the rest of the pack? The longer we wait, the greater the chances of Zane getting caught. What will the rest of the wolves think of us if they find out themselves before we tell them?" Alex asked.

"We'll show the rest of the pack at the pack graduation party. You'll be okay, Zane. I see your anxiety. We'll all be there to support any outcome," Steven said.

But Zane stiffened up anyway. *I know it will be better when everyone knows, and I no longer have to hide it,* Zane thought. "Pyrox will be okay. He has time to learn who his pack is. As long as you are with me, all should be fine."

Graduation day finally arrived for the chosen group of the Moon Goddess. The pack was preparing for the after-graduation party.

Before the graduation ceremony, Valerie was with Bluey in the girls' locker room, touching up their makeup that had run from all the crying and feeling the weight of the celebration. *Growing up, you always say 'I can't wait to graduate,' but when it finally arrives, you think, 'I never thought this day would come,* Val thought. Her life had changed so much in the past two months.

The girls heard the announcement to go to line up in alphabetical order. Bluey and Val locked arms, heading toward the door.

"Isn't this exciting, Val? We did it," Bluey said cheerfully.

"What do we do now?"

"Don't worry so much; you'll give yourself wrinkles," Bluey said, booping Val's nose.

"Oh, Bluey. What would I do without you?"

As the girls sat on stage with their fellow graduates, Val scanned the crowd. Something wasn't sitting well with her nor Iggy.

Is something wrong, Iggy?

You relax. I'll be upfront, keeping watch.

What's wrong?

I don't want to alarm you, but I feel a family member close by. I can't tell who. Just relax. I'll keep watching.

Iggy turned Val off mentally, but Val still felt her presence keeping watch. She mind-linked Bluey, *Is Sassie on edge by any chance?*

'We aren't used to feeling vulnerable' is all Sassie said. She told me to relax, that she'll keep watch.

Really? That's the same shit Iggy said to me.

We'll be done here shortly. We'll be out of here in no time.

Val scanned the crowd cautiously and got an incoming mind-link from Zane, *I feel your anxiety, love. Are you okay? Do we need to leave?*

I'm fine, babe. I love you.

You're my world, Valerie.

It had been an hour listening to "goodbye and happy future" speeches, and the time had come to get their diplomas. Afterward, Zane and Val found Zane's family, and there were tears, hugs, and kisses all around even for Val. *I'm blessed now to have a loving family. It hurts a little knowing my family sucks though, and the only one who gets love is my brother,* she thought.

Zane picked Val up and twirled her around—when she spotted someone who shouldn't be there. "Zane, we have to go."

"What's wrong? I feel your panic."

"Let's get Bluey and Rocky and head back to the office."

The group ducked into the alpha's office for privacy. "Sorry I dragged everyone out so fast, but there was someone from our old pack who shouldn't have been there," Val explained.

"Who?" Alex asked.

"Our pack witch's son, Quin."

"Are you sure it was him, Val?" Bluey asked, concerned.

"Yes, I'm certain. I need to know why he was there," Val said, uneasily.

"We won't leave your side nor Bluey's. You don't need to worry, Val," Rocky said.

Zane took Val upstairs to change and get ready for the after party, but clearly, he had other things in mind. He led her into the room, locking the door behind him. When he cast a seductive, predatory look at Val, her floodgates opened.

She stood still, shaking with anticipation. Staring unblinking, deep into her soul, Zane slowly lifted Val's dress up and over her hips. His hands dropped down to reach her ass, cupping her cheeks, lifting her to his waist. She happily wrapped her legs around him and held on, then he spun her back to their bed and slowly laid her down. His hands glided under her dress, over her torso, up to her breasts. Suddenly, Zane put his lips to her flat stomach, using his other hand to slightly lift her up to take her dress off instantaneously. Then he raised his lips to meet hers. Dragging his lips down her neck, he pinched one of her nipples and suckled the other. Her now-soaked panties were ripped right off, and a warm moist mouth was on her clit.

As her clit was being assaulted in the most pleasurable way, Val panted like a bitch in heat. Her orgasm was near when his mouth left her clit to go back on her mouth. A hard thrust made her see spots, and a pleasurable scream left her throat. She was finally able to see his eyes and how possessive and animalistic they were. Hard thrust after hard thrust and growls of pleasure left her mate. Feeling high from unfathomable bliss, her orgasm washed down in waves. Zane grabbed her hips and drove deeper, until they both let out a roar.

As they came down from their sex session, Zane dropped down, and they put their foreheads together and kissed.

"I love you so much, Valerie."

"You're my world, Zane."

Bang! Bang! Bang! Came pounding at the door.

Completely spent, the pair had dozed off, and both jumped to the roof from being startled awake. Zane leaped off the bed stark naked and growled, "What the fuck do you want!?"

"Ah come on, Zane! The party starts soon," Rocky called through the door, then pushed it open without a care.

"Do you have a death wish?" Zane asked.

"Come on! Get dressed! We have to prepare you for your big reveal," Rocky said.

Zane gave Rocky a shove out the door, slammed it shut, then hopped back on top on Val. "Can't we just stay here, love?" he asked with sad puppy eyes.

"I'd love nothing more, but we have to do this."

Zane grumbled and rolled off Val, and they both dressed. They met everyone downstairs in the living room.

"You ready, Zane?" Alpha Steven asked.

"If I must, Alpha."

Everyone left the pack house to go to the outdoor stage that they had put up at the training grounds. Evan and Trudy held each other nervously as they watched Zane take his place at the podium with the pack leadership and the goddess-chosen group. Alpha Steven stood tall and proud at the center and bellowed, "Good evening."

Oh, Goddess, here we go. I hope no one is frightened. I'm not trying to mentally psych myself out, but I can't help what the Goddess gave me, Zane thought.

"We're gathered tonight to celebrate our recent graduates. Welcome to hard work and discipline. We also have something amazing to disclose to you all. We have with us, in our own pack, werewolves who are to fulfill our Moon Goddess's prophecy. Zane, step forward please." Steven said.

Zane looked over the crowd, stomach in knots. Valerie appeared beside him and grabbed his hand.

Steven continued, "The Reborn Lycan was born a part of our pack, as prophesized. We have trained hard for months to control what the Moon Goddess blessed us with. There's no reason to be afraid. He's ready to be revealed!" Steven nodded to Zane to shift.

Ready, Pyrox? Zane began shifting, freeing Pyrox from his human cage. Val released Ignisara to welcome Pyrox and set him more at ease. Zane's bones cracked and popped into his Lycan form, and his human consciousness retreated to the back of his mind.

Pyrox saw the crowd before him, some frightened, others slack-jawed.

Alpha Steven put his hand on Pyrox's shoulder to show the pack he's not afraid, so they shouldn't be either. "Please welcome Pyrox with open arms. I assure you he's no harm to you."

Questions were yelled from every direction, so loudly Zane's head spun.

Alpha Steven put his hands out and yelled, "Silence!"

Zane realized the crowd didn't know he could speak in this form. He stood a bit taller. "I'm on the side of our mother Moon Goddess. If you're also on her side, we can be friends. If you choose to go against her and those I love, then and only then will we have problems."

The crowd looked shocked.

Chapter 25: Uneasiness

After Zane revealed his Lycan, the rest of the party went fairly smoothly. Because most of the pack hadn't heard of the prophecy nor of Lycans, they needed to be reassured that he was truly one of them, not an abomination.

"There will be a time in the near future, when I'll explain the entire prophecy and offer a demonstration of his gifts," Steven told the pack. The crowd went back to celebrating the graduates without further thought—or so they thought.

Thoughts of the reveal crept through Alex's mind. He heard impure thoughts from a few pack members. In the past, he could only hear thoughts like that through mind-linking. *Is my gift getting stronger? Why me? How will I control this and not wolf out on my people?* Alex turned to his wolf, Heim, for some kind of answer.

Heim, what's going on?

The goddess has yet to speak to me directly like when she gave us this gift. I believe our mother gave us this for a reason.

Can we turn it off? It's driving me nuts.

I'll do my best to focus and filter what you hear so you can concentrate. You know how to tune me out, right? Try to do that in your mind with incoming thoughts too. For now, that's the best advice I can give you.

I'll try. Thanks, buddy.

After the party had broken up, Alex sat in his room, trying to focus on Heim's advice. It felt like he had been sitting for hours, trying to shut that shit off. With a massive headache, Alex went to find his dad. *He has powers to help control the others for now. Maybe he can help me too.*

Without knocking, Alex barged into his father's office. Big mistake! He screamed in horror and ran for his life. Now on top of his headache, he wanted to melt his eyes out and have his memory wiped. Witnessing your father pound your mother from behind, bent over a desk is not what any kid wants to see, ever.

Alex ran smack into Mark, and they both hit the floor so hard Alex flipped right over him.

"Ahh, fuck!" Mark exclaimed.

Still holding his head, Alex groaned in agony.

"Are you okay?" Mark asked. Alex couldn't answer; he was seeing cartoon birds flying around. Still lying flat on his back, he felt the floor vibrate with incoming footsteps. *Great. Here come my parents. I can't look at them after seeing that shit.*

"Alex? Alex? What the fuck, man. You all, right? Come on, man. Open your eyes."

Alex felt Mark tapping his face. He heard his mom yell for him and felt his father pick him up. Assuming he was being taken to the infirmary, Alex blacked out.

He must have been out of it for a while. When he woke, his mom, with her pixie-cut black hair, was hunched on his legs, fast asleep. Gently, he pulled his legs out from under her, got up, picked her up, and laid her down on the bed. Just as he was covering her with a thin blanket, a concerned nurse came in and said, "Alpha Alex, you're up. How are you feeling, dear?"

"Fine now, thank you."

"May I check you over and let you be on your way?"

"That sounds fine, just don't wake my mom," Alex said as he eased down into the chair his mother had been sitting in. When the nurse came closer, he noticed her scent, calling to him but not in a mate way. He let her finish her tests, then asked, "What's your name?"

"Veronica. I'm a little new here. My mate, Ellis, is one of the pack warriors."

"Which pack did you come from?"

"I was in the Royal Kingdom."

"Do you have any sisters?"

"I do. Why do you ask?"

"No reason. Am I good to go?"

"Yes, sir, should I wake Luna Tessa?"

"No need. I'll take her home. She was probably up all night watching over me. Thank you for everything."

Alex and his mom returned to the pack house. Alex vowed to get some sleep and worry about everything tomorrow. When he awoke, his headache was gone, and he was not hearing anyone's thoughts. He found his way to the kitchen, where the group was chowing down on Trudy's breakfast. She made the works this morning: French toast, sausage, bacon, dippy eggs, and hashbrowns.

"Good morning, sunshine. How are you feeling? More importantly, what the fuck happened?" Mark asked.

"Long story short, I was hearing everyone's thoughts all at once since Zane's reveal. Plus, my head was pounding," Alex said.

"Is that what had you screaming and running like a madman?" Mark asked.

"That's a different story, one I'd rather have burned out of my memory, thank you very much."

Rocky laughed, "You caught your parents having sex, didn't you?"

"How the hell did you know that?"

"Same shit happened to me," Rocky confessed.

Everyone laughed, while Alex groaned.

"Ya well, at least you didn't catch your father cheating on your mom and have to keep it a secret. Not that I think it's actually a secret," Val said.

"Let me guess. Was it, Opal?" Bluey asked.

"Yup," Val popped the "P"

I guess my shit wasn't so bad after all, Alex thought, then tried to lighten the now sour mood. "I think my mate is in the Royal Kingdom Pack."

"How do you know that?" Mark asked.

"Did you have a vision of her like I did with Val?" Zane asked.

"No, but when I woke up in the hospital, a nurse came in. Her scent called to me, but not in the mate sense. She said she's from the Royal Kingdom and mated to warrior Ellis. If her scent smells good to me, I figured she might be my mate's sibling."

"Unfortunately, you have to put that on hold. We leave for training in two weeks. At least the Royal Kingdom is on our rotation. From what I heard, the first and last days are parties. Hopefully you can meet her then," Mark said.

"I hope so. Anyone want to head out to train?" Alex asked.

"Val and I are going to visit my parents, but maybe later," Zane said noncommittally.

Bluey and Rocky headed to his house, while Mark and Alex went to the training grounds.

"You ready to spend time with my family?" Zane asked Val.

"You bet. It would be great to feel a sense of normalcy."

They walked hand in hand toward Zane's house, enjoying the summer day. When they entered the house, they saw Zane's mom crying on the couch. They rushed to her, sandwiching her in a hug.

"You guys are the best. I needed that," Trudy said.

"What's wrong, Mom?" Zane asked.

"Your father must go on a mission all summer and take Robert with him. They said they need to start training Robert to take over for your father when he retires since it will no longer be you, Zane. All my boys are leaving me." Trudy started crying again.

Val and Zane held her. His sisters came into the living room, rolling their eyes. Zane scolded them with a look, and they shrugged and went outside.

"Trudy, it will be okay; they're both excellent at what they do. They will be just fine. I'm sure of it," Val reassured her.

"Ya, Mom. Dad has been gone longer before, and he's always come back."

"Let's go to the kitchen. I need coffee," Trudy said.

Even though they had just eaten breakfast, Zane raided the kitchen for food to share with his mom and mate. *I can't help but have thoughts of what our future holds and the prophecy. I hope we don't have a grim future, but I feel there's a war coming.*

"Zane, are you ever moving back home? If not, can you at least live here for the summer?" Trudy asked.

Val answered before Zane could get a word in, "Yes, of course we will. I bet Bluey and Rocky will end up at his parent's house for the summer too."

"Okay, then I guess that's settled. I still have my room here, right?" Zane asked.

"Yes, of course. Your brother has temporarily moved in there for the sake of the shower, but he won't be here," Trudy said.

"Won't Luna Tessa be lonely this summer?" Val asked.

"Sofia is coming home this summer, so Tessa will have her daughter back for more mother-daughter bonding. She'll be just fine," Trudy said.

"Alpha Steven has a daughter? I didn't know that," Valerie said.

"Alpha daughters attend different schools until they're sixteen, then they transfer back home," Trudy explained.

"Bluey was never gotten sent away," Val said, confused.

"You'll have to ask your former luna about that. I'm just a chef, dear. We'll more than likely have a barbecue to welcome Sofia home, hopefully before her brother leaves. I'm usually one of the first to know about those things so I can prepare the food," Trudy said.

"It will give us a chance to spend time with Bernie and Erica here this summer. I've been so busy ever since my birthday I feel like a horrible brother," Zane said.

"You aren't a horrible brother, Zane. The twins need to understand it's part of being a werewolf. They do miss our family game nights though. It will be good for the girls to have you back this summer and get to know their new sister."

"We'll be back later, Mom, with our things, but I need a run. I don't know if I'm allowed to release Pyrox in front of everyone yet, so we're going to drive to our normal spot for now."

When Zane opened the front door to leave, he was bombarded with a crowd. "Um, can I help you all?"

They started yelling at once, and Val jumped in front of Zane. She repeated Zane's question, "Can I help you?" receiving the same reaction.

Zane mind-linked Rocky straightaway, because Pyrox was about to let loose it on the idiots. After a few minutes, Zane saw Rocky and Bluey running toward the house, with Alex and Mark hot on their tails. Rocky jumped in front of Val and let out a roar of anger. That got the crowd to shut up, so Alex could do crowd control.

"Why are you all here? My father said he'll address everything further, very soon."

Everyone was still silent, not even crickets. Mark made the crowd take a few steps back, then he shifted and let out his beta growl. He turned to Zane and Alex and said, "Well?"

Zane saw Alpha Steven standing far in the distance, listening to everything unfold.

A random person, yelled, "We wants answers right now!"

"To what fuckin' question?" Alex asked.

"Friend or foe!" another random person called.

"Did not one of you listen the first time? He's on our goddess's side. If that is where your heart lies, then friend. If not, foe. If you're against our goddess, you're also foe of this pack!" Alex yelled.

The group heard clapping from a distance coming closer and louder. Alpha Steven parted the crowd like a wave. "I couldn't have said it better myself, son. Now what should I do with you all? Hmmm?"

"What do you mean by that, Alpha?" yelled a wolf in the crowd.

"When did my pack stop trusting me to keep you safe? When did my pack start harassing families? I think fending for yourselves would work, since you all live in the pack house and Trudy cooks for you all ungrateful wolves. You come to her home for what? Something I'm going to give you next week? I'm waiting for my daughter to come home. Now go home!"

Before the alpha left, Zane stopped him. "Where should I to let Pyrox out? He is now very agitated."

Steven shrugged, "You know what, Zane? Let him out where everyone can see. If that's what they want, give it to them. I'm sure if Pyrox has issues, he'll do the right thing to these ungrateful wolves. Just don't use his powers. Not yet."

With permission from Alpha Steven, the friends shifted and headed to the forest. Iggy zipped by Pyrox, playfully nipping at his feet. He sensed eyes were on them as they let out steam. With an idea, Zane mind-linked Rocky, *Hey, want to put on a brutal show for the on-lookers?*

Fuckin eh right, brother!

Zane and Rocky nuzzled their mates and let them know what they were about to do, so they didn't get the wrong idea and tried to interfere. At full speed, they collided, snarling, snapping, and clawing at each other. Rocky's wolf, Carrick, got behind Pyrox's legs and head-butted his knees, thinking Pyrox would go down. Nope, Pyrox swatted him away like a pesky fly. Rocky shifted back to human form for a better chance on two legs with the fight.

Using all of his might, Rocky managed to bear hug Pyrox and wrestle him down. Then he linked, *Stay down for the spectators' sake. Maybe they'll stop fearing you can't be stopped.*

Then Zane shifted back, and the friends hugged and shook it out, laughing the entire time, showing the crowd they're not a threat—but will hold their own in a fight.

The younger wolves who were watching had unreadable faces. Mark and Alex shooed the crowd away.

With Val and Bluey under Zane's and Rocky's arms, they walked to the training grounds. Rocky and Zane leaned against the nearest tree and watched the girls spar. Though they were opposites in height and body stature, their fighting technique was the same. The two friends played off each other like a dance. *I wonder if their entire pack is trained like that. Looks efficient,* Zane thought.

Of course, the beautiful mates began to draw attention, guys looking lustfully, girls in admiration. Oddly enough, Pyrox nor Zane felt jealousy. Zane surmised possessiveness and jealousy issues depend on insecurities in the relationship. *I'd die for her in a heartbeat. That's all I need. I trust her completely.* Once the ladies finished sparring, the friends went their separate ways. Zane and Val showered one last time at the pack house, packed up, and moved to their new home for the summer.

Chapter 26: Hello/Goodbye

The pack was in full swing, preparing for the return of Alpha Steven's daughter, Sofia and the farewell-for-now for Alex and Mark.

Alex was finishing packing for the next six months of training and travel, when Mark burst into his room, looking like he had just seen a ghost.

"It's not my fault! Don't kill me!" Mark panted.

"What did you do?" Alex growled, balling up his fists at his sides.

"It's the Moon Goddess's fault."

"You're not making sense, Mark! Out with it!"

"Sofia is my mate," Mark sighed in defeat.

Alex was stunned into silence. *My sister and my best friend? Guess it could be worse.*

Mark snapped him out of his thoughts, "Alex!"

"Please don't hate me, bro. It's not my fault, but I'll love her and protect her to my last breath."

"Guess we really are brothers now, aren't we?"

"I guess so, but now we leave tomorrow. I'm not going to be able..." Mark tried to say.

"Mark O'Connor," his father screamed from downstairs. "Get your ass down here *now*!"

"Shit," was all Mark could say, then he visibly gulped.

Alex gives him a smack on the back, "Well, good luck, brother."

The friends headed downstairs to find both of their parents waiting for them. Beta James wore a stern, stoic look. Beta Female Nora tried not to look so happy, but her eyes couldn't hide it. Alpha Steven and Tessa stood together with Sofia between them, each one having a hand on her shoulder. *She really has grown since I've seen her last,* Alex thought. Her face was neutral.

"Took you long enough, Mark. What do you have to say for yourself?" Alpha Steven demanded.

Mark bowed as he spoke, "I'll love her with all I have. I'll protect her to my dying breath."

"That's all I wanted to hear. You may rise," Steven said.

Everyone looked tense as Steven read the room. Then he dropped his sternness, smiled, and grabbed Mark in a bear hug. "Welcome to the family. But if you hurt her, everyone will kick your ass, son." He joined Mark's and Sofia's hands as howls of joy and clapping erupted throughout the room.

I haven't seen her in two years, and she ignores me for my best friend. That just won't do, Alex thought as he stormed over and pulled them apart.

"Hey!" Sofia whined.

Alex bear hugged her—like it or not and said, "I missed you too, Sofia."

"Oh, brother," she responded.

"Now there's even more reason to celebrate tonight before your training begins," Steven said, then turned to Mark. "If you mark my daughter before she turns eighteen, I'll hurt you badly. Understand?"

Mark nodded.

"What training?" Sofia asked.

"Alex and I go to alpha/beta training this year," Mark said. "We'll be gone around six months. I'm sorry."

"That's not fair. I just returned and found you, and you're leaving? How soon do you go?"

Mark sighed, "Tomorrow. We leave tomorrow." He put his forehead to hers. "We have our entire lives together. Don't fret. This training will make me a stronger beta, mate for you, and father to our future pups."

Alex walked away and headed back to his room to finish packing. *I'm happy for them. I really am.* But envy reared its ugly head. *I know I'll find my mate in the Royal Kingdom, but it's so frustrating having to wait. My first priority is first and foremost being a strong alpha. I have to remind myself of that.*

Val and Zane moved back to his old room at his parents' house at least for the summer. It did have its own bathroom, but it was so much smaller than the room at the pack house. The couple already felt cramped. Zane planned to move some of his brother's things out and talk to his mom about what would happen when Robert and their dad return from their mission. Turning to Val he asked, "I'm going to shower. Do you want to join me, my little mate?"

"Your family is in the house; they will hear us."

"We're just going to shower. What's wrong with that? You know we need to save water," Zane said playfully.

"It's never just a shower with you, mate. Do you promise just washing—no funny business."

Zane raised his hands in defense. "Only washing."

They got in the shower, and as promised Zane washed Val, starting with her hair. *I love her long, soft, silky-smooth hair.* Zane massaged her hair from root to tip. She moaned, making him instantly hard. Zane lightly growled in her ear, "Valerie, you moan like that and expect just a washing?"

"I can't help it; your hands are magic."

"You think so, don't you, my little vixen?"

"Mmmmmm."

Zane lost control, and his hands traveled down her perfect, wet body. He gave her a slight slap on her tiny, fine ass. She gasped. Engulfing her from behind, Zane plunged his fingers into her hot core. He leaned with her slightly back to get a better angle, but she was so small compared to him, he held her easily. She panted heavily as he slid his fingers in and out of her. Val's panting got louder and louder the longer he finger-fucked her. Zane gently placed his other hand over her mouth to muffle her moans, but she took that as a signal to get even louder.

Zane's dick was diamond-hard hearing her pleasure-filled moans. He couldn't take it any longer. Repositioning them in the shower, he replaced his fingers with his rock-hard dick, shoving into her hard. He was rewarded with a growling moan in his hand. Throwing his head back in pure bliss, Zane thought, *Did we just crack the shower tile?* but without a care, he continued. *She's too satisfying to stop.*

Val started to move with Zane in a blissful rhythm, making him penetrate her deeper. Her inner walls got slicker and tighter. Zane sensed she was about to cum, and so was he. The mates released together.

Val sank back toward Zane with him still inside her. "That was wonderful, Zane. But I'll be so embarrassed if anyone heard us." She slid off him with a slick *pop*. "How will I face your family?"

"Baby, you have nothing to worry about. I promise. We're all werewolves here. It's our nature. They all know that." Zane said, kissing her forehead.

Later that night, with the party going well, Alpha Steven scanned the room to see his daughter getting reacquainted with everyone. *She'll be in a world of surprise when she finds out everything tonight,* he thought. *Better go gather the troops for the main attraction.*

"Pack Silver Stone, who's ready for a show?" he bellowed out over the crowd, which erupted in cheers. "Ladies, please start us off like we discussed." Steven opened his alpha link to the entire crowd to keep an ear out for traitorous thoughts. *I love my pack and people, but fear and greed can turn some of the most loyal members.*

After gathering most of the pack members, Steven explained the prophecy. Some were suspicious, others curious, still others disbelieving. Steven kept his explanation simple and reassuring, hoping the pack would understand more when they're done.

Alex also scanned the crowd with his goddess-given gift, which Steven had told him to keep secret, as he had Rocky's. Watching Alex, Steven thought, *He makes me such a proud papa. He'll lead our pack better than I have when he's ready. He has learned to control his gift better since he found out his mate is in the Royal Pack.*

Next Val and Bluey began to demonstrate their gifts, simply calling on their powers and holding fire and water out in front of them respectively. The pack gasped. Then Val and Bluey juggled the fire and water skillfully in their hands for a few minutes, backing up from one another, then gently shooting their powers toward each other. Their aim was to show the pack that they could easily neutralize one another to help the pack be at ease and not been seen as a threat.

Alpha received some mind-links from the pack:

Oh goodness! They're going to kill us!

Wow! Extra protection for the pack.

It sucks they have to leave to protect the king.

We'll cross that bridge when it comes.

They're so hot! Those mind-links came from unmated men and teens. *I didn't need to hear those,* Alpha disregarded.

Alex linked his father that a few girls were flooding him with jealousy. *We need to keep them in check.*

Get with Sofia to plan for her to keep an eye out while you are away.

I don't see her at the moment, but I will find her.

Teen she-wolves could be the worst when it comes to jealousy, especially the snotty ones who thought they were more special than they really were. Steven had sent a few families to other packs because they tried starting scandals involving Mark and Alex. Steven might come across as a pushover alpha, but it's for good reason: It lets people show him who they really are. Steven rarely let people get away with things and live, but it was always hush-hush. Alex had convinced him to let those families live and just send them elsewhere. With all the issues that go on in the werewolf world, Steven didn't have time to deal with petty pack teens.

Alex went to find Sofia as his father had asked. He couldn't find her, nor Mark, anywhere, and both of their links were shut off. Suddenly, Alex felt a new connection to the family mind-link band: *I'm going to kill the fucker.*

Alex caught his my dad running toward the pack house, Beta Jones hot on his tail. They raced straight up to the alpha floor to Sofia's bedroom, and by the time Alex got there, his father had Mark up against the wall by his throat. Mark was already turning blue. Sofia was screaming at their father and pounding on his back to get him to let Mark go. Beta Jake sat on the edge of the bed, breathing hard, knowing he couldn't interfere. Sofia's mom and Nora quickly entered, and her mom worked her mate/luna magic to get Steven to release Mark.

Once he finally let go, Mark fell to the floor with a thump—crumpling into a heap on the floor. Tessa pulled Steven out of the room, and Nora and Jake were by Mark's side in a flash.

Alex turned to Sofia, "What the hell, Sofia? You know the rules. Did you want Mark to die because that is what almost happened?"

"We didn't do anything like that. He wanted *me* to mark *him* before you left. That's all."

"That's an incomplete bond, Sofia, and it will fade away. Sofia, you can't complete the bond yet. Did you not learn a damn thing about mates or packs in school?"

"Yes, I did. I know it will fade, but it should at least last while you are gone. Because I'm of alpha blood, it will last longer than most."

"What about when his heat comes because of the unfinished bond? What the fuck were you two thinking? That had to be the dumbest thing you could have done. He wasn't going to cheat on you, Sofia. We're going to be too busy training. You might as well have signed him a kitchen pass now—and his death certificate."

Sofia blanched pale. She went to Mark to comfort him, kissing him profusely, saying *sorry* over and over. Mark regained his color, but Alex had to break things up. "All right he's fine now, and we have other things to talk about, Sofia. We have no choice but to do it now."

With a huff, Sofia asked, "What is it?"

"During the demonstration, which you missed, a group of girls were projecting extreme jealousy. You need to keep an eye on them while Mark and I are gone."

"What's the big deal? It's just stupid teens being stupid teens."

"Stop, Sofia. If you learned anything about packs, you know about the damn politics and inner workings of a pack and how jealous bitches can cause major problems. Since you're back home now and an alpha's daughter and new female beta-to-be, they will try to befriend you for who you are and who you're mated to.

Trust me when I say it sucks to find out people only want to be your friend because of your rank."

By the time Alex stopped talking, Mark was back on his feet. Alex turned to him next, "You should've talked to me. We could've avoided this damage."

"Sometimes things happen so fast, brother, you can't help it. You'll see when you're at the Royal Kingdom. We didn't have sex. We didn't fully mate."

"You'd be dead if you had, and at my father's hand," Alex said, smirking. "Have fun going through heat now while trying not to get your ass kicked for six months."

"Yea, yea. Can we be alone now, so we can spend..."

Mark was interrupted by a loud "No!" in unison with his parents, Alex, and Steven, who had appeared back in the doorway.

The group calmed down and headed back outside, with Alex determined not to leave his sister's side. *Shit. By the attitude she came home with, I don't trust her not to make Mark finish the mate bond. Girls always use sexuality to get what they want, and we men can't cave into it.*

After the girls finished their show, Zane and Rocky went to get them food to replenish their energy. A group of girls approached them as they ate and drank. Instantly, Pyrox got on edge.

Rocky slapped Zane's shoulder, "Why so tense, brother?"

Zane mind-linked him instead of speaking aloud, *As soon as that group came over and approached Val and Bluey, Pyrox tensed up. Something isn't right, Rocky.*

They seem harmless. But I'll call for Alex just in case.

The friends waited a few minutes for Alex, keeping a close eye on the girls.

The second Alex arrived, he stopped dead in his tracks. "Who that fuck is that?"

Zane and Rocky looked at him quizzically.

Alex dashed toward the group of girls, grabbed one by the throat, and screamed in her face, "Who the fuck are you?!"

Alpha Steven appeared instantly, and he and Beta Jake took the girl away immediately. The other girls tried to scatter. Zane, Rocky, and Alex jumped into action, capturing the girls and following Steven with them firmly in hand.

The party was pretty much shot now, with the leaders in the dungeons with the warriors. Alex was in a half shift and pretty pissed off. After the prisoners were secured, Alpha Steven calmed Alex down enough to speak. "Magic. One isn't a girl. No scent. Possibly spies."

No wonder Pyrox was on edge, Zane thought. Before his eyes, the "girl" vanished out of the cell. *Well fuck!*

Alpha Steven released everyone except Alex and Zane to go home and sleep.

"What did you see, Alex?" Alpha Steven asked.

"I saw that group of girls Rocky mind-linked me to observe. One had a ruse around her. The closer I got, I could see *him* clearly, wearing a cloak of sorts—just like when we had the fire at school." Alex answered.

"Rocky called me because Pyrox was edgy the minute that group of girls approached Val and Bluey," Zane said.

"Good instincts, Zane, and amazing work, Alex, as always. Let's interrogate the others to see what their role was or is."

After about two hours in the cells, Alpha Steven let Zane and Alex go home and sleep. Alex and Mark were leaving in the morning, which was coming quickly. Alex determined they were being influenced by the now-missing boy. But Steven let all the prisoners go with only a warning, escorted out of the pack's territory by warriors until they were back in the control of their parents.

Chapter 27: Darkness Revealed

Around a month passed quickly. Alex and Mark were training hard and keeping an eye on Roman and Ricky. Every third or fourth day, they reported back to Alpha Steven, but so far Roman and Ricky were keeping to themselves and just training—nothing suspicious thus far, which brought a little joy to Steven's heart. *I truly don't believe they're bad kids,* he thought.

Zane's Lycan hadn't reported any more issues involving magic in the pack. Sofia was successfully reintegrating back into the pack. *She's learning her new role as female beta, working with Beta Female Nora. It's just as important a role as a luna,* Steven thought, proud that Sofia still got to enjoy being a sixteen-year-old at the same time. She's trying to keep her eyes and ears open on the troublesome group of girls.

Zane had been working hard at being Rocky's right-hand man. They started taking patrol shifts within the pack ranks, transitioning seamlessly from high-school students to contributing, working pack members. Val and Bluey requested to join warrior training. They said they used to train by themselves, learning how to take down a fully grown male wolf. After watching them spar, Steven created a new, separate training for females.

Val and Bluey learned to use their size as an advantage—rather than a hindrance—in battle. Steven was blown away watching them fiercely, fearlessly train the other she-wolves. *I wouldn't expect anything less from an alpha-beta daughter pair. I'm happy they're part of my pack,* Steven mused.

Steven decided to make Zane a gamma in training—though he had never had one before, never needed one before, but now it felt right. Steven gave word to the royal council about having a Lycan in the pack. He couldn't keep the secret any longer. *I don't know where that warlock came from nor who he reported back to. King Sidious could have sent him, for all I know. If I was caught keeping a secret like a Reborn Lycan from the king, I'd be hanged for treason.*

Steven's thoughts were interrupted when Jake walked into his open-door office. "Hey, boss."

"What's up, Jake?"

"I have Raven and Lucius here, requesting an audience with you. Do you have time?"

Steven spotted the wife and son of the pack's warlock. Back when Steven's father was the alpha, their entire coven was almost wiped out, by one of their own. He managed to get in between their battle and rescued as many survivors as he could. The Hammon family was the only family that decided to stay within the pack's borders.

"Of course, please show them in," Steven said.

Raven and Lucius bowed and sat.

"Is everything okay? Everyone treating you well?"

"Absolutely, Alpha. But we would like to know: Why haven't you come to us for help?" Lucius asked.

"What do you mean? Are we in danger that I haven't handled?"

"I'm not questioning your competence, Alpha. You take care of our family. You let us live in peace like we're your wolves within these borders, like we're your family too. You let us openly practice and teach our magic. We would not be treated so well anywhere else. Let us help you protect the pack," Lucius said.

"It's nothing we can't handle. I don't want to put you and your family at risk." Steven replied.

"Thank you for that, but our boys are old enough now to protect themselves. We have taught them well. A lot has happened since the prophecy came to be realized. We have felt the use of magic that isn't ours, like at the graduation party. Lucius's parents used to help put protection spells in place to detect magic use, like the alpha vault. Let us do the same. We'd love to help," Raven said.

Steven knew he had no real reason not to trust them. He sat back in his chair, ran his hands down his face, and turned to Jake. "Jake, close and lock the door and sit."

Steven explained everything that has happened since Zane received his Lycan, with Jake filling in details along the way. Steven realized, *I should have Delta Curtis here too. This involves his family.* They took a break to wait for Curtis, who was currently on a patrol rotation, a protection detail for the territory borders. They scheduled a time after dinner to reconvene.

After dinner, Steven finished explaining to Lucius and Raven. They took it all in with great interest. They sat in silence for a few moments, then Lucius mumbled something to Raven, who looked at him and nodded.

"Alpha, I'm taking a shot in the dark when I say this. It seems a witch named Opal is an issue," Lucius said.

"Who's Opal?" Steven asked.

"She's the oldest, most powerful witch. Legends say she was one of the first witches and doesn't age because she was given eternal life by the goddess herself. She's the one who tried to wipe out all covens. She wanted to be the only witch left. Your father, Alpha Steven, weakened her, so she took refuge with the Shrieking Moon Alpha after the battle ended. That's the last we have heard about her," Lucius said.

Steven sat in silence. *It figures Alpha Van is involved.* He looked at his beta and delta, sighed, and said, "I believe you, Lucius. Are you willing to cast protection spells?"

"Yes, Alpha. Of course."

"Thank you. I grant you permission to cast whatever you deem necessary for protection. Please don't speak of any threat just yet. You can freely speak about protection should anyone ask, but tell them a half-truth. Report anything suspicious back to one of us three or the chosen gifted," Steven commanded.

King Dominic Sidious's council had just informed him that one of his loyal former guards, Alpha Steven Gibbson of Silver Stone Pack, had a newly shifted tracker who he believes is a Lycan. *That couldn't be possible,* the king thought. *The Moon Goddess took us away because they were monsters.*

The king day dreamed, remembering how it all happened: She wanted the Lycans to happily protect her creations, and we were fine with it for quite some time, as long as we were respected.

But generations passed, and that respect went down the shitter. We watched and protected as they loved and were loved and had families. Our Mother Goddess, our creator, seemed to forget we even existed. We received no love from her, no one soul to match each of our own, like she gave the werewolves, witches, dragon shifters, and all the other creatures she made for us to keep watch over and protect stopped respecting us, forgetting what we were truly capable of.

We got sick of it all—the thousands of years of what seemed like complete emptiness. We started stealing power and beautiful creatures and destroying their mates. We raped. We killed. We didn't care anymore. We were finally living again. But no matter what we did, no matter what species we mated with, we couldn't reproduce. We formed our own pack and stuck together.

Then the goddess came in all her power and glory, finally remembering we were still here, but she came not with grace, but with vengeance. Speaking not a word, she separated our Lycan souls from our bodies and absorbed them all. Then she spoke, "I gave you indestructibility, eternal youth, eternal life, strength, and power. But you hurt my creations you were meant to protect. Now you're human. Live out the rest of your human lives."

The king spoke against her, "You forgot to give us the one thing you gave all others: someone to love. We wanted fated souls too. We watched, and we protected your other creations for a thousand years. But we received shit in return."

"I gave everyone free will, Dominic. You might not have had fated souls, but you were always free to find love," the goddess said, then left. The king never saw her again.

The former Lycans tore each other apart. The king was the last former Lycan standing. In his lonely travels, he came across a witch. He was tired and bloodied, and she nursed him back to health. We stayed together as a sort of couple or so the king thought for many years. Although the king had lost his Lycan, he was still a strong human. He told the witch everything over the years many times over. She was powerful and taught herself many things.

One day, she returned to the king and said, "I'm developing a way to become a powerful beast again. She called it a Skin Walker of the Becoming." Her spell failed the first few attempts, and so she adjusted the spell. Her solution to the spell and secret to unlock the dark power was to sacrifice.

The king and witch experiments on different shifters and tried again and again. Nothing worked. They fell in love, and she became pregnant with his child. For the first time in the king's long life, he was truly happy and told her, "We should give up now so we can raise our family. I don't need a beast anymore."

"You need a beast to protect me and our unborn child to help me raise him in this world," the witch said.

When their son was born, the king was so happy.

"We did it," the witch told him. "We created the ultimate sacrifice."

The king's heart dropped. He loved their son.

But the witch reminded him of everything they were trying to accomplish. "It must be done," she said.

They performed the brutal ritual. The king had to kill his first-born son, then consume his still-beating heart. He wept from the depth of his soul, but he did it. And it worked.

The king became the ultimate Skin Walker, possessing infinite power, eternal youth (still looked 30 at age 900ish), and the ability to shift into any being or split his soul to occupy any other creature. They went into hiding, living deep in the forest.

The king and witch waited 150 years before he stepped back into the world because they discovered they needed to reenact the ritual every ten years for him to retain his power and youth. Some of his children challenged him, but they all died. After having to consume so many of my children, the kind had no mercy nor heart left. Leaving no one alive in my path. I've been king ever since.

Snapping out of his reverie, the king got back to the matter at hand: Steven's so-called Lycan. On one hand, the king thought, *I could use him as a personal guard. But on the other hand, he could expose me—even kill me. I need to protect my secret.* The king was in conflict, knowing all his options made him look weak.

Alpha Steven was about to train to blow off steam when he received a direct call from the king. "It's an honor, your majesty," he answered, trying to sound happy about his call.

"I received a message about a possible Lycan shifter in your pack. Are you sure he just isn't a one-off, off-breed werewolf?" the king asked without pleasantries.

Steven hadn't expected that question. "His new form called himself a Reborn Lycan, sir."

"What qualities does he possess that other werewolves don't?"

"He's much faster and stronger than even me, sir. Every one of his senses is heightened."

"Very well. I'll pay your pack a visit in three days to see if I want him as a royal personal guard, as is my right."

"Of course. That is why I informed you of this matter."

The king ended the call without even a goodbye.

Steven assembled the chosen gifted group immediately. He knew the king had said three days, but that really meant two days, or even one day. He had seen the king look through the eyes of birds and animals to gain information to use it against people. Steven did not tell them of the others as it seems the king doesn't remember the prophecy or know about the Goddess scrolls.

The teens rushed in breathlessly from training.

"Sit. Catch your breath," Steven said, then explained what he needed them to do. "The king said he'll be here in three days, but expect him to arrive early. He doesn't seem to know about the prophecy nor powers. From now until he leaves, use no magic and be extra cautious of animals that seem to stare at you. There are things he's capable of. Don't trust him. Zane, he'll try to fight you in Lycan form. As much as Pyrox would want to beat the king, he can't. If the king sees how strong you are, he'll kill you."

Steven continued, "Val and Blue, take Sofia to the human city for four or five days. Make sure he's gone before you return. If you need to fight the king, fight him like a tracker would fight.

I'm not saying trackers are weak, because Evan is a strong wolf, for example."

And he concluded, "Lucius and Raven will be here soon. They will mask all your mating marks—but not remove them. If the king saw your mating marks, he would use them against you all. Any questions?"

"Why do you seem panicked?" Zane asked.

"Long story short: In my youth, I was a Royal Guard. I've seen and heard things. The king isn't alright. We must prepare and proceed with caution. Remember when you let the pack watch you lose your fight with Alex and Rocky, so they didn't see you as a threat? I need you to do that once again as much as I know you don't want to."

Two days later, Lucius called Steven. "Alpha, we've detected dark magic a half-mile from pack borders."

"You're serious? How worried should we be?"

"From the signature, very. It has a very old, dark feel to it. My family is on high alert. We'll keep a good distance away but close enough to do our best to intervene if necessary."

"Thank you, Lucius."

Not fifteen minutes later, the border patrol guards mind-linked Steven that the king had arrived and would be at the pack house in about ten minutes. *It can't be a coincidence that Lucius warned me of old, dark magic, and the king is here not moments later,* Steven thought. He gathered his best guards Jake, Curtis, Zane, and Rocky in front of the pack house and waited for the king and his entourage. They bowed low as King Sidious exited his vehicle. He gave a small nod to acknowledge their respect.

Pyrox is going nuts! Something isn't right with the king, Zane mind-linked Steven.

Hold down your power! Hide it, Steven replied.

"Get up! Get up," King Sidious commanded. The group shook hands, then the king continued. "Alpha Steven, pleasure to see you again. Doing well for yourself since departing from my kingdom, I see."

"Not as well as you, your highness. We were expecting you tomorrow, but we'll prepare the feast as quickly as possible."

"You want me to stay for a feast after I check out your Lycan member? Most packs want me to do my business and leave."

"I even prepared rooms for you and your guards. You're our king and deserve respect and to be celebrated."

"Ever so loyal to me, Alpha Steven. That's why it was so hard to let you go. I see your son is in this year's rotation."

"Yes, sir. He is. I taught him almost everything I know. Hopefully he does me proud, and you consider him a candidate for a few years within your Guardsmanship."

"We'll see. I've had plenty of rest in the car. Is the Lycan ready to spar with me, Steven? I want to make my decision before the feast you're preparing."

Zane stepped forward, keeping himself as small as possible but showing no cowardice. King Sidious assessed him carefully. "What's your Lycan's name, boy?"

Zane stiffened and lied, "Payton, sir."

"Are you afraid of me, boy?"

"A little bit, sir."

"That's to be expected. I'm king after all. I can't hold that against you. Let's go see what you can do. No holding back on me. I can take it."

The group headed toward the sparing area. Pyrox talked directly to Sunka, so Zane didn't look suspicious. He wanted everyone not to react when he shifted—no sounds nor body language. Alpha explained that he had moved most pack members away, on border patrol, or preparing the feast, to defray any questions the king might have about the lack of members around due to his "unexpected" arrival.

When Zane shifted, Steven was surprised. Pyrox still looked like a Lycan, but not the one they had come to know. His fur was now light brown, almost blond, instead of midnight black, and his claws weren't as sharp nor long.

The king nodded, and the fight began.

Zane started off strong, holding his own against the king. Quickly he feigned fatigue. He managed a few direct hits on the king, making him slightly mad. King Sidious kicked Zane in the chest, and he fell back, hard. Zane faked a huff and puff, attempted to get up, but didn't submit to the king. They fought for only about twenty minutes, but then the king stopped the fight. He grabbed a towel and gave Zane a friendly gesture to help him up. Zane grabbed his hand and stood, hanging his head down, to show the king he was upset he lost the fight in such a short period of time. The king smirked. Zane walked off to the showers with Rocky in tow.

Sidious went over to Alpha, quietly mumbling, "They don't make them like they used to." He said, "He's a Lycan for sure, but he's weak. I don't need him in the Royal Kingdom. He's free to stay in your ranks. No offense, Alpha."

Thank goodness, Steven thought, then said, "None taken, your highness. I have you and your guards in a suite on my floor with its own shower. Let me show you, so you can clean up before the feast."

Then Steven went to his office to call Sofia. "Stay with Val and Bluey in Silver Line City for three more days to be safe. Enjoy yourself, but stay out of trouble."

After that, the pack feasted with the king. For once, a celebration went well with no problems. The king left after breakfast the next morning with no issues. Waiting two hours for him to be totally clear of the pack territory, Steven asked Lucius, Raven, and the security team to thoroughly sweep the pack house and everywhere else the king and his guards had been, searching for anything suspicious left behind or any lingering magic.

With pack members busy performing their assigned tasks, Steven called Zane, Rocky, Jake, and Curtis to the magically protected vault for privacy.

"Zane, can you explain or can Pyrox talk through you, to make things easier?" Steven said.

"It'll be easier for him to talk through me."

Pyrox came through him. "Alpha Steven, as you know, I'm a Reborn Lycan, meaning I had another human host before Zane almost a thousand years ago now give or take. That first human host was Dominic. I didn't want him to recognize me because he knew of my power firsthand. I sensed an old, dark magic radiating off him, something sinister. I'm surprised our Mother

Goddess hasn't figured out by now that his human soul was still alive or that's why she's allowing a Lycan like me to walk this Earth again to redeem my kind and to rid the Earth of evil once and for all."

Pyrox continued, "After the goddess removed me from Dominic, she retrained my soul and promised to give us the love we need and someone to keep us in check. The other Lycan souls will only be born now through my seeds of generations to come. She also explained that Opal, her first witch creation, was who severed Evander and Trudy's first true mate bond, and that because they overcame that obstacle and still are truly madly in love that their divine love was born. Theirs is a true love that can never be broken, and with that my soul was bonded to Zane. Because true love runs in our blood, Zane and I can never be used for evil."

Chapter 28: War Games

Zane felt relieved that Alpha Steven's plan worked. Having been so up close to the king, he wondered, *It's weird how old the king is. He isn't a Lycan anymore, so I wonder what kind of dark magic it took to stay looking that way for so long.* Zane was now officially a gamma in training, among the top four ranks of the pack. *I'm going to have to give orders once in a while, not what I'm used to doing.*

Zane and Rocky were finishing their six-hour patrol and helping the warriors get set up for their turn with alpha/beta training rotation. They took root by a tree and watched their mates train, flawlessly throwing and dodging kicks and punches, tossing water and fire magic here and there. *It makes me hard, so very hard,* Zane thought. Glancing over to Rocky, Zane noticed his eyes were black, indicating Carrick was very present. Out of nowhere, the girls both did flips and shifted midair. Zane and Rocky both lost it to their beasts within and shifted mid-dash toward their mates.

Without a care who was around, they mounted their mates. Everyone nearby scattered. Rocky engulfed Bluey's wolf, pounded vigorously into her. Pyrox did the same to Iggy, not caring they were out in the open doing it side by side with their best friend. It was pure animalistic mating, a full-on animal display of claiming what's theirs. They rode them hard for at least a half-hour and simultaneously released their satisfaction in howls and roars. Oddly, they heard howls in response from the pack.

The friends shifted back, panting hard. Zane was still rock hard. He looked over to Rocky, then they both smirked with confidence and started fucking their mates in human form too. Another half-hour later, they released again. Pulling their mates close, they grabbed some clothes, then headed home.

Zane let Val bathe in their bathroom while he took the bathroom in the hallway. Pyrox was quiet and satisfied, as was Zane, who thought, *I can't believe we did that, outside in front of whoever was there. I can't lie to myself and say it wasn't a thrill because it was. Valerie doesn't seem upset about it. Our beasts within can't be controlled all the time. When they want out and want their mates, they will play.*

"What the hell was that all about, Rocky? Not that I'm complaining. That was hot," Bluey said.

"Carrick couldn't help it. Once you shifted like you did, he had to have you. He thinks he caught the scent of arousal coming off other pack members while you and Val were sparring. I think he and Pyrox needed to show dominance and claim you for all to see, show them all to back off, you're taken. Period. You made him horny as hell. He hadn't gotten to claim Sassie yet."

"Well, the pack certainly answered our howls during climax. That was sexy as hell, like they understood. What made you continue in human form?"

"Rick was sated, but I was still horny for you, so I said, 'fuck it.' Then Zane and I shared the same thought with a smirk. I knew we were on the same page."

The couple laughed together and walked back to Rocky's house. They weren't quite done fucking yet and had another round in the shower, then slept until Blaze woke them for dinner.

For Rocky, the day before had been a great day. He woke with that satisfied fresh day feeling for himself—and for Carrick. They were getting ready for the alpha/beta rotation to arrive, and Rocky had a brilliant idea not just for training, but for fun too.

Now that King Sidious has let Zane stay, he doesn't have to hide anymore, but our girls still have to hide their magic, Rocky thought.

Bluey and Val were off doing their own thing, so Rocky met up with Zane. The friends didn't any patrols that day, just the task of finishing up tent city. They sparred a bit, then Rocky ran his idea past Zane. They sat and watched Alpha Steven and Beta Jake go at it, then Rocky's dad added into the mix. It was awesome and inspiring to watch their leaders train.

Rocky was built like his dad, and while his didn't have Rocky's gift, no one would know it by watching him fight. They went at it for a while. When they finished, Alpha Steven was barely breathing hard or sweating, but Curtis and Beta Jake were on their backs, panting hard. Alpha Steven helped them both up with a smile and back slap. Rocky and Zane approached them while they were drinking and wiping down with towels.

"That was awesome to watch. Can I run an idea by you guys since you're all together?" Rocky asked.

"Of course, son."

"Since the rotation will be here soon, I was wondering if a few of us could do a practice sneak attack war game? I know you said they usually get the first day to get settled in from traveling, but the enemy will attack at your weakest," Rocky said.

The fathers looked at each other, then back at Rocky, nodding in approval. Jokingly Alpha Steven slapped Curtis's shoulder and said, "Well, Curtis, looks like you can retire now. You taught him too well."

The men laughed.

"No way; not yet," Rocky said.

After dinner, Rocky and Zane gathered in the war room with the other trainee warriors. The alpha thought it was the perfect opportunity to help Rocky and Zane train their youngest warriors in training. Rocky and Zane came up with a sneak attack training plan for around midnight. All the alphas and betas in training should be mostly asleep by then. Alpha Steven wanted to see what they had already learned or what they were ready for when the time came.

Everyone participating in the war games had been sleeping to adjust for the games. The day came, and they were preparing. Zane was excited because he got to sneak in first. His job was to sneak around the campsite in his Lycan form and kidnap as many of the trainees as he could before anyone caught on. *It's great not having to hide Pyrox anymore,* he thought. With Zane's heightened abilities and tracker training, he set a goal to catch at least fifteen out of forty in the group before anyone catches him. However, he knew he had to avoid Alex and Mark for as long as possible. *They will for sure sense me and Pyrox quickly.*

Alpha Steven came into the war room, slapped Zane's shoulder and asked, "You ready, Zane?"

"Pyrox and I are both excited actually."

"Pyrox knows it's a game of capture and not to harm or kill, right? Not even the girls' brothers?"

"As much as he wants to rip into them, he understands."

"All right then. You're up. Let the games begin. To your positions."

It feels so good to be free and do what I do best: hunt, Pyrox thought. He circled the camp, trying to stay a good enough distance away not to be detected as he scented out Alex and Mark first so he could avoid them, at least for now. Their tents were on the edge toward the western side, bordering the forest. *Check.* He traced his steps back toward the east side of the camp. He let his senses take over and picked his first victim. Their tent inhabitants and surrounding tents, were all asleep, making his first few victims easy prey.

Pyrox kidnapped two at a time for the first six. Poor guys didn't even put up a fight. He took them to the makeshift holding area. While Alpha Steven and the others waited with Pyrox's first six captives, he brought in seven and eight. Those two were loud, almost had woken up the entire camp.

Pyrox proceeded with more caution now and headed southeast of the camp. Some of the trainees were now standing about, but Pyrox could tell they were not fully with it. *I've been hunting for a while now and wanting to stir things up a bit. I have not met my personal goal just yet, but fuck it,* he thought. When Pyrox spotted a pair of alphas and their betas sitting on a log, half asleep around a dying fire, he released a low grumble roar. It was faint, but loud enough to perk up their heads. Pyrox scrambled behind a tent and roared again, prompting the trainees to stand and look around with noses in the air. *Good luck sniffing me out, fellas,* Pyrox thought. *I'm holding in my scent.*

The trainees turned their backs from where Pyrox was. He stood to his full height behind the tent, then let out a louder grumble and started dashing behind tents, knowing damn well they've never seen a Lycan form before. He could smell their fear. He made a mad dash to snatch the more powerful one and zigzagged through the trees. The trainee put up a fight—kind of. Pyrox dropped him off and said, "Well, guys, it's your turn. I managed thirteen of forty. Now you guys get to play."

The other trainers set off with smiles, all eager to play games and train. Pyrox released himself back to Zane so he could hunt and play too.

Once Pyrox gave Zane back control, he changed and went back out hunting. It was still his job to capture the trainees. It was still fun, even though all of the trainees were awake and out of the tents with their practice weapons in hand. They didn't catch on to what the real agenda was until they realized their numbers had significantly dropped. At first, they thought it was to protect the camp and drive out the "enemy."

Zane next focused his sites on Mark. As he did, Mark understood what was really going on, and like the good beta he was, he mind-linked Alex to warn him, who then of course warned the remaining alphas and betas, which at that point were only twelve. After the trainees were warned, Zane wasn't able to capture any more, so Alpha Steven ended the games. Everyone was brought back to the camp.

"Good job, Zane! That was fun to watch. I haven't had that much fun in a while," Alpha Steven said, chuckling.

"It was definitely a good exercise for us all," Zane said. "Rocky had a good idea. I know for sure Pyrox scared the hell out of several trainees. I hope it was a good lesson for them. They need to understand there are things out there that they don't yet know exist."

With a nod, Alpha Steven addressed the group of wolves. "You all weren't taking your training seriously enough. I know you're tired, but enemies don't care. They will strike when you're at your weakest, always. Go to sleep. Always remain vigilant, especially when you're not in your own territory. I'll explain more tomorrow."

When Alpha Steven returned home after the war game, he woke Tessa. *I know my beauty was asleep, but I was wound up and needed a release.* The pair cuddled, and right before he passed out, Sunka told him Tessa smelled different.

Knowing Steven disrupted her sleep last night, he let his Luna sleep. He headed downstairs to find Trudy already cooking with her staff, along with extra people to make enough food for the trainees too.

She's such a gem, Steven thought. *I'm starving. I'm not going to work the trainees hard today physically; the rest of the week is more about knowledge and mental awareness training.* Steven mind-linked Alex to have everyone make their way to the pack house for breakfast.

He finally got to hug his son after him being gone for months. "How have you been, son?"

"Honestly, bored really. All we really did was learn how the other two packs train physically. I learned a few different techniques, but that's it," Alex said.

"Unfortunately, that's all some alphas know how to do, son. That's about to change, at least here. I know for sure my cousin and the royals' training will be similar to mine, if not more advanced."

"I can see that already, Dad," Alex said, laughing.

All the trainees made their way to the pack's theater room, which Alpha Steven had set up to be the classroom for the month. They sat in their friend groups, chit-chatting and waiting for Alpha Steven to arrive. A few guys tried to get Alex to spill the beans on what happened the night before, but Alex reminded them that his father was treating him like a normal trainee at the moment. "I don't have the info you're searching for," he said.

Alpha Steven walked in with his top two, Rocky and Zane, noting how everyone was situated in the room, figuring he'd fix that a little bit later. A few trainees noticed Steven had arrived and stopped talking, stood, and slightly bowed out of respect. Steven noted them and nodded for them to sit.

Steven, Rocky, and Zane stood in front and waited to see how long it took the rest to notice their presence. Alpha released a bit more of his alpha aura, letting it consume the room. Curtis and Jake patiently kept watch, while Rocky timed with a stopwatch. He shook his head and turned the stopwatch so Zane could see it. Zane nodded, knowing Jake was writing down names for Steven.

After fifteen minutes of the bullshit, Steven let out his dominance roar, yelling, "For those of you who have not learned an ounce of respect, you'll be taught! Do you think acting this way will fly in front of King Sidious? Trust me, it will not." He took a deep breath. "Did anyone learn anything from last night?"

One trainee stood.

"Victor, what have you learned?"

"We were caught off guard, too relaxed on foreign land. If it wasn't training, we would have all died most likely, sir."

Steven smiled inwardly, thinking, *Finally, someone besides my people is actually eager to learn and understand.* "Very good Victor. Anyone else?" He waited. "No one else? Really? Fine, I'll tell you what I observed then. One, Victor was right. Two, even after everyone was finally aware of what was going on and only one at a time was being captured, only one alpha/beta, Alex and Mark, communicated with one another. By the time Zane captured Mark, there were only twelve trainees left. Rocky, please give everyone a notebook and pen."

With Zane's help, Rocky passed out the stacks, which prompted the trainees to groan like typical teenagers.

"Now I know so far all you have done is train physically," Steven continued. "Alphas and betas must be the strongest to defend their loved ones. Is the lack of communication during the game a lack of trust between alpha and beta, laziness, or because no one wants to take this seriously?" Steven let them stew for a bit on that one and went to get coffee. By the time he returned, the arrogance was gone, which was exactly what needed to happen.

Most alphas didn't understand how to train others—without revealing their pack secrets—but Steven did. It was a basic thing the younger ones need to know to survive. They needed to be taught about what war is really like.

"I feel the atmosphere here has finally changed," Steven said. "Good. The answer wasn't any of those possibilities I just mentioned—for some of you anyway. The answer really is arrogance. I'm not oblivious to the fact that some of you are supposed to be sworn enemies."

Steven scanned the room in silence for a few seconds before continuing. "I want you all to ponder some questions without answering them out loud. Why? Was it because it's what you're told to do? Or is it because of something you've personally witnessed or heard? What's more important to you: your pack, power, or control? I'm not asking for world peace or new allies. Every alpha holds his own reasons for everything in his own heart. I'm going to make this a short day, so you'll have time to reflect on last night and the questions I've given you today. This month with my pack might or might not have created more than you bargained for. Dismissed. Stay in the designated area."

With that, Steven let them go, but he had his warriors keep constant account for them all to simulate war conditions. In two days' time, more games were to begin.

Being here is overwhelming. We haven't done much of anything, but train and spar, Roman thought. Last night was an eye opener on how lax the first two pack programs had been. Alpha Steven had made some excellent points that morning and inspired Roman even. *During our training time here, we're supposed to be in a battle-style mode, strictly tent city. When we learn what needs to be learned, we'll earn free time,* Roman pondered.

Ricky broke him out of his thoughts, "No one asked about the thing that was taking us last night."

"What do you mean 'thing'? It was Val's mate," Roman said.

"At the beginning, it wasn't him. It was something else. I wasn't quite asleep yet when the game started. It looked like a deformed werewolf on hind legs," Ricky answered.

"Why didn't you say anything when it started or ask in this morning's lesson?"

With a sigh, Ricky responded, "Alpha Steven was right. I was arrogant and slightly tired."

"I think now is a good time to speak up, while he's giving us a break to rest to make some allies," Roman said. "Let's find Alex and Mark to see if they will talk to us. I don't know if they get special privileges or not because it's their home pack—like has been the case in the other packs we've been to."

The pair set off, and to their luck they found Alex and Mark shooting the shit with some other wolves. Ricky and Roman inserted themselves into their gathering. Alex looked Roman's way and nodded. Roman nodded in return, and the four headed toward the forest for privacy.

"What's up, guys?" Alex asked.

"Alex, Mark, I know we haven't been on the best of terms," Roman said. "But I feel like after what your dad said, well, we feel our fathers made us enemies."

"What are you trying to say?" Alex asked. "You don't hold yourselves accountable for your own past actions? Are we not enemies anymore? What you guys have done is unacceptable. How do you explain your actions?"

"Can we talk in private, or do we have to stay in this area?" Roman asked.

"It depends if I can convince my father," Alex said. "I get no leeway here just because it's my pack."

Roman replied with one word: "*Prophecy.*"

Alpha Steven received a concerning mind-link from Alex about Roman and Ricky needing to talk in private.

They know about the prophecy.

Steven was already in a meeting with plans for another war game, so he told them to meet him in his office. He figured it was a good opportunity for his warriors to come up with a plan of their own, giving them some trust since it's just a game, but practice for them all.

Steven mind-linked the main players of the prophecy, **Come to my office.** Zane, Rocky, Jake, Curtis, and also Val and Bluey arrived and pondered what Ricky and Roman could know about the prophecy or if there's another one at play. Roman, Ricky, Alex, and Mark came in as Steven gestured for them to sit.

"What needs to be discussed, boys?"

"We know Bluey and Val are in danger," Roman said.

Zane and Rocky growled immediately.

"I assure you, they're more than safe here under my care and with their very strong, protective mates," Steven said aggressively. "After what you and your fathers have done to them, what's your sudden interest in their safety? How do we know you guys aren't going to pull other stunts like in the past?"

In unison, Ricky and Roman said, "We didn't have a choice."

"Everyone makes their own choices," Steven said gravely.

"We want to make amends, Alpha Steven. We want to protect them from our fathers' clutches."

"Alex said you mentioned a prophecy. Does it involve them?" Steven asked.

"Yes, sir." Roman said.

Steven let Curtis take over for an intimidating factor, with Alex feeling for lies as Roman explained the prophecy his father had let him read. Alex nodded because so far, Roman was telling the truth. Then Ricky explained how his half-brother, Quin, Opal's son, was involved.

We finally have a name, Steven thought. *I'll pass this information on to Lucius and Raven, so they'll have all the pieces they need to protect our pack, and also themselves.*

Once Roman finished, Steven piped in, "Let me summarize. Your fathers know about the girls' powers. They believe they're the key to becoming royalty. Alpha Van has been trying to get me to see Althea and Valerie as more of a headache, so I send them back to Shrieking Moon. They want you two to force your seed to grow inside of them..." Steven was cut off as Curtis burst over and lifted Ricky and Roman both in the air by their throats and roared in their faces, "NO ONE IS TOUCHING THEM, BUT THEIR MATES!"

Steven had to release his alpha aura at Curtis to get him to let them go. *Can't have him killing them. Can't blame him. His pappa wolf came out,* Steven thought, then called for refreshments, sending Curtis out to wait for them to come. *I don't need anyone else to know what's going on inside my office at the moment.*

Once everyone had collected himself and calmed down, Roman continued, "Not to make matters worse, but what you guys don't understand is that our fathers are so sick and determined that if we don't get the job done, they will."

Steven felt physically ill as the blood drained down his body. Looking at everyone else in the room, he could tell they felt the same. Zane's eyes glowed, and he was shaking with anger. As calmly as possible, Steven asked, "Is that the only prophecy he has?"

"That is the only one he has shown me," Roman replied quietly.

Feeling that everyone needed a break from the tension, Steven released them to go run, especially Zane. Pulling Alex aside before he left, Steven said, "We need to discuss with everyone if we let

Ricky and Roman in on our prophecy or not before we bring everyone back. Take them back to the camp, and you, Mark, and the others will meet back here in an hour or so."

I can handle a lot of situations, but this? This is too much, Steven thought. He went to his room and heard Tess throwing up in the bathroom. Knocking on the door, he asked, "Tess, baby, are you all, right?"

There was no response, just more puking, so Steven went in to see Tess hunched over the toilet. Gently, he pulled her hair away from her face, rubbed her back, and asked, "What's wrong, baby? What can I do for you, my love?" He cooed with that last question.

Beyond worried she wouldn't answer, Sunka piped in his link excitedly, **We're having another pup!** He yipped in happiness.

Alpha knelt beside Tess, stunned. "Shhh, baby" was all he could get out.

Tess sniffled from a combination of throwing up and crying and said, "I'm too old for this, Steve."

"Baby, you're only thirty-seven, still just a pup in our world. I love you so much," Steven said and brought her to his chest.

"Alex just turned eighteen; Sofia is sixteen. I thought the next diapers I'd have to change would be our grandbabies," Tess said tearfully.

"I know, my love. We'll be okay. We have love and support, literally all around us. I love you so much."

With that, Tess jumped out of his arms and yelled, "You! You did this to me again!"

Steven smiled, embraced her, and said, "Yes. Yes, I did."

He got her in a bath to soak, then ran down to the kitchen to grab crackers and ginger tea. Thankfully Trudy was in there still preparing for the pack's next meal. Alpha told her about the Luna and what to expect with her new pregnancy, not that Trudy needed it because she has four pups.

Steven returned to Tess's side. He set the tray of snacks on her nightstand and finished helping her wash and relax. He laid down with her head his lap and massaged her head until she fell asleep. He sighed in contempt. *I don't want to leave, but damn it, I have to,* he thought.

As planned, Steven sat with everyone, weighing the pros and cons of letting Roman and Ricky in on the prophecy. It took a while, but they all agreed to tell them everything. Steven sent Mark to the camp to retrieve Roman and Ricky, then he turned to the rest and asked, "Before Mark returns, and we spill our secrets, are there any objections? Last chance?"

No one answered.

"Good, so there's some good news today," Steven said. "Tess and I are having another baby."

Everyone in the office smiled, and the girls said "aww."

Alex slapped Steven on the shoulder. "Damn, old man. You still have it in you, eh?"

"I still got it, son."

The wolves laughed, lightening the mood before they got down to more painful business. When Mark returned with Roman and Ricky, the wolves got situated.

"First, we have issues that need to be resolved," Steven began. "No more violence. Keep your wolves under control." He saw Zane smirk, so he added, "And *your* Lycan. Ricky and Roman are telling the truth about Val and Bluey being in danger, but not by them." Steven looked at Valerie and Althea, "But by your own fathers. They want the throne, and they think they can get it through you two. Due to what we now know about King Sidious, I feel you two might be in even more danger by him too, if he finds out about your powers. I don't want to start a war with anyone, but if I must inform the king of all this, I'm not sure if he would steal you two, destroy Shrieking Moon, or both. I'm at odds at the moment. Zane with that out there, we can start with you."

"What? You want me to shift right now?" Zane asked. "I'm having trouble with Pyrox at the moment. If he's out, blood will be shed."

"Well, shit. We can't have that," Steven said. "Take Valerie and go to the falls. Let loose and get calm. I'll notify patrols and the warriors to get a head count in the camp to make sure no one sees you just yet." Steven mind-linked out that message, then turned to Ricky and Roman. "Roman, Richard, Zane is a Lycan."

The rest of the group shifted around in their seats to get comfortable, figuring it was going to be a long meeting. Ricky doesn't seem surprised, but Roman did. For the next hour, Steven explained everything to get them up to speed about what had happened during the king's visit.

"So, if the king isn't a werewolf or a Lycan, what the hell is he exactly?" Ricky asked.

"My sources point to it being Opal's magic involvement," Alpha Steven explained. "That is all we know so far. Now Roman and Ricky, you must take a blood oath."

After swearing their allegiance, Roman, Ricky, Alex, and Mark returned to their camp to rest, while the rest of the wolves parted ways for now, still having their normal duties to fulfill.

To say Zane was livid about this new information would be an understatement. After he and Val reached the falls, he let Pyrox loose to enjoy time with his mate. That calmed him down. Thank goodness. He was taken aback that Val didn't seem surprised her father and former alpha were that sick in the head. *Pyrox and I want to go to Shrieking Moon and tear them limb from limb slowly and make them suffer,* Zane thought. After Pyrox and Iggy had their time together, Zane took Val home and had his time with her.

When Zane woke up, Val's head was on his chest.

"Your heart is my lullaby," she said.

Her beautiful hair splayed around Zane like a soft, silky hug. He brushed his fingers through her fiery locks, gently absorbing all the softness through his fingertips, admiring each strand and her naked, sleeping figure. Captivated by her beauty, Zane graced his lips to her forehead. Engulfing her tiny sleeping body, he slowly shifted their positions, spooning her from behind. Her plump ass was rubbing his cock, making it harder than he already was. Zane glided his hands gently up her side from her legs to the curvaceous hips then her torso, and then rounding his hands to her full, tight breasts. She moved her eyes to meet his, full of need. Taking her lips hostage to his, Zane dug in.

Her leg stretched over his hip as his arm snaked teasingly slow down her taught abs to her wet hot core and plunged his fingers into her wetness, moving them slow but hard. With hooded eyes, she continued to stare into his eyes, reached down for his hand, and brought his fingers close to their mouths, and they shared the sweetness with passion. Zane slammed his cock into her so hard, and they roared with pleasure. Val arched her back, opening her hips wider as Zane slammed into her harder, faster, deeper. She was a moaning, panting mess, and in love with the fact it was him doing it to her. He held back his release, so she got hers first, as his hardness memorized her inner walls with every thrust, every muscle, rippling as she was the sheath to his mighty sword. Her slick walls started throbbing, clenching, and pulsing with release. As her juices coated Zane, he let loose his own pleasure, making their fluids combine into one.

"Very good morning to you, my sexy beast," Val said, giving Zane one last peck.

"Good morning, my fiery goddess."

"I sound like a broken record, but a girl could get used to this kind of treatment."

"I'm nothing but a servant to my Fire Goddess. Your wish is my command," Zane lowly growled into her ear.

"Flattery will get you everywhere, my not-so-humble servant," Val said, then sat up and asked, "Are there any more war games?"

"Yes, tonight."

"Bluey and I want to play. Why do you guys always get to have all the fun?" Val pouted.

"Come with Rocky and me to the meeting tonight after dinner. I'm sure the alpha won't mind throwing some curveballs in tonight's games," Zane said, smiling.

The other wolves relaxed to preserve their energy for the night's games. Because Alpha Steven had occupied the theater room with the trainees, they took refuge at Rocky's house. Blaze enjoyed the company. She joined them for movies and relished the time with the group before they had to play the games.

Then Zane, Rocky, and the other pack leaders gathered in the war room to hand out assignments. Turned out Alpha Steven wanted to use Valerie and Bluey anyway, so the girls got their wish. Neither Rocky nor Zane were the least bit happy about that, and their mate protectiveness and jealousy kicked in.

He's our alpha, and we must obey, Zane thought. *He's using them as capture pawns and splitting the groups as protectors and aggressors.*

Then Steven told Rocky and Zane to go hang out in the game room. "You're not going to be involved tonight," he commanded.

Zane and Rocky were complete wrecks. They tried to play pool and video games to keep their minds busy, but to no avail. The girls cut their mind-links off, thinking, "Let them have fun with the games." Zane's and Rocky's inner beasts were not happy, though they knew they can take care of themselves if anyone got handsy.

"Zane, we need to do something, or we'll drive ourselves crazy," Rocky said.

"We were told to stay in the pack house. What are we supposed to do? All I want is to keep an eye on those alphas and betas. I don't trust horny men with our women. Not much is going to calm me or Pyrox down at the moment," Zane replied.

"I'm with you, brother. What was he thinking, using our mates instead of other she-wolves? We have plenty here for him to choose from. Maybe he *wants* us to get involved," Rocky speculated.

"It's not training for us, Rocky," Zane replied.

"Maybe that's a yes and no, but maybe we provide the expect-the-unexpected portion of their training," Rocky said.

"I love your thinking, Rocky. Fuck it! Let's go play," Zane said, jumping up.

Zane and Rocky ventured out of the pack house, sensing the trainees in the forest already. They stripped and shifted. Since the king knew about Zane, he has been shifting more freely, and it made him less tense. Carrick and Pyrox were both dark as night, so it was easy to hide their physical forms. Pyrox and Zane masked their scent. The pair stealthily made their way through the forest, avoiding the trainees and playing the role of aggressors who have yet to capture their mates.

Pyrox with his masked scent, crouched down a bit next to Carrick, making Carrick look like he had a shadow in the night. They moved in tandem, knowing the aggressors saw them, but they thought they only saw one entity. They waltzed straight to camp with no problems.

Zane and Rocky spotted the girls standing around a fire.

Val smirked, knowing they were there. *Nice of you to come out and play baby,* she finally opened her link back up to Zane.

Oh, my spitfire goddess, we'll have a repeat in front of these trainees, little mate, Zane mind-link replied.

Come and get me, big boy, Val linked before closing Zane off again.

Growling lowly, but loudly, everyone jumped into a protective circle around the girls. Zane decided to have a little practice of his own with his powers, so he shifted back. Because the girls used water and fire, he mainly practiced with earth and wind. He started with a breeze, focusing it to act like a creepy snake, weaving it in between their feet, trying to get them off balance, but they were in solid stances. While continuing the wind with Zane's hands, he used his feet to make the ground beneath them rumble and shake. He then moved his arms, so the wind went to the trees to make as much noise as possible.

Sneaking around was fun and all, but now Zane just wanted his mate. After everything that had transpired today, he needed her. He started flipping tents, sniffed out Marks and Alex's, and set it on fire. *Chaos now caused. Perfect.* As expected, the aggressors' group stormed the camp with Alex in the lead. *Of course, he knows what was going on, but that's okay,* Zane thought. With everyone engaged and not watching the girls, Rocky swooped in, grabbed the girls, and bolted. Zane and Rocky with the girls met up far enough away from the now uprooted camp site.

"Alpha said you guys wouldn't be able to stay away for too long," Bluey stated with a laugh.

"Their faces and reactions were priceless. Even with all the chaos Zane created, as expected, they left the girls unguarded," Rocky said.

Chapter 30: Wrapping Up

This month was wonderful, thought Alpha Steven. *Learning I'm going to have another baby and having the training here was a great time. Rocky and Zane screwing with them during the war games was hysterical. They finally caught on after the first two games. Never did tell them how or what they were up against. They thought I got my pack witches involved. Come to think of it, I should have involved Lucius and Raven's kids. I'll have to talk to them to see if they would like to join in on some pack training.*

Mark ended up not being able to control himself nor Steven's daughter for that matter. They had finished their mating bond. Sofia's parents wanted them to wait until she had finished high school at least, just in case she got pregnant. They wanted her to have her teenage years being a teenager—not a mother. They let Alex do the honors and beat the hell out of Mark. It's done and over with, and now the parents move to the next step, acceptance. Steven headed to the theater room for one last meeting with the trainees.

"Good morning, gentlemen. I hope you had a bit of fun and also learned vital lessons during your time here. Take what you learned here and use it to better your futures for yourselves and your packs. I truly enjoyed teaching each one of you," Steven said, then paused and looked at them. They nodded back at him. *I hope it's because they approve their time here was worth it,* he thought.

"I want to explain what you were all up against. I'm not sure who King Sidious informed, but we have a Lycan shifter in our pack. He's faster and stronger than us normal wolves, but just not strong enough yet to be the protector of the king. King Sidious came here, assessed him, and let him stay, until we get him trained," Steven explained.

"I knew it! I knew it wasn't your witches. Is he the first one since the beginning of our heritage?" Victor asked.

"As far as we know, he's the *only* one. Any other questions?" Steven asked.

"The alpha scrolls I read states he's supposed to be the king's guard. Why did the king allow you to keep him here instead of training him himself?" Keith, another trainee, asked.

"You'll have to ask the king, Keith. I notified him of our Lycan and didn't keep him a secret. He's very busy, so he's probably relying on me as the Lycan's alpha to train him up," Steven said.

"Was it the Lycan or your witches who were using powers?" Keith asked.

"I gave my witches and kids in my pack time to stretch their powers and have some fun too. I also wanted to show you that if you must battle, there are more than just us wolves out there. Plus, not every wolf has good intentions, but not every witch has bad ones," Steven said.

"Everything makes sense now. Thank you, Alpha Steven," Keith said.

"I don't want to keep you all here much longer, so I'll leave you with a final speech," Steven said. "Hard times are hard, while the easy pass you by. Don't believe everything you see or hear. One's gut intuition just might set the truths you seek free. A friend might be a foe, but a foe might be a friend. See you all tonight for your final feast. Mingle with my pack this final day. You have all earned it. I'm proud of you."

Once Steven dismissed them, he went to the kitchen. Tessa was helping Trudy clean up breakfast. He snaked his arms around her, kissed her neck, and whispered, "Hello, sexy momma."

She swatted him, spun around, pointed at him, and yelled, "You did this!"

Steven smiled back at her, "Yes, I know, my love." He yanked her back to his and kissed her so deeply she blushed. He grabbed a leftover sandwich off the plate she was holding and headed to the training yard.

Watching the men and women spar, Steven made mental notes on who needed improving. Rocky was upping Zane's hand-to-hand combat training. Steven's Alpha instinct told him that they needed Pyrox to improve quickly. The dark feeling of war coming was settling into his bones. *Pyrox takes orders well, but he's still not used to getting people to listen to him or giving orders. He doesn't want to use his fear factor on his own pack,* Steven thought.

Wanting to see his son for a few moments, Steven went to their campgrounds. Everyone seemed to be packing or have already finished. To Steven's surprise Alex, Mark, Roman, and Ricky were laughing with each other. *I'm certain I can cross Roman and Rocky off my sworn enemy list. Their fathers, on the other hand, are a different story,* Steven thought.

"You guys all done packing?" Steven asked.

"Hey, Dad. Yes, Dad," Alex said.

"How did your training go? Did you learn anything?" Steven asked.

"A little heads-up would have been nice, you know."

"Now what fun would that have been? 'Not like an enemy is going to have a sit-down with you and say, 'I'll kill this guy and that one, so on and so forth.' I couldn't favor you or Mark in the training for a reason. No hard feelings, I hope. I love you guys," Steven said.

"Of course not, Dad. What brings you here anyway?"

"Just wanted to see if everyone is doing what you need to do and how everyone is doing. How do you feel about your next step? White Fang."

"That's Pete's pack right, Ricky?" Roman asked.

"Yup, his sister isn't too shabby to look at..." Ricky said.

"Well on that note, I'm out of here. See you guys at the feast," Steven said, then they all laughed as he walked away.

Roman and Ricky were on the final stretch of the training rotation. Ricky found his mate at White Fang, Pete's sister, Courtney. The White Fang rotation had been a piece of cake, like the first two, but because Strong Hold's Alpha Charles is Alex's cousin, that one was hard work. Very excellent training. He did in fact use his witches, having made that known from the get-go. The trainees were now on the road to the Royal Kingdom.

Quin had visited Roman and Ricky while they were at White Fang, warning them his mom left the pack to give birth at the

Royal Palace. Knowing what they knew, Roman and Ricky found that concerning. They didn't know what her connections or intentions were with the king, but they knew she kept him young looking at the very least. Quin mentioned last time she was pregnant and gave birth at the Royal Palace, she came home empty handed, claiming she lost the child during childbirth. "Shit like that happens in our world more than we talk about," he said, but he explained he wanted to mention it anyway.

Ricky and Roman finally made at least an alliance, if not a truce, with Alex and Mark. Roman knew Alex and Mark were still wary of Ricky and his past actions, but they were trying to fix it. Not to mention they were blood oath bound and couldn't say anything to anyone. It didn't help that the pairs always seemed to be pinned against each other during all this training.

Alex and Roman were just shooting the shit, both happy for their betas for finding their mates, but both just a hint jealous.

"I think my mate might very well be in the Royal Kingdom," Alex told Roman, then proceeded to tell him about one of his warriors' mates.

I pray my mate might be there too, Roman thought. *Fingers crossed, so I don't have to go to those stupid mating rituals.*

Not many wolves actually traveled to the Royal Kingdom. The Royal Kingdom sent their merchants out to make money. It made one wonder what secrets the king was hiding. He kept only the best of the best for his royal guards and let their families stay. Therefore, everyone who resides within the kingdom had alpha and beta bloodlines. If they produced insignificant heirs, the king forced them to return to their original pack lines.

Roman's wolf (Ourln) was feeling uneasy and wanted to shift. They had been stuck in this car for hours. No sooner did he think that when they saw the kingdom walls ahead. *Holy shiny walls,* Roman thought. *It looks magnificent, but it sure doesn't have a warm feeling about it.*

As they approached the Royal Kingdom, Alex felt dread. His wolf, Heim, was uneasy. He looked out the window, and at first the kingdom seemed shiny, but when he concentrated with his gift, all he saw was a rundown, crumbling mess. *Odd. It's a ruse, like what the fuck*, he thought. Alex had been warned by his father about the king that no matter what he saw he had to keep it to himself until he got home. The king had loyal people everywhere and would not hesitate to kill on site. Also, he will butter up the alphas and betas to convince the ones he wants to stay. *I pray to our goddess I make it out of here with my life and my sanity*, Alex thought, pulling out his cellphone to snap a few keepsake photos.

As they pulled into the kingdom gates, Alex observed that everything within the gates seemed well kept. The castle was huge, and even the guards were intimidatingly huge. Alex and Heim began mentally preparing for their time here. The trainees were shuffled through the castle and shown to their rooms, alphas and betas paired. *I would not want to be left alone in this castle*, Alex thought, noticing that Mark seemed quieter and tenser than usual. "You all right, Mark?" he asked.

"Something isn't right, Alex," Mark replied. "Xeris is screaming at me for us to leave. You being an alpha, it's probably even worse for you. Do you think we're all experiencing this?"

"I'm certain we aren't the only ones feeling the dark vibes about this place," Alex said. "Remember my dad's warnings: Keep our eyes open, but our heads down, work hard, but not too hard so as not to catch the king's interest. He'll manipulate strong alpha and beta wolves to stay here and work for him. If you text anything negative, delete it immediately and don't talk about it until we leave or else our lives will be in danger."

"Basically, don't say anything bad. There are eyes everywhere," Mark concurred.

"You got it, man. We're in this together; we watch each other's backs. No question."

"Until death, my brother. Until death."

Four days later, the trainees had yet to meet the king. They had been trained how to march like Royal Guardsman and been used as extra eyes on patrols. *It's like they're trying to condition all of us to blindly fall into place as guardsmen*, Alex mused.

Mark and Alex were sent to the outskirts of the castle walls that border with Strong Hold pack territory. *I don't understand why, but here we are none the less,* Alex thought. Looking left, he saw a bored Pete and his beta, and to his right, Roman and Ricky chit-chatted away. When Alex looked straight ahead in the trees, all he saw were eyes. Heim's hackles raised, and he was ready to shift, but he keep quiet. Looking closer, Alex saw the eyes stared at the trainees, but they didn't move. Remembering what his father had said, it dawned on Alex that it was the king spying on them through others eyes.

Alex elbowed Mark and jerked his head toward the trees, "Does it look like those birds are watching us? They are not moving or blinking." It was innocent enough to say, knowing what Alex knew. Mark held his breath and stared into the trees for a little while until he confirmed what Alex saw.

"I bet they've been there the entire time, like it's a test to see who notices first," Mark speculated.

"Watch my back. I'm going to try and catch one," Alex said. He called on Heim's stealth and speed to climb a tree and capture one of the birds. Once Alex got on a limb, the crow creepily turned its head to him, cawing and causing the other birds to fly away. It scared the shit out of Alex, and he almost fell out of the tree. He climbed back down, and as soon as his feet touched the forest floor, he heard a thunderous bellow laugh behind him, followed by clapping. *Oh, shit it's the king,* Alex thought.

"I knew you'd be the first, Alex son of Alpha Steven Gibbson," King Sidious said.

Alex bowed low and closed his eyes. Darkness radiates off the king, burning Alex's eyes. "My king," was all Alex could reply with.

"You and Mark were the only ones with eyes open and aware. I figured it would take about four rotations, but just like your fathers before you, it took only one, before you realized I have enchanted spies. Please rise, my boy," the king said, putting a hand on Alex's shoulder. "Since you and Mark passed my first task, you both have earned the rest of the day off to explore my kingdom, followed by dinner with me. You both may go relax back at the castle."

"Yes, your highness. Thank you, my king," Alex said, standing.

King Sidious gathered the remaining trainees in a group. Mark and Alex went back to the castle, both forcing positive vibes but dreading their dinner with the king. With their free time, they decided to see if they could find Alex's mate.

The king had been keeping a close eye on Steven's boy more than any other trainee. *His father was one of my most loyal guards and a great fighter too,* the king thought. *I've caught him on more than one occasion defending my honor and punishing those who were against me. He's the closest thing I ever had to a friend.* The king was sad when Steven had asked to leave the kingdom to look for his mate, but the king had let him go. Even though Steven called the king occasionally to check up and inform on things, the king was unsure he wanted Steven's son in his kingdom. *He's very observant,* the king thought, knowing it was the time of the decade when he would have to consume another child to keep Opal's spell Skin Walker of the Becoming intact to retain his youth and life. *Alex is so aware of things going on around him that it's scary. Normally, I'd be proud, but right now, I'm concerned that I don't know where his loyalties lie.*

Only Opal and the king knew about the ritual. The council knew the king was not a werewolf, but it still didn't know exactly what he was. He kept their bellies full, pockets heavy, and dicks wet, so they turned an eye.

The king had a gut feeling that he should find a reason to send Alex home before Opal arrived here to give birth to yet another sacrifice, fearing Alex would notice something was different. His wolf will smell it. *These other alphas and betas seem to be dimwits,* the king thought. He looked forward to his upcoming dinner with Alex and Mark to see what they knew and where they stood.

Chapter 31: Witness

Being away from Sofia is hard, Mark thought. He was so distracted that he was just going through the motions, no longer caring about the training. His wolf, Xeris, kept clawing at his mind, *mate, mate, mate.* It took strength for Mark to push Xeris down so he could function.

Alex clapped his hands in front of Mark's face to bring him back to reality. "Yo, bro, you ready for dinner with the king?"

"Sorry, man, X won't leave me alone. He just wants to get back to his mate. I do too, but we have to finish our shit," Mark said.

"We do indeed. Heim seems to have been wrong about our mate being here because I have not scented anyone the least bit appealing. Now he seems to have gone into hibernation and won't even talk to me," Alex said.

"That's weird..." Mark was interrupted by a guard's knock for dinner. "Well, it's time to go eat."

Mark and Alex followed the guard through the castle, and Mark reached out to X to get him to mind-link with Heim. It would give him something else to do, besides nag Mark about their mate. Let him focus on helping Alex and Heim.

"You, okay, Alex?" Mark asked. "You should be happy. We get to eat with the king, though we still have to put on a show."

"I don't know, Mark. All of sudden, I have an empty feeling, like I'm mate-less," Alex said.

"I doubt you're mate-less, Alex. Our goddess wouldn't do that to an alpha who's also a good person."

"I pray you're right, brother."

"I say this as your friend, brother, and beta. Get your shit together quick, before we get to the dining hall."

"You're right."

As Mark and Alex finished their short journey to the royal wing of the castle, Mark noticed that Alex was walking taller with his chin held high. *That's my alpha,* he thought. *I hope he can reel in his gift because who knows what he sees. It's game time, and I see him in all his glory.*

"Gentleman, glad you could join me this evening," King Sidious said as Mark and Alex entered the hall.

In unison, they replied, "Your majesty."

"Pick a seat, any seat, and the servants will bring in the first course," the king said, then gesturing to Alex, "How's your dad?"

Poor Alex has to make small talk, not one of his strong suits, Mark thought.

"He just recently found out my mom is pregnant again. She's so mad."

"That's great news! Why would she be mad?" the king asked.

"She figured at her age, not that she's old, the next set of diapers she would be changing would be her grandpups, not that I've met my mate yet, but Mark here is my sister's mate."

Oh, gee, thank you, Alex for putting the focus on me, Mark mind-linked Alex, who gave him a side smirk.

"That's great, Mark. Congratulations are in order then."

"Thank you, my king. It means a great deal coming from you, sir."

Thank goodness the first course arrived, so Mark and Alex could eat instead of chit-chat. The longer Mark sat there, the more nauseated he became. *I've had a few bites of food, and it smells like death,* he thought. Unfortunately Mark and Alex had to endure more small talk before the main meal arrived.

As soon as the plate landed in front of Mark, X took over for a split second and whacked his plate to the floor, while Mark started vomiting harshly. In a panic, Mark wiped his mouth and began to profusely apologize. The servants quickly appeared to help clean up the mess, so Mark excused himself to the nearest restroom.

A few seconds later, he heard a knock. "Someone is in here. I'll be right out," Mark called.

Undeterred, in walked a servant boy.

"Sorry, sir, but I brought you a fresh set of clothes. Don't worry. You aren't the first beta that's happened to," the servant said, handing Mark the clothing.

The servant turned to leave, but Mark quickly grabbed his arm. "What do you mean I'm not the first one?"

"I'm not allowed to talk about anything that goes on inside this castle. Excuse me," the servant said, pulling his arm free, then darting back out the door.

Mark changed into the clothes he was given. The creepy part was the clothes were his, like the king's staff somehow knew what was going to happen. After Mark finished cleaning himself up, he got his shit together and went back to dinner. "I don't know what happened, sir. Again I'm so sorry," he said to the king at the table.

"You're fine, boy," the king replied. "Your father reacted the same way. He said it was my powerful aura. Only alphas can handle being around me at first."

"That makes sense, your highness."

"Your father, Jake, was a loyal guard to me, just as Steven was. He did get used to my aura eventually. Alas, when Steven left to start a family, Jake left with him, and they both found their mates less than two months later."

Mark and Alex ate dessert in peace and silence, though X tried to break free again. *I don't know why he's so agitated,* Mark thought.

King Sidious broke the silence. "I have an offer to both of you. Would you consider becoming part of my Royal Guard, following in your fathers' footsteps?"

Mark and Alex had anticipated this question.

Alex spoke first, "It's a true honor you'd ask us, but I speak for the both of us and have to regrettably decline. My dad is going to need me to take on extra responsibilities since he's having another kid. Plus because Mark is mated to my sister, I can't let her suffer the pain of being away from her mate. She's only sixteen, so she has to stay and finish school. However, if something is needed, you have our full support."

"Very well put and understood completely, Alex," the king said, nodding his approval.

Alex was grateful when the painful dinner ended. He could tell the king was fishing for guards, but he wasn't having any of it. Alex kept his head down as much as possible because the king smelled like death, and because of his gift, Alex could see his black death aura too. Alex needed to talk with his dad badly, but it wasn't an option right then.

Alex and Mark were doing walking patrols with Roman and Ricky. When they were at the front gate, they saw a vehicle approaching. Roman gestured to the driver to stop the car. The woman driver rolled down her window, and Roman called loud enough for the others to hear, "Hey, Opal, what brings you here?"

Oh shit, the witch is here, Alex thought. As he watched, Roman talked to her like they were old friends and let her pass.

Mark came up from behind Alex and said, "Something bad is going to happen while we're here. I feel it in my bones."

Alex nodded, and he and Mark kept moving while Roman and Ricky stayed at the gate. Alex and Mark ran into a Royal Guardsman and asked where he would like them to patrol next.

"We need extra coverage tonight," the guard said. "Go back and nap. The patrolman in charge of tonight's rotation will collect you and Alpha Pete and his Beta Toby."

As Alex and Mark returned to the castle, they saw Pete and Toby. Together the trainees shot the shit all the way back to the castle.

The guards retrieved the four at 2100 hours. Heim was fully awake and seemed to be revitalized, but he still wouldn't tell Alex what's wrong. The guards instructed Alex and Pete to switch betas, implying it was for training purposes. The trainees had learned from their Strong Hold training rotation that it's good to be able to communicate with someone else near you and have someone's eyes you trust elsewhere.

Alex tried to strike up small talk, "How has this place been for you, Toby?"

"I haven't really seen anyone else lately. Have you?" Toby asked.

"Come to think of it, neither have I. Mark and I have had patrols with Roman and Ricky and now you and Pete."

"How was your dinner with King Sidious?" Toby asked.

"He was very easy to talk to. But Mark vomited everywhere. He couldn't handle the king's aura."

Alex mind-linked Mark, *Something might be wrong here! Watch what you say to Pete.*

Toby seems to be trying to dig up information about the king or for the king.

I'll be careful, Mark mind-link replied.

"No offense, but that is pretty fucking weak. When the king approached me and Pete to do patrols with you tonight, I was just fine," Toby said.

"Mark's also missing his mate and all. It's okay. No offense taken. Wonder why they needed extra patrols tonight?" Alex changed the subject.

"I'm just doing what I'm told, Alex. I don't ask questions."

Well, his attitude just took a 180. Now he's trying to get under my skin. Time to shut his arrogance down, Alex thought. "True betas have to do what they're told. Don't they?"

That did it. Toby shifted fast and took off in his wolf form.

"Get back to your assigned patrol with me!" Alex yelled, but Toby kept on going.

A Royal Guardsman came over to see what all the commotion was about. Alex told him, which instantly made the guard upset. The guard went off to find Toby, mumbling to himself, "Fucking betas, fucking kids. I don't have time for this shit."

Alex was now alone in unfamiliar territory all by himself. He continued his patrol when he heard faint screaming coming from deep within the forest. He was diligently looking for the creatures the king had possessed, but he saw no eyes. He heard no other patrols nor smelled any other wolves. He approached slowly and cautiously, knowing he still had a job to do while he was here. He smelled smoke before he saw a fire. And he heard screaming. The closer he got to the screams, he could see flames dancing in the trees. He spotted two figures huddled inside a ring of fire. He halted his approach to watch, making sure he stayed downwind.

Alex realized he was witnessing a woman giving birth. It seemed normal, until he recognized the king, who was suddenly holding up the child, as if to make a sacrifice. *Awww, the king finally has an heir to the throne,* Alex thought.

The woman who had just given birth was now kneeling with her arms upraised, holding plants Alex had never seen before and chanting. The longer she chanted, the higher the ring of fire grew. The woman threw the plants into the ring of fire. As Alex watched, the king roared, then inhumanly, unnaturally opened his jaws and with one swallow, consumed the child.

Alex was in shock, but he knew he had to leave—fast! He quietly rose and headed back to his patrol route, doing his best to keep his breathing regulated and to slow down his heart rate before anyone saw him. He continued on his path for about twenty minutes before he found Toby, who was being held by the Royal Guardsman. "Where have you been, Toby?"

"I don't answer to you, Alex," Toby snarled.

"Take him to the cells, Alpha Alex. He seems to be going feral," the guard ordered.

"Yes, sir. Let's go, Toby. We both have to listen to him," Alex said.

Alex grabbed Toby from the guard. He walked in silence with the grumbling Toby. "What the hell has gotten into you, Toby? Why does the guard think you're going feral?"

"Just shut up, Alex. Leave me the fuck alone."

Where are you and Pete? I need Pete to come deal with his fuckin' beta, Alex mind-linked Mark and Pete.

Pete doesn't understand. I can't even mind-link him, Mark replied.

Tell him the guardsman thinks Toby's going feral, Alex linked, tightening his grip on Toby, who kept trying to break free. "Just knock it off, Toby," he said.

The pair reached the side of the castle where the prisons were, and Alex gratefully handed Toby over to the guardsman at the door, then headed back toward his route. Suddenly, he saw Pete running his way, followed by Mark and yelling, "What the fuck, Alex?"

"All of a sudden, Toby's attitude did a 180, and he started getting very testy with me. We exchanged words, and he bolted. A Royal Guardsman went to look for him while I stayed on my route and came across them about twenty minutes later. The guard thought Toby might be going feral and told me to take him to the prison."

Alex looked at his watch, then continued, "Let's finish our patrol. We have three hours left."

The trainees started back on their route and were startled to run across Toby. Alex stared at him for a second, then used his gift and discovered the figure before him might *look* like Toby, but it was actually the king in disguise. "Toby?" Alex finally spoke.

"Hey, guys," the king said, in Toby's form.

"We just took you to the prison. How did you escape? Let's get you back," Alex said.

"I'm fine. My wolf just needed a good long run. That's all," the king said.

"Let's go find Pete so he can keep an eye on you at least. We can't have bad behavior on the king's watch. We have to train hard here."

"I'm tired now. I'm just going to go to bed," the king said, then took off toward the castle. Alex looked at Mark and shook his head. Without words being spoken, Mark understood that was the king not Toby.

Keeping the gruesome baby sacrifice secret was killing Alex on the inside. This training has been disappointing to say the least, nothing but patrols. To keep his mind occupied, Alex counted down their time left here. The atmosphere seemed to have shifted since that day to heavier air, making it harder to breathe.

For the next few days, Mark kept trying to get Alex to open up, but he couldn't just now. "Have you seen Toby at all? It's been like a week now," Alex asked.

"No, I can't wait to go home to my mate—if you know what I mean," Mark replied.

Alex knew what he meant, and he felt the same. He just didn't have a mate to go home to. They both just wanted to get the hell out of there. "Man, that's my sister you're talking about. You want another brotherly beating?" Alex said, winking at Mark.

"Man, we used to talk girls all the time, and now I can't with you. Guess I need a new best friend," Mark said laughing.

"Keep telling yourself that. No one wants to put up with your ugly ass, and my poor sister is stuck staring at it for the rest of her life."

"She already loves this face and body, buddy. Don't be jealous. It wasn't you who got all this."

Alex couldn't help but laugh. It felt good to laugh and get his mind off things. The friends kept up their banter for the rest of their patrols. They finally crossed paths with other alphas and betas, which was a relief because they were beginning to think they were the only ones left out there.

Finally, the trainees were approaching their final week when it was announced that there would be no final feast nor ball this year. They were all very disappointed with this news.

I swore my mate was here because of our warrior's mate, Alex thought. *Guess I was wrong, but we're finally getting the hell out of here.*

Chapter 32: Welcome Home

While the trainees were at the Royal Kingdom, Zane had been having one-on-one training with Alpha Steven, learning how the Royal Guards fight and tips to counter their moves. Steven's advice was to save strength to use his powers against the king.

Alpha Steven had stopped hearing from Alex since he had left for the Royal Kingdom for his training. Zane could tell Steven was worried about his son, but he distracted himself by focusing on getting his pack ready for war with the Royals.

Pyrox was getting super antsy because he knew he would have to face his former human host. He knew it was his destiny to kill the king.

Zane and Steven were leading group training when Alpha Steven received a call from Alex. From across the room, Zane could read the relief on Steven's face. Steven gestured to the group to wrap up their training so he could talk to Alex.

Zane and Rocky walked over to the corner of the room where they had tossed their water bottles and sweatshirts. Having ended his call, Alpha Steven came over and said, "Go take a quick shower and have a snack. Grab your mates and meet me in my office." Then he was off.

"That didn't sound good at all," Rocky observed.

"My gut is telling me war prep is over, and the real war will begin," Zane said.

"See you in a bit, brother."

Zane mind-linked his fiery redhead, *Meet me at home,* knowing she was at the pack house with his mom.

The couple met at home, then got ready and went back to the pack house. They greeted Alex and Mark and made small talk until Alpha Steven called them all into his office. Mark and Sofia were almost ready to take off to spend time alone after Mark has been away, but they refrained and waited. Alpha Steven, Beta Jake, and their mates came into the room, also grateful for their sons' return. After about fifteen minutes of meet and greet, it was time to sit down with Alpha Steven.

"Don't worry. We'll have a welcome home shing-dig," Alpha Steven said. "For now, we need to listen to what Alex and Mark have encountered at the Royal Kingdom. The shit up there's worse than I thought. Alex, you have the floor."

With Val perched on Zane's lap, the group listened intently to what Alex and Mark experienced. After hearing all the disturbing details, Pyrox confirmed the king must die, and Zane relayed, "How the hell can someone do that? He can turn into different people and consume babies? How do we even fight that?"

"Those are good questions, Zane," Alex said.

"We must work together and train to take him down. We're relying on you, Zane. Is Pyrox up to the task?" Alpha Steven asked.

"Yes, he is. He agrees it is time for the king to go. Seems he no longer has any soul. He's forgotten about right and wrong. Killing him is what's best for our kind," Zane said, shaking his head.

"I'll meet with Lucius and Raven to see if they know a way around whatever it is the king and Opal have done. I think it is also time for Opal to meet her end," Steven said.

The meeting adjourned. Winter left, and spring passed them by. The pack did nothing but train.

Because there was no winter celebration that year at the Royal Kingdom, Alpha Steven decided to hold one at the end of spring. With help from the upper females of the pack, they got the invitations out in two days' time. Even the king was invited. The head females start planning the party while Alpha Steven made security plans. Knowing what King Sidious was capable of, he trained his pack relentlessly.

Steven met with Lucius and Raven, bringing them on board with plans to assassinate the king. Lucius and Raven left to travel to an undisclosed location to discover how to get around Opal's spell.

Because the chosen group knew this assignment was for reconnaissance, they volunteered for security, except for Alex and Mark, being the alpha and beta. Plus, Alex still hoped his mate would show up somewhere. As the RSVPs to the celebration began arriving, acceptances included Strong Hold, Summoning, White Moon, White Fang, Shrieking Moon, and King Sidious. Long before the celebration, the pack secreted away any incriminating information in Alpha Steven's vault.

Steven sent everyone to their assigned security posts once Alpha Charles arrived, thanking the goddess he was the first. Steven met briefly with Charles, his beta, and Jake. Evander and his son Robert relayed good information on Alpha Van. Basically, the guy was insane, and Steven hoped Roman would be able to take him down.

Steven wanted his pack and the other guests to have a good time, holding his breath that there wouldn't be any drama. He headed down to his Luna to help with the meet and greet. When he arrived, he saw he was just time to greet the king.

"Luna Tessa, my dear, you're more beautiful than I remember," King Sidious kissed her hand and bowed. Tessa blushed.

Steven greeted him, "Your highness, it's more than an honor you came tonight. I hope you get to enjoy yourself."

"I'm hoping to find a companion tonight," King Sidious said.

"As long as it isn't my Tess or any other already mated wolf," Alpha Steven said.

"I wouldn't dare, Steven."

Steven shook the king's hand and escorted him to the party room, telling him the pack had his usual room made up for him in the alpha wing of the pack house and let him meander about.

Steven returned to Tessa to find her greeting none other than Alpha Van and his Beta Jones. Steven and his wolf, Sunka, both growled internally but put on a happy face. "Welcome, Alpha Van. Glad you could make it, Beta Jones."

"Thanks for the invite, Alpha Steven. Where are our daughters at? We miss them dearly," Alpha Van said.

"They're around. If I see them before you do, I'll let them know you're looking for them because you miss them so much. Please greet our king. He has already arrived," Alpha Steven said.

"I didn't know the king would be here," Alpha Van said, looking surprised.

Steven nodded and moved him along. He mind-linked Rocky and Zane about their mates' fathers' arrival and that they were already asking for them. Steven and his cousin Charles were keeping an eye on things. So far everyone seemed to be happy and laughing.

Steven didn't want drama, but Sunka opened their hearing more, and they caught Alpha Van talking about King Sidious, "Contact Opal so she can zap some poison to us. We can make it look like Alpha Steven is trying to kill the king."

Oh, hell no. We might be planning a war with him, but I don't need my name dragged through the mud. We don't even know if that would kill him or just piss him off and cause more problems, Alpha Steven thought, then called, "Guards! Royal Guards!"

Everything and everyone stopped. King Sidious approached Steven and asked, "What's wrong, Steven? You don't call for my guards unless... Who?"

"Alpha Van and his beta, sir," Steven replied.

"Seize them!" the king commanded.

"What!? We didn't do anything!" Alpha Van protested.

"Bullshit! Did you forget we're a bunch of wolves with hearing to match? Did you or did you not have your beta contact someone named Opal to zap you over some poison?" Alpha Steven asked hotly.

"No, why would I do that?" the indignant Alpha Van replied.

"To make our king sick and make it look like I was trying to kill him," Steven replied.

"Did you just say 'Opal'? Well, then that's easy clear up," King Sidious said, taking out his phone. Then speaking into the phone, "Opal, were you just contacted by Beta Jones? That's all I need. Thank you." Turning back to Van, he asked, "Would you like to try again, Alpha Van?"

"You know my pack witch on a personal level?" Alpha Van asked.

The king laughed in his face. "Please lock them up and continue on with the festivities. Don't let this damper our evening."

Alpha Steven took great personal pleasure in doing as the king requested. Even though the king terrified many, they tried to have a good time. But the atmosphere in the hall remained thick, despite how relaxed the king looked. It didn't put anyone at ease—except maybe the younger wolves.

King Sidious approached Steve and demanded, " I haven't seen your Lycan. Zane, was it?"

"He chose security detail, your highness, with his mate, who happens to be Beta Jones's daughter," Steven replied.

"He found his mate already? How did he meet her when Alpha Van's pack is far from yours?" the king asked.

Oh shit, Steven thought, then said aloud, "She's actually the niece of Delta Curtis; her mom is Curtis's sister. He hasn't seen her in a while, and we invited her to Zane's birthday. She doesn't go anywhere without Althea, and she ended up being Rocky's mate, Delta Curtis's son. I sent the council an immediate notification to have them transferred."

"Wow, that's a hell of a love story. Why the immediate transfer?" the king asked.

"That, sir, is going to be a long conversation meant for privacy. Can we sleep and have that conversation tomorrow?" Alpha Steven asked.

"That bad, eh? I wasn't planning on staying, but you piqued my interest, Steven."

"I didn't expect drama with Alpha Van," Alpha Steven said, not looking forward to the conversation with the king and knowing that he had to cover his tracks for keeping things that involve him, from him.

Steven left a note for Alex to prepare the chosen group for what might come from today's conversation. *He'll do me proud,* Steven thought, then went down for breakfast, where he saw King Sidious eating and flirting with Remmy. *Seems like he found a companion for the evening.*

"Good morning, Alpha. Just sit. I'll fix your plate," Trudy said.

"Good morning, Trudy. Thank you. Good morning, your highness," Alpha Steven said.

"Good morning, Steven. Think I'll steal Trudy from you too. Her food is fantastic," the king said without warmth.

"I'd wither away without her cooking," Alpha Steven said, then promptly was whacked by Tessa.

"Ouch! Tessa baby, you know I love you and your food too," Steven said to his mate.

"Ya, ya, Steve. You just like to knock me up," Luna Tessa said with a smirk.

Steven pulled Tessa to his lap and peppered kisses on her. "That's not true, my love, simply not true. I love all of you—your beauty, fierceness, love of everyone, mothering to our pups and also our pack, and most of all for keeping me grounded and in check. Not to mention your wolf is a magnificent beast."

"Flattery will get you nowhere right now. I've pups to go coo in the nursery. Enjoy your day. I love you," said Luna Tessa.

"That was something to witness," the king said.

"Can't help but love her. I take it I have to find Trudy a new cooking helper?" Steven asked.

"If you don't mind," the king said with a nod.

"As long as she agrees to make the move," Steven said, looking at Remmy.

"I do, Alpha Steven," Remmy answered seriously.

"I'll do the paperwork before we start our colorful conversation, so she can leave with you when you head home," Alpha Steven said.

Steven finished his food and headed to his office. He mind-linked Alex when he closed his door. Alex received the message and understood what Steven needed. Steven reluctantly started Remmy's transfer paperwork. He didn't want her to go because he was afraid for her. The king walked in as Steven was finishing up Remmy's papers.

"So, what needed to wait?" the king asked.

Steven took a deep breath before answering. "When Valerie and Althea were contacted and invited over, Rocky was talking to Valerie, who explained some problems she and Althea were having with their brothers—constant unwanted sexual advances. So, I sent my tracker Evan, Zane's dad, and Delta Curtis to escort them both here for the party and their safety. Alpha Van and I had already agreed to send our unmated back and forth after school in the summer, so Roman and Ricky came too. Later I found out Alpha Van and Beta Jones were using the girls because of a prophecy he said he has," Alpha Steven explained.

"What prophecy?" the king asked.

"I believe they said it's called Prophecy of Water and Fire. They think it involves the girls because of the way their wolves are colored," Steven said.

"Do you know anything about it?" the king asked.

"I searched what old ass scrolls I have and found nothing, so I sent Evan, his son, and a young warlock to find me the information. They returned with this," Alpha Steven said, handing the king the scroll they stole from Alpha Van.

The king took some time to read through it. "So two female wolves are said to protect me like the Lycan?"

"That's what they think, but I don't take much stock in a piece of old paper," Steven said.

"I feel ya. So what are Alpha Van's plans?" the king inquired.

"What I got out of their sons is they want to be royalty; they want your throne. They wanted their sons to impregnate each daughter to activate "powers" and hoped you'd want them for your kingdom. Then Alpha Van could take the entire pack with him and make them royalty because their sons would be force-mated to the girls," Steven said.

"Do they have powers since they found their mates?" the king asked.

"I didn't ask, but I haven't noticed any powers from either of them. Also my wolf, Sunka, hasn't felt anyone more powerful than me—other than you, of course. The girls are amazing fighters. They started a she-wolf-driven program. They teach my she-wolves how to fight people bigger than them. I assume their pack life wasn't good growing up," Steven said.

After their long conversation ended, King Sidious bid his farewell to Alpha Steven. Remmy said goodbye to her pack to leave with King Sidious, and the king had his guards take Alpha Van and Beta Jones back to his prison at the Royal Kingdom.

Chapter 33: Sudden Invasion

Zane felt relieved that the king had gone, taking with him Val's and Bluey's imprisoned fathers. Alpha Steven gave the pack a few days off from training, and they took advantage by blowing off steam in the city.

The wolves found it interesting how humans bundled up when the slightest chill hits the air, while they would be warm walking around in sleeveless shirts and shorts. The wolves started getting the munchies and found a quaint hole-in-the-wall restaurant. When they walked in, they were stared at like they all had two heads and tentacles. Alex cleared his throat to gain the hostess's attention.

It smells off in here and has a weird vibe, Pyrox mind-linked Zane, who tried to ease his mind. *We don't come to the city very often. But I trust your judgement and will keep Val close to us at all times.*

Because the group was large for the small restaurant, the friends were seated in the very back corner far from the entrance. As they were seated, eyes followed their every step. Bluey let out a low growl of annoyance, and Val elbowed her. Zane saw the girls mind-linking, then laughed and relaxed. The waiter brought menus and some starter water. Pyrox started growling now too and mind-linked Zane.

What's wrong buddy? Zane asked.

Old blood is near.

I know you're our goddess's first protector, but I don't know what that means." Zane said.

It's not human, wolf, or witch. I can't remember which creature smells like this. Our creator created so many back then.

Are we in danger?"

At the moment, I'm unsure, but it might be best to leave.

Then Zane mind-linked Alex to catch him up on what Pyrox just said. Alex nodded, and they got up to leave.

Before they got far, an odd man approached them asking, "King of wolves, what brings you here?"

"No one here is any of that, sir. I assure you," Alex said, looking confused.

"Nonsense, I can feel power here," the odd man said.

"We're all powerful in our own right because we're all together. We're leaving," Alex said, turning to go.

"No one will bring harm here. Please sit. It is an honor to have you here," the odd man said, gesturing to a chair.

"We're seriously confused, sir. What might we call you?" Alex asked.

"Names are unimportant at the moment," the odd man said. "Stay here. I'll be right back," he called over his shoulder as he started walking away.

Pyrox is still unsure. Alex, what should we do? Are you picking up on anything? Zane mind-linked Alex.

I don't see anything other than a blue hue around him, Alex linked, scanning the rest of the room. *No one will look over here now so all I see are hints of greens and yellows. Stay put but remain vigilant. Even if things go south, we're wolves. We're strong, and we'll prevail in a situation like this.*

Zane and Alex waited for the odd man to return. When he did, he was carrying a gold-trimmed, purple-and-black box.

Pyrox mind-linked Zane, *I haven't seen that in a very long time. It contains something special, or at least it did.*

Contained what exactly?

Another mistake our Moon Goddess created and didn't know would go sour. The soul she couldn't contains in her realm because she was still needed on earth's realm. Pyrox linked.

Alex pulled his alpha out and finally tried to command the odd man to give up who he was.

"I mean you no harm," the odd man said. "This box contains something I'm supposed to give to the true king of wolves."

"And who exactly do you think that is?" Alex asked.

"You seem to be the commanding one, but I can't pinpoint where the power I feel is coming from. There's so much power emanating from this group that I can't tell who is the most powerful," the odd man said, looking frustrated.

"We have a king, and it's none of us here, I assure you." Alex said.

"We shall see in all due time. In the meantime, I'll put this box back, and you guys can carry on with your day. Whatever you all order will be on the house if you choose to stay that is," the odd man said, picked up the box and walked away.

The chosen group left the restaurant as well. They did not want to take any chances of more oddness happening, so they went back to the main street of the city to find a better place to eat.

Later that day, Zane was still feeling very uneasy about their encounter with that odd man. He asked Pyrox many times if he understood anything besides his knowledge of what was in the box. He assures Zane it was not us he was talking about, because our goddess never groomed him for such a task with his time with her. Zane was unconvinced.

Back at home, Zane couldn't sleep a wink, so he left Valerie snuggled in their bed and let Pyrox free. They headed to the waterfall in the middle of pack territory, which was always beautiful when the moon twinkled in the water under the moon light. Pyrox let out a roar of frustration. The trees shook, the ground rumbled, and the wind blew. He let it all out, and they passed out.

Zane and Pyrox entered a dreamlike state:

"Zane... Zane... Pyrox... Pyrox..., I need you two to wake up now, we need to speak... Come on now up, up with you."

Zane opened his eyes, feeling like he was having an out-of-body experience. Bright blue and white light surrounded him. To his astonishment, he looked over and saw Pyrox, looking to be passed out! *We're no long one, what the hell!* he thought and sat up in a panic.

Zane heard a soothing voice, "Relax, Zane. Breathe. It's not what it seems here."

"But Pyrox is unconscious, and we're no longer one. What am I supposed to think?" Zane asked.

"My dear son, I sensed so much distress I needed to come and help you prepare for what's needing to be done," soothed the Moon Goddess.

"Where are we and what needs to be done?" Zane asked.

"Son, you know the answers already that you seek. You and Pyrox just have to accept the truth," the Moon Goddess said.

Zane sat silently thinking, unsure for how long. *She's right. I know who she is, and I know what she needs from us. I was right all along. I just didn't want to be.* He finally spoke, "I know you, my Moon Goddess, my mother. I know we need to kill King Sidious, remove him. His time is over. I've never killed before; I've never led before."

"But Pyrox has," the Moon Goddess said. "I wiped his bad memories of his first time on Earth. Sidious corrupted Pyrox after time. I had pulled my Lycan spirits back to me and retrained them for the reason I created them in the first place. I was just waiting for the right circumstances for their return."

"My parents..."

"Yes, Zane. Their story is a rough one, but in the end all love, true love, divine love created a perfect soul to handle a Lycan spirit. You're strong enough to handle what Sidious could not. Yes, I made mistakes, not just with the Lycans, but at the time I thought I was doing the right thing by not giving them chosen mates. I was trying to follow in other footsteps and let love happen freely. I learned it's not likely, but it is possible —just like with human souls and an animal spirit."

"Will Pyrox ever remember what happened in his past?"

"I've released his memories to him. That's why I brought you both here. He's processing them as we speak."

"You'll return us to one, right?" Zane asked.

"Yes, of course. Spirits need a commanding soul. Your parents have raised you and your siblings well."

"What's that supposed to mean?"

"You'll understand soon enough. I've given you everything I can at this time. Sleep now, Zane."

Zane woke up being slapped repeatedly in the face by Valerie.

"What the fuck, Zane! I wake up to you gone! It felt like my soul was incomplete. I thought you were dead!"

Without a word, Zane snatched her to him and held on tight. "I'm sorry, my love, oh so sorry."

"You better start talking."

Zane hold her close and explained what had happened while walking home. Pyrox had yet to come through since the Moon Goddess reawakened his past memories. Zane explained he needs time to process. The couple fell back to sleep once they hit the bed.

All of a sudden, they were woken up by chaos. The pack was under attack. Val and Zane ran out of the house toward the sounds of the fighting to see it was the king and Shrieking Moon! Alpha Steven was locked in battle with the king, Alpha Van, and Beta Jake all ganged up on him. Royal Guards had ahold of Alex and Mark by their necks, while the rest of the pack was fighting all around.

PYROX, I need you NOW! Zane called to him. ***It's time for us to fight! You can finish processing later.***

Zane saw a ball of fire zoom past him to meet Bluey and quickly subdue their fathers, giving Alpha Steven a chance to recover and back away from the king. *He knows he's mine to take down*, Zane thought. To Zane's horror, King Sidious went for the girls, but Rocky, well Carrick, smashed into him. Pyrox finally decided to break free and show his need to protect his mate, with a roar mightier than he had ever let out before that seemed to bring time to a standstill. King Sidious recovered from Rocky and stalked toward Zane with malice.

"So, it has been a long time, old friend," the king snarled. "I should've guessed she would bring you back."

"Seems we were never friends, Sidious," Pyrox said.

"That's King Sidious to you!"

"Hardly! Leave now or die, Sidious."

"I can't die, you fool."

Opal stepped to the king's side, "That's right."

"Then you shall both die this day," Pyrox said.

Pyrox locked in a fierce battle with Opal and King Sidious. The more Pyrox clawed and punched, opening wounds, the quicker they healed. The king was so ungodly fast that Pyrox didn't even have time to use his powers. The king morphed into different creatures to heal his wounds, plus Opal did God knows what to keep him alive.

The entire pack was up in arms, fighting off Shrieking Moon Pack fighters and Royal Guards. No one seemed to be fighting to kill, rather to establish dominance. Steven was protecting a now very pregnant Luna, who wanted to fight but couldn't and wouldn't risk her pup. Rocky fought his heart out protecting his mate, giving the girls time to finally come together and fight.

Althea, love, you and Val need to break free to help Zane with the King and Opal! Rocky linked.

I'm trying, love, having a rough time at the moment, Bluey replied.

Be right there, my love. These Royals are tough.

Alpha Steven, in Sunka form, came barreling toward Rocky. "I got these chumps. Go to the girls!"

Rocky quickly took off. He found Bluey locked in a fight with her own father. Rocky shifted back to human form, wrapped his arms around Alpha Van's neck and growled, "How could you do this to your own daughter?" He squeezed Van's neck harder. "What kind of father are you?" Alpha Van began turning purple. "I'm not going to kill you. It's up to my mate to decide your fate." Then Rocky turned to Bluey and said, "I'll be right back, love. Help Val."

Bluey headed toward Val, who seemed to be enjoying herself. "It smells like a wolf barbeque over here. It's making me hungry. Should I get some steak sauce?" Bluey joked.

"I'm thinking Worcestershire sauce," Valerie quipped.

"I can't spell nor even say that, so A1 sauce it is," Bluey said, looking down at her old beta. "What do you think, Beta Jones?"

"Fuck you, Althea!" Beta Jones scoffed.

"No thank you. You get to decide his fate, Val. Fry him some more or have him locked up with my father for now?" Bluey asked her friend.

"We don't have time to mess around anymore, Bluey. We need to get to Zane and entrap Opal so Zane has a chance."

Fortunately, Rocky returned just in time to take Jones off the girls' hands. In desperation, the Shrieking Moon fighters surrendered, and the girls headed to Zane's fight.

"Remember what we practiced, Bluey?" Val asked.

"Yes, you put her in a fireball while I enclose it in a water ball," Bluey said.

"No, the other thing," Val said.

"That is scary to do, Val."

"Trust me. She's powerful. It's going to be the only way to stop her."

The girls finally arrived at the main battle between Zane, the king, and Opal. Everyone around seemed to just be watching rather than helping. Pyrox was battling what looked like a mix of wolf and eagle. Both were a bloody mess, but because Opal was helping heal the king, most of the blood was Pyrox's. Seeing all the blood, Valerie screamed to Bluey in a panic, "NOW, BLUEY, NOW, PLEASE!"

In that instant, Opal was no longer moving and powerless. Bluey used her water-controlling abilities to seize up the liquid within Opal's own body to stop her in her tracks. "NOW permafrost her ass from the inside out!" Bluey commanded, then with all the strength she had left, she froze Opal from the inside out, and the witch fell to a heap on the ground.

Once Valerie saw Opal completely frozen, she blasted the witch with a huge fireball, shattering Opal into a million tiny pieces. Bluey collapsed from the effort of using her powers.

With Opal out of commission, Zane gained the upper hand on the king. Zane was tiring, but he knew he couldn't let up.

Val stood in the shattered remains of Opal. Blaze, who had been observing the battle from a safe distance, rushed in to tend to Bluey.

Val mind-linked Zane, *It's almost over, baby. Opal's gone. Knock the king's his fucking head off! One last push! I love you.*

With Val's words of encouragement, Zane used his Earth power to bend the king motionless. Without words or hesitation, Pyrox pierced the king's neck with his claws straight through to his spine and ripped his head clear off his shoulders.

Val stood right behind Zane and with all her strength created a blue flame. As the pack watched, she burned the king to ashes.

It's over.

Everyone stopped.

The Royal Guards fell to their knees, with the Silver Stone Pack behind them.

Pyrox released control back to Zane, who stood in all his glory, covered in King Sidious's blood, looking like a ferocious beast, master of death. With Zane's remaining strength, he half-shifted to Pyrox and let out an all-mighty roar of pure power.

With the sky now dark, pure energy of light was before Zane and the others still involved in the attack. It manifested into a beautiful ghostlike form as the Moon Goddess descended before them. Zane knelt as she reached out to touch his shoulder, "It's done, my son. Thank you." She kissed his forehead and said, "Rise."

The Moon Goddess turned to address the field of wolves before her. "My children, here is your new king, King Zane Montgomery. It's up to him now to guide my creatures to happiness. My brothers and sisters don't all share love and peace for creations in their hearts. There will be challenges ahead. Stand by King Zane, and when the time comes, I'll be here once more."

The Moon Goddess then walked over to the ashes of King Sidious. His ashes rose into the air and swirled, silently being absorbed into the goddess's own body. Then she moved over to Opal's scattered remains. Her slivered remains flew up, spiraled, and soaked into the goddess. And then the Moon Goddess left.

Chapter 34: New Beginnings

Zane told the Royals to gather their injured and leave, explaining, "I'll be up there to deal with the Royal Kingdom." He helped his pack with their injured people before taking Valerie home. They barely spoke before going to bed, exhausted.

Zane thought, *Apparently, I'm a king now, but I don't know a thing about leading anyone. I was born to be a tracker. I have to rely on Pyrox now. We planned to bring war to the king, yet he brought it to us. We need to know why. I was keeping up with the fight pretty well, but after all the blows and cuts we were taking, I was getting worn out and tired. Val and Bluey are an impeccable team. I'm happy no one was killed.*

Holding Valerie while she slept brought Zane and Pyrox peace, but now they knew it was their job to get answers from her father and former alpha. Zane wasn't ready to move from his queen, who was tucked comfortably on his chest. As worn out as they both were, he wanted to worship her like the queen she was. He internally laughed because he'd been calling her his queen for some time now, and now she literally *was*.

Slowing rolling Val onto her back, Zane grabbed her nipple with his mouth, sucked on it, nibbled a bit, and woke her with a pleasurable moan. "MMMMM" he rubbed her clit while he switched nipples, getting her wet and ready for him. She batted her gorgeous eyes open, and he plunged deep into her as he muffled her gasps and moans with his mouth. She made him extra hard, and she got it harder and faster. She clawed at his back and met his every thrust. He grabbed her hands, pinned them above her head, and marked her again as his queen. In an instant, her walls got tighter and clenched his stiffness like she was milking him for everything he had. While his teeth were still in her neck, she stunned him by flipping them over, and she dug deep with her canines and hips. In one moment, their tension and frustrations were released. Zane looked up at her beautiful face, "Good morning, my queen."

She giggled, "Now it's actually true, my king."

The couple got up, showered, and met Zane's family in the kitchen.

"Good morning," Zane's mom was the first to greet them, but she skipped Zane and hugged Val first.

Then he get tackled from behind, and he chuckled. "Erica, Bernie, good morning, my beautiful sisters."

"So, are we princesses now since you're king?" Bernie asked with a beaming smile.

"I'm not sure how that works exactly, but why not? Robert, you're a prince, I hereby declare," Zane said with a flourish of his hand.

"Oh, gee thanks, brother," Robert smirked.

"Man, I don't know how any of this works. It's not like I asked for it. You can blame Opal for all this mess."

"She's dead now. Bluey and I took care of that bitch," Val bluntly stated, and for the first time ever, *thwap*, Zane's mom smacked the back of *her* head.

"Sorry. Trudy."

"It's all right, dear. Just don't let it happen again, or you'll get more like everyone else in this house," Trudy said affectionately.

"She does it a lot. I think I have a callus on the back of my head," Robert joked.

"Well, watch your mouth in my house and around your sisters and any other nonadult, and it won't happen, son," Trudy said.

"Yes, Mom."

"Let me get you all some food, then I've to get to the pack house," Trudy said.

Zane made them all breakfast, and they made small talk and got caught up. Unfortunately, their time was cut short when Zane's dad linked him to get to the prison section of the pack house. Val and Zane helped load the dishwasher before heading out. Zane hugged his sisters and fist bumped his brother. He didn't do man hugs but loved Zane just the same.

As Zane and Val walked to the prison to meet everyone, he confessed, "I don't know much about leading, Val. How am I supposed to lead anyone, let alone nonwerewolves?"

"Good thing for you I'm a beta. We'll figure it out together, but our first task is getting answers from my father," Val said.

"You're right. You're always right. I love you so much," Zane said, hugging her to his side while they walked.

The minute they reached the prison, Zane hugged Rocky, and the girls embraced each other, like they hadn't seen each other in ages.

"How are you holding up, Rocky?" Zane asked.

With a smirk on his face, he bowed, "I feel fine, my lord. Thank you for taking me into consideration."

"Good grief, Rocky. Stop that."

"As you wish, my king."

As much as Zane hated hearing it, it did break the sour mood of the prison and what they had to do. "You ready to get some answers? Alpha Steven and his party are waiting and ready for us."

"I call dibs on my father; he needs a good beating from me," Bluey piped up, happy to volunteer for the task.

"I get mine!" Val added.

The group headed into the meeting room, which was now filled with monitors.

"Good morning, Alpha Steven."

"Morning, my king."

"Not you too."

"You have to get used to it, Zane."

"Maybe, maybe not, just not from you guys. You're my family."

"Yes, my..."

"No, stop it."

"Fine, fine. Who do we interrogate first?"

"The girls want to take on their own fathers."

"Fair enough. They put their children through enough hell. Just keep an eye on them," Steven said.

"I think the girls will do just fine on their own. Besides if Rocky and I go in there, we just might kill them off the bat and not get any answers at all."

"Sounds good. Let the guards at least escort the girls in."

Bluey and Val smirked at one another before entering their fathers' cells. The rest of the group sat in the room, watching the monitors and listening. Before any questions were asked by either of them, Bluey froze one of her father's feet, while Val set one of her father's feet on fire. Neither Alpha Van nor Beta Jones made a peep; it's like they knew what was coming. The girls were setting the stage on how powerful they really were compared to their fathers. Bluey and Val just stood in front of their fathers in silence, linking each other, knowing they had to ask the same questions to get answers.

The men knew the girls were more than capable of handling this situation, but it still sucked to watch from a monitor. They heard Beta Jones start whining.

Val combined with Iggy said, "Shut up, you piss-poor excuse of a father and beta. It's just a little burn. You'll heal if I let you. Now why did Sidious attack us?"

"You're nothing but a little whore of a mistake. I don't answer to you," Beta Jones bluffed.

Val started laughing something fierce. She pretended to wipe tears from her eyes. "I'm the queen now, you little bitch. How do you like that shit! Bluey is my beta queen. You wanted royalty so bad, and now here you are. So yes, you do answer to me."

Jones tried to answer. "You're no queen, AHHHHHH!" as Val set another body part on fire with a smile.

"You were saying?"

"FUCK YOU!"

"Ewwww no. It's bad enough you and Van tried to have us ruined for our mates." Val proceeded to burn his feet to straight ash. He passed out, and she called for a medic.

Zane ran in there so fast. "Are you hurt, my love? Where? I'll kill him!"

"No, no nothing of the sort, my love. I need him awake. He didn't answer my question."

"Don't scare me like that. I'll leave, and you can continue as soon as they wake him up."

"Can you stay please? Maybe if you release your powerful aura, it will get him to talk. Torture isn't working."

"I'll do as my queen wishes." Zane released his new aura into the cell. Jones winced. Val asked again, "Now are you going to answer me?"

"Never," Jones tried to squeak out.

Zane calmly knelt beside him and whispered, "Answer her."

"Why did Sidious attack us with some of your pack alongside him?" Val asked.

"We told him we know you and Bluey had powers, that you were mated to a Lycan, and that we would get you both to mate him and have powerful babies. We also told him our pack was at his disposal for whoever wanted to fight for the king," Jones said weakly.

"You're a sick fucker. You know that? Besides he already knew Zane was mated," Val said.

"He didn't know I was mated to you, Val. We wanted to keep you safe. We didn't know if he had the prophecy or not. We needed to keep you and Bluey under his radar," Zane said.

"Are you sure it's not because I'm just beta born, and you're embarrassed to be mated to me?" Val asked, concerned.

"How could you even think something like that? You're mine. You have been mine, and you always will be mine. Understand that? I love you," Zane said, gazing into her eyes.

Val blushed.

Zane thought, *Awwww how adorable and beautiful she is.*

"You know I can hear your thoughts, right?" Val asked.

Zane put up his hands in defense. "I like my limbs thank you very much."

They both smiled.

"I really do too," Val said, then turning back to her father, she scowled. "Now back to you, Father. Why would he attack based only on your word and no proof?"

"We had proof. We had Quin go to your school," Jones protested.

"Quin who? He doesn't ring a bell," Val said.

"Oh, you know, your half-brother. Opal's son. Our pack's witch," Jones said.

"WHAT! All this time Opal was your lover? Honestly, I didn't even know her name. What about Mom? Wait, you mean the time that student made me start a fire at the school?" Val asked.

With an evil grin, Jones clamped his mouth shut and didn't say anymore. Val was ready to burn him to a crisp, but Zane had some questions too. So, he grabbed Val's hand and asked her to wait. "Jones, you're a foul piece of shit. What exactly did he promise you in return?"

"He would deem Shrieking Moon a Royal Extension."

"You'd whore me out for a title, Father? How well did that work out for you?" Valerie asked with a smirk.

With Valerie's last words a tear ran down her face and started burning him to ashes from the legs up. Zane hugged her tight as soon as she was done and let her cry. When she let it all out, they walked out of the cell. Val let go of Zane and went right to Bluey and Rocky, who engulfed Zane too. They finally let go of each other, and Zane could see Rocky and Bluey covered head to toe in her father's blood.

"Got answers, did you?"

"Oh no, not me. It was all my Althea." Rocky sniffed, "Smells like you got your answers too."

"What the hell happened in there?"

"He said he was trying to whore her and Val out to the king. She lost it. Used his own blood against him and made him explode from the inside out."

"Bet that was awesome to witness."

"Bro, it *was* awesome. Good thing Alpha Steven records everything that happens in here."

"Nice."

The friends returned to the pack house, got cleaned up, and went to lunch. Zane hugged his mom and thanked her for everything she did. He saw his sisters and hugged them closely too. He told them not to be so hard on their parents, then pulled Robert aside, gave him some brotherly advice and pulled him in a hug even though Robert hated them.

With the king gone, the girls' fathers dead, and the Moon Goddess declaring Zane King of not only werewolves, but all her creations, Alpha Steven had more fears of safety for the pack and Zane. *Zane doesn't realize how much he now has on his plate. King Sidious might be gone, but the corrupt council he kept still remains. Zane is going to have to deal with them too. I know*

some things to help him, but I don't know if I truly know enough to be all that helpful.

Steven feared for Alex because he knew he was going to be needed to assist Zane with the ongoing corruption within the Royal Kingdom. He taught them every fighting style he knew, which in return he hoped would help keep them safe—at first. Power struggles would happen once word spreads about King Sidious being dead. The word would travel about the girls' power, and who knows who would try and take that from Zane and Rocky.

For now, all Steven could do is prepare, plan, wait, and continue to pray that the Moon Goddess will keep an eye out on her children and answer their calls of prayer at a time of dire request. *We'll need it.*

About the Author

Holly Hiller grew up in the Lehigh Valley, Pennsylvania. She graduated from Whitehall-Coplay High School, then served in the Air Force as an AMMO troop from 1999 through 2008. In the Air Force, Holly traveled all over the world. Her favorite duty station was Germany, and she still misses her time in the service. Today, Holly lives in Slatington, Pennsylvania, with her husband, Sean. They have four children and ten reptiles: four bearded dragons, three water dragons, two leopard geckos, and one uromastyx.